THEY WERE LIKE FIRE AND GASOLINE.

"Look, we need to stop disagreeing over every little thing," Jack said. "We just have a basic personality conflict."

"Right," Tess agreed. "No reason we can't deal with it; we'll work on it." She looked into the salad bowl. "What did you do to the lettuce? It looks like it was beaten to death."

He looked over her shoulder. "So I cut it instead of tearing it. No big deal; it doesn't change the taste."

"But it's all mangled! It looks all bruised."

Jack muttered an oath under his breath. In no time flat, she had him ready to stuff a gag in her mouth. And her expression said she knew it—she had an almost satisfied look.

Well, he'd be damned if he was going to give her that satisfaction.

SUE CIVIL-BROWN

Tempting
Mr. Wright

AVON BOOKS
An Imprint of HarperCollinsPublishers

This is a work of fiction. Names, characters, places, and incidents are products of the author's imagination or are used fictitiously and are not to be construed as real. Any resemblance to actual events, locales, organizations, or persons, living or dead, is entirely coincidental.

AVON BOOKS
An Imprint of HarperCollins*Publishers*
10 East 53rd Street
New York, New York 10022-5299

Copyright © 2000 by Sue Civil-Brown
ISBN: 0-380-81179-0
www.avonromance.com

First Avon Books paperback printing: October 2000

Avon Trademark Reg. U.S. Pat. Off. and in Other Countries, Marca Registrada, Hecho en U.S.A.
HarperCollins® is a trademark of HarperCollins Publishers Inc.

Printed in the U.S.A.

WCD   10   9   8   7   6   5   4   3   2   1

After the bleak November landscape of Chicago, the bright greens of verdant Paradise Beach seemed garish. Tess Morrow paid the cab driver, then stood blinking in the blinding sunshine with her bags at her feet. Her mother and stepfather's house looked the same as it always did, a one-story stucco structure with a red-tiled roof and an enclosed, gated courtyard full of flowers and palms.

The landscaping was lush, almost voluptuous, and Tess suddenly had a negative reaction to it—the kind of reaction she would have had to a large-breasted woman in a see-through blouse. By contrast, she felt almost virtuous for living on gray city streets in a third-floor walk-up.

And right now, she could have used a good dose of the Windy City's trademark, the chilling wind off the lake. Lord, she was going to melt if she stood here any longer.

Picking up her carry-on and her cosmetics case, she let herself through the tall wrought-iron gate into paradise. Well, it might have been paradise for some people. To her, it seemed almost sinful that bougainvilleas and hibiscus were still blooming riotously and that palm fronds were rattling in the steady sea breeze when the trees at home were lifeless gray fingers.

Her reaction was abnormal, though, and she knew it, but at the moment she wasn't prepared to consider it. She had more important things on her mind: her mother and stepfather had disappeared.

Crossing the red brick driveway in the punishing sun, she walked up the narrow path to the front door, grateful for the shade of the porch. Fumbling in her purse, she sought the special key ring on which she kept the keys to her parents' house—a key ring she hadn't needed in years.

God, it was hot. Her wool skirt was prickling her even through the nylon slip, her pantyhose were chafing and making her even hotter, and she could feel sweat rolling down her back between her shoulder blades. Already her dark hair was plastered to her forehead.

Where the hell was that key ring? Dropping her bags, she dug through her purse, finding old tissues, a receipt from two years ago for wine she couldn't remember buying, a bottle of ibuprofen, and a half-dozen crumpled business cards. Sweat dripped off the end of her nose, soaking the tissues and cards.

Aha, there it was.

She pulled the ring from the bottom of her purse and started to insert the key in the lock. Just then the door popped open and she found herself staring into the face of her nemesis: her stepbrother Jack Wright. Worse, he was grinning.

"Well, well, well," he said, leaning against the doorjamb, his voice hinting of foreign climes, with just a touch of a Caribbean lilt. "It's Shorty."

"Oh, God," she said. Tess reached out, grabbed the knob of the outward-opening door, and slammed it in his face.

Then she shoved the keys back in her purse, picked up her suitcases, and started back to the street.

Halfway across the courtyard, the sun and common sense drew her up short. What the heck was she doing? She had as much right to be here as he did. And what's more, her mother and stepfather were still missing.

Swearing under her breath, she did an about face, nearly twisting her ankle as her three-inch spike heel caught in a groove between the bricks. She swore again and marched back to the house. He had absolutely no right to keep her from coming into the house.

Dropping her suitcases again, she had to fumble once more for the key. By this point she was so annoyed that her jaws ached from clenching her teeth. Perspiration, rolling like rivers now, burned her eyes, and she wanted to scream.

Just as she started to insert the key in the door, it swung open again, and there was Jack lounging against the doorjamb, a grin on his face. "Hi, Shorty," he said, just as he had two minutes ago. "Change of heart?"

All the dislike she felt for him rose until her throat burned with it. "Don't call me that," she said sharply. She was painfully self-conscious about only being five-foot-one, but she didn't think Jack had any business gloating, since he wasn't all that tall himself, maybe five-nine. "What are *you* doing here?"

"About the same thing as you, I bet. We're missing some parental units."

"And you wouldn't know anything about that, would you." It wasn't a question.

His grin faded, to be replaced by a look of mock dismay. "Your confidence in me is amazing."

"The only confidence I have in you is that you're probably in some kind of trouble." He was still blocking the doorway, and she was getting hotter by the second. "Are you going to let me in?"

"Why not?" He stepped back with a grandiose wave and invited her inside.

It was hardly any cooler inside, because all the windows were open. Tess dropped her bags on the terra-cotta tile and fought her way out of her wool suit jacket. Her long-sleeved jacquard blouse was sticking to her skin, and she plucked it away, trying to ignore Jack's patent interest in the view and the strange way it made her tingle.

"Wrong climate for that outfit," he remarked, his tone lazy. He was wearing khaki cargo shorts and a loose white shirt with rolled-up sleeves, showing off plenty of tanned skin, not to mention some really phenomenal legs.

"No kidding." Count on Jack to say the obvious. "It's cold in Chicago."

"Duh."

She tossed him a glare and reached for her bags, but before she could grab them, he had moved swiftly and snatched them up.

"I suppose you're planning to stay," he said in tones of long-suffering resignation.

"Until we find Mom and Dad, yes."

"I thought so."

"Well, you're welcome to leave."

"Me?" He lifted his eyebrows. "I came riding to the rescue first, Shorty. I've got squatter's rights."

She made up her mind right then and there to ignore his provocations. "So you're stuck with me, doofus." Turning sharply on the heel of her navy pumps, she headed for the bedroom wing and the room she was always given when she came to visit.

It gave her a small feeling of satisfaction to know that Jack had to follow her with her bags. For all she knew, when he had picked them up, he may have been planning to toss her out on the street, but now he was trotting after her with her suitcases like a lackey—his appropriate station in life, she thought irritably.

Jack had been driving her crazy ever since

their parents married fifteen years ago, and in the last few years she'd decided that for the sake of her sanity, she wouldn't come home for holidays anymore. Much as she would have liked to spend the time with her mother and stepfather, she couldn't stand Jack's constant needling. He got under her skin faster than a chigger, and was every bit as irritating.

And it was so very *lowering* to find herself, a woman now thirty, arguing with him as if she were still a five-year-old.

He dropped her suitcases on the bench at the foot of the bed. "Anything else, madam?" he asked with mock courtesy.

"Yes. Get out. Now."

He cocked his head to one side and didn't move. And damn him, he was too solid and big for her to pick up and move bodily. "Don't you even want to hear what I've learned about the folks?"

Her heart stopped. Oh, God, she couldn't believe she had forgotten her worry about them in her annoyance at finding Jack here. "What? What, Jack?"

"Not a damn thing." He tossed her a salute and sauntered out of the room.

Tess slammed the door after him, and then became even angrier when she heard him laugh.

God, he was awful! From the minute they'd first met and he'd asked her why she had a dumb name like Tess, they'd been squabbling and he'd been making her miserable.

Stripping off her blouse and skirt, she tossed

them on a chair, then peeled off her sticky underwear. To be fair, though, she thought as she stepped into a cool shower, he hadn't really started it with the comment about her name. *She'd* been the one who first had asked him, rather nastily, why he was still living at home when he was a senior in college.

All right, she'd been a bitch. But she'd only been fifteen and really angry that her mother was remarrying, which meant she would never get her father back. But that was no reason for Jack to have kept it up all this time.

She toweled off, feeling a whole lot better, and dressed in some of the summer clothes she hadn't had much opportunity to wear since her last visit here. She wanted to put on a gaily printed sundress that always made her feel like someone else, but decided not to give Jack an excuse to say something she wouldn't like. Instead she pulled on a pair of white Bermuda shorts and a hot pink tank top, shoved her feet into some white canvas shoes, and headed out to face her self-designated tormenter.

Jack was sitting in the living room, a phone pressed to his ear, talking in a low voice. Behind him, through a wall of glass doors, the Intracoastal Waterway was visible, a tranquil scene in the afternoon sunlight.

Why did a man so irritating have to be so gorgeous? The way his brown hair was sun-streaked ... she found herself wondering if he spent his entire life on a beach with a surfboard. But nobody knew what Jack did with himself, leading to the inevitable conclusion that he was up to no good. Reminding herself of that enabled her to overlook the fact that he was gorgeous.

As soon as he saw her, he said good-bye and hung up.

"How long have you been here?" she asked.

"I got here a half-hour before you."

So much for his squatter's rights. "You got the same phone call?"

"From the neighbor? Yeah."

"Wait a minute." She pushed her damp, dark hair back from her face. Since moving to Chicago five years ago, she'd let it grow longer, but now, back in Florida again, she had a sudden urge to chop it all off. "What neighbor? I didn't get a call from a neighbor."

"Who called you?"

"Mom and Dad. Well, actually, Mom. Two days ago. I was out of town on an audit for a week, and when I got back, there was this message on my machine—something about how they were trying to get a flight and get home. They didn't say where they were, and I didn't even know they were gone until then."

"Me neither. But you heard from them two days ago?"

"That's when I got the message. I don't know when they called."

He lifted his eyebrows. "Why not?"

"My machine doesn't have a date stamp."

"God, Tess, are you ever going to come out of the Victorian age? Get a new answering machine."

She felt her temper flaring again. "It won't help *now*. And I'm not Victorian."

"You could fool me." He stood up and started pacing the floor. "So you might have heard from them as recently as two days ago?"

"I don't think so, because there were some other messages on my machine after Mom's, and I'm pretty sure one of them was from last Thursday, so that would make it at least..." She paused to count backward. "At least six days."

"Did anyone ever tell you you ought to be a detective?"

She thought she detected sarcasm in his voice, and as usual she flared. "I'm an auditor. I have a brain. I reason well."

"Hmph. Seems to me it would be easier just to get a new answering machine with a date stamp."

"I'm not anal about my personal calls."

"That must be the only thing you're *not* anal about."

She ground her teeth. "Let's get back to the problem, here."

"Right. The missing parental units. So you got the message two days ago telling you they were trying to get a flight home, a message that didn't say where they were, a message that is *probably* six days old. Two days ago, I get a call from a neighbor telling me they're missing. Does that pretty much sum it up?"

"Yes." She was still talking through her teeth because she didn't like the way he had emphasized the word *probably*, but she refused to tell him where he could stick it. "And by the way," she said, "how did the neighbor call you? Nobody has your number."

"*You* don't have my number."

She resisted the urge to snap his head off. Reminding herself that she dealt with more difficult people all the time without losing her cool, she said, "Mom said you're unreachable."

"Mom's primary language is French. She occasionally fractures her meanings."

"So you *do* have a phone?"

"Well, no."

"Oh, hell." Getting more frustrated by the minute, Tess folded her arms under her breasts and tapped her toe. "Just tell me how the neighbor called you."

"I have a kind of voice-mail thing. Like paging."

"Oh." Well, Tess could understand how her mother's explanation of that might have gotten messed up. Brigitte LeBlanc Wright got a lot of things messed up, and not all of them had to do with language. But it still bothered her that a neighbor had his number when she didn't. Not that it really mattered.

"This is bad," he said after a few moments.

"No kidding." She loaded as much sarcasm into the words as she could. "Who called you?"

"Mrs. Niedelmeyer—you know, the old bat who lives three doors down and seems to spend her whole life watching the neighborhood?"

"Yeah, yeah," she said impatiently. "Old Nosy. What did she say?"

"That Mom and Dad disappeared a week ago. They didn't tell anyone they were going away, and she was getting worried."

"God." Tess flopped into an armchair and stared glumly at the floor. "Oh, jeez, Jack, you don't think they went to Cuba, do you?"

"Cuba? Why Cuba?"

"Because Mom has always wanted to go there. I don't know how many times she's mentioned it."

"Lovely." He stopped pacing and put his hands on his narrow hips. "Well, she's Canadian."

"So?"

"So, she could go. Dad couldn't."

"Of course he could. Americans can go to Cuba. You just have to fly to someplace outside the country to get a flight there. And there's all kinds of warnings, mainly that there's no embassy there to help anyone who gets into trouble."

"But if they were going to do that, wouldn't they have told someone?"

She had to admit he was right. Their parents never took a long trip without telling Jack and her that they were going away. "Should we call the police?"

"Not yet. God, Tess, we don't have anything to tell them. A neighbor who says they've been gone for over a week without telling her where they were going, and a phone call to you, date unspecified, that says they're trying to get a flight home. They'd laugh us out of the station."

Tess felt her heart sink even more. She hated to admit he was right, and a dozen arguments sprang to her lips. She swallowed them, though, before she could make a fool of herself. "We've got to do *something*."

"I agree. I'm going to do it right now."

"What's that?"

"I'm going to talk to Nosy, see if she knows any more than she told me on the phone."

Tess hated to admit it, but it sounded like a splendid idea. "Let's go."

He arched a brow. "You, too?"

"Yes, me, too," she said hotly. "Of *course* me, too. I want to hear it from the horse's mouth."

He sighed, then gave her a crooked grin. "Not a bad description of Mrs. Niedelmeyer."

"How can you make a joke at a time like this?"

"Humor's great for relieving tension."

She rose from her chair, shaking her head. "You don't take anything seriously, do you?"

The smile vanished from his face, and for a moment he looked utterly grave. "I take a lot of things seriously. Get a clue, Shorty. Just because someone doesn't meet your specifications for the perfect human being doesn't mean he or she's a jerk."

She sniffed, refusing to answer, and headed toward the door. He followed, practically breathing down her neck. She had half a mind to turn around suddenly and throw him off balance, then decided against it. What if he grabbed on to her for support? She couldn't bear the thought.

The house had evidently been cooler than she thought, because the instant she stepped outside, she wanted to melt again. "Man, this place is humid."

"It's right on the water," he said mildly enough.

"I know it's on the water. It's still humid. And hot. I don't know how anyone can stand to live here."

"News flash: a lot of people would disagree with you. It's actually a perfect day. Couldn't be much above eighty-five."

Perfect? It would take a bonehead like him to think that was perfect. She could feel her skin shriveling under the assault of the sun, and wondered if there was someplace nearby where she could buy some SPF 50 sunblock before she burned to a crisp.

They walked down the quiet street past other homes, no two alike. Tall palms lined both sides of the street, giving it a very tropical feeling. Tess couldn't understand the fascination for palms, because they sure didn't make any shade.

The Niedelmeyer house was two doors down, on the other side of the street. It was much smaller than the Wright house, a bungalow from the fifties with much-patched stucco painted bright pink with turquoise trim. The garden was showing signs of neglect, but a few hardy hibiscus bushes still blossomed.

Mrs. Niedelmeyer opened the door to them. She was a small, wizened woman of indeterminate age with thin, tightly permed white hair and sharp brown eyes. She greeted Jack with a big smile. "Jack, my boy, how good to see you." The look and greeting she gave Tess were noticeably cooler.

Why did Jack elicit such warmth, when she knew for a fact he didn't care for Mrs. Niedelmeyer any more than she did? But then, Jack could charm the rattles off a snake when he put his mind to it. It was one of the reasons she distrusted him. On the other hand, he'd never tried to charm her, not even once—which, irrationally, bugged her.

Inside, potpourri burners were clogging the air with the scent of roses. The living room was small, the furniture old and worn. Mrs. Niedelmeyer invited them to sit as Tess wondered if she was going to asphyxiate. Not even one window was open to let out the overwhelming aromas, and the room was hot besides.

"Let me get you some tea and cookies," Mrs. Niedelmeyer said, clearly ready to settle in for a long visit.

Tess felt panic rising in her throat, but Jack spoke.

"Thanks, Mrs. N., but we don't have time. We're trying to figure out what happened to Mom and Dad."

"Oh, I'm sure they just went on a vacation," Mrs. Niedelmeyer said.

"Really? Then why did you call me and tell me you were worried about them?"

The elderly woman looked momentarily confused. Then she said, "I *did* do that, didn't I?"

"Yes, you did."

"Well, I *am* worried. They always mention when they're taking a trip. Are you sure you wouldn't like some tea and cookies?"

Tess exchanged a look with Jack, who gave an almost invisible shrug.

"Why," he said, turning to Mrs. Niedelmeyer, "do you think they're on vacation?"

"That's where people usually go, isn't it? When they go away for a long time."

"So why are you worried?"

Again that look of confusion. "Because they didn't tell me?" It almost seemed like she was seeking the right answer.

"Did you see them leave?"

"No." She looked pleased, as if at last she was sure of herself.

"How long has it been since you saw them?"

She cocked her head thoughtfully. "A week? Maybe a little longer." She gave an embarrassed laugh. "It's sad to admit it, but I rarely know what day of the week it is anymore. When you're retired, one day is like the next. I even have to ask the date when I go to write a check at the grocery. But let me get Mr. Niedelmeyer. He's better about dates than I am."

She rose and left them in the living room while she disappeared to some other location in the house.

"I'm suffocating," Tess said.

"It's overwhelming, isn't it?" he agreed. "I'm going to need a shower when we get out of here. It smells like a funeral parlor."

For some reason, the simile sent a chill racing down Tess's spine. "She doesn't know anything."

"It seems like it."

"I don't remember her being this ditzy."

"Me neither. But it's been a while."

"Yeah."

Tess was suddenly overwhelmed by an urge to get out of there; a sense that if she sat in this living room for another minute she was going to explode. And it wasn't only the suffocating odor of rose that was making her feel that way, it was fear and worry.

"I suppose we could be making too much of this," Jack remarked. "Maybe they *did* just go on vacation."

"Without telling anyone?"

Their eyes met, his deep brown, hers bright blue. "I guess not," he said. "I'm clutching at straws."

For a treacherous instant she actually felt something like human warmth toward him. She got a grip on herself quickly. Being in the same boat didn't mean they were members of the same species.

Mrs. N. returned with Mr. N. The man, balding and portly, was wearing a white T-shirt and old slacks held up by suspenders. He was covered in sawdust.

"Sorry," he said, shaking Jack's hand and nodding to Tess, "I was working in my shop. Madge said you want to know about your folks. 'Fraid

I don't know anything. One day they were here, the next they were gone."

Tess spoke. "Did they say anything about taking a trip?"

"Not to me."

"Do you recall when the last time you saw them was?"

Mr. Niedelmeyer's expression grew thoughtful, and his eyes lifted to the ceiling. "Can't say that I do, exactly. A week? Maybe a little longer. Steve was out working on the front gate, talking about putting a lock on it." He shrugged. "We've been having some prowlers. And there was a robbery a couple of doors over about two weeks ago. Or maybe three. Anyway, Steve was talking about putting a lock on his gate, and maybe getting a security system. Don't know that he ever did it, though. You don't think burglars killed them, do you?"

Tess's heart lurched.

"No," Jack said swiftly. "We're pretty sure they went on some kind of trip. Brigitte called Tess a few days ago and said they were coming home."

"Well, if that's so, where are they?" Mr. Niedelmeyer asked.

"That's what we're wondering."

"And why are you asking me when I saw them last? You think I did something to them?" His face was flushing red.

"No, of course not," Jack hastened to say. "It's just that we're wondering—"

Tess interrupted him. "Mr. Niedelmeyer, we're

just trying to find out if they ever got home after they called me. Or where they might be stranded. That's all. They called me about six days ago and said they were trying to get a flight home. That's the last I heard. But you haven't seen them in the last six days. That's all we wanted to know."

Niedelmeyer leaned forward, poking a dusty finger at her. "I can tell you one thing, young lady. The grass hasn't been cut."

"The grass hasn't been cut?" she repeated blankly.

"The grass hasn't been cut," he said firmly. Then he turned and disappeared into the rose-scented bowels of his house.

Tess looked at Jack, utterly at a loss. He gave her a similar look back. Mrs. Niedelmeyer said, "Are you sure I can't give you any cookies or tea?"

Tess thought she would barf if she had to swallow anything while she was strangling on rose perfume. She declined politely, then asked, "Mrs. Niedelmeyer, what did he mean, the grass hasn't been cut?"

"It hasn't been cut," the elderly woman answered with a shrug. "What else could it mean?"

Outside in the heat, Tess gulped air gratefully. "God, I thought I was going to suffocate."

"Me, too." But Jack sounded thoughtful as they walked back toward the house. "The grass hasn't been cut. What the hell did he mean by that? It sounds like a bad password from a third-rate spy movie."

She pointed up the street toward the house. "It's getting kind of shaggy and long. Probably all he meant was that they've been gone awhile, or the grass would have been cut."

"Maybe."

As they drew closer to the house, she studied the grass along the street and around the courtyard walls. "At least a week, don't you think?"

"A week for what?"

"A week since it's been cut?"

He looked at the grass. "Maybe. I'm not an authority on the rate of grass growth. Guess I'd better cut it before the neighbors get irritated, though. It *is* kind of long."

"No, don't cut it."

They were at the gate now, and he looked at her with a lifted brow. "Don't cut it? Why the hell not?"

"Because we need to figure out how long it's been growing."

"You're crazy, you know that?"

"I'm not crazy. If we can figure about how long it's been since it was cut . . ." She snapped her fingers. "Hey, don't they always hire a lawn service when they're going to be gone more than a week?"

"Do they?"

"I think so. I seem to remember Mom mentioning it." She stood looking down at the grass. "We can tell how long they've been gone if we can figure out how long it's been since the grass has been cut."

"Brilliant, Watson. So what are you going to

do? Ascertain the average growth rate for this type of grass in this climate? Figure in the watering—or lack thereof—the amount of fertilizer in the soil, not to mention the height to which it was last cut, and *voilà*, give us the exact number of hours since it was last cut? Never mind that they may have cut it days before they left. Never mind that we already know they've been missing for six days, at least since they called you. But I forget, your answering machine doesn't have a date stamp, so we're *assuming* it's been six days."

She glared at him, deciding that she really hated him. *Sincerely* hated him. "You got any better ideas, you overgrown beach bum?"

"Beach bum?" He appeared struck by the description. "You think I'm a mere beach bum? Can't you do any better than that?"

"All right. You're uncouth. Useless. A parasite on society."

He nodded, an odd smile curving his very nice mouth and glittering in his usually warm eyes. "A parasite on society. That's pretty good. I suppose that doesn't apply to you IRS auditors. I suppose you see yourselves as Robin Hoods, stealing from the poor to make the rich richer."

"You have no idea what I do!"

"I know you work for the IRS. I know that when you were out of town last week you were probably turning some poor schmuck's life into a living hell. Does that make you feel good, Tess? Do you sleep well at night? Because I'm damned if I know how you can."

"Why, you arrogant, useless *bum*. People owe

their taxes for the good of society. That's how roads and dams and *welfare* get paid for!"

"Sure. And I pay mine willingly."

"You pay taxes? On what? Your surfboard?"

His smile broadened a shade. "Sorry to disappoint you, Ms. Morrow, but I don't own a surfboard. I also don't charge people huge penalties for making little mistakes. Now, if you'll excuse me, I'm going to cut the goddamn grass while I try to figure out what harebrained idea your mother dragged my father into, and what kind of trouble they're in now."

"What do you mean, my mother dragged your father? Are you saying he can't think for himself?"

"Come off it, Tess, you know your mother. She's a drama queen. She can arrange a scene a minute until she gets her way. It can be fascinating to watch, but it could also wear down the Rock of Gibraltar."

He walked through the gate and headed for the garage. Tess looked after him, her mouth open, wanting so badly to defend her mother and tell him what a slug he was, but the words wouldn't come.

Because deep inside, she knew he was right. Whatever was going on here had probably started as some fertile little idea in her mother's brain. It may have gone all haywire through no fault of Brigitte's, but it had almost surely started with some idea of hers.

Now Steve and Brigitte were missing, and the

only clue they had was that the grass hadn't been cut.

And Tess was suddenly feeling very scared and very lonely.

2

Beach bum. The words rankled as Jack pulled the lawn mower out of the garage and filled the tank with gas from the can sitting on a shelf. Once or twice, he glanced back to where Tess was standing, looking like a lost waif.

God, a beach bum! And he couldn't say a word to defend himself. He swore under his breath and put the gas can back on the shelf, then screwed the top back on the tank on the lawn mower.

In spite of himself, he glanced again toward Tess and felt an unwelcome protective tug. He'd always felt that toward her, and he resented the hell out of it. But she was so tiny, and—if he was going to be honest about it—very cute, too. Blue eyes too big for her delicate face, dark hair that sometimes looked as black as a raven's wing, and other times, like now when she was standing in the sun, lit up with fiery red highlights. She looked lost standing there at the gate, lost and small and alone.

And he didn't want to feel any of the things he was feeling right now. Except that he always had, from the day he'd first met her when she'd been fifteen and he'd been twenty-one. He hadn't been happy about the marriage, hadn't been happy about having a child foisted into his family, a child he was told to consider a sister—but he'd been prepared to accept it until she opened her sweet little mouth and dripped scorn all over him.

She'd thrown the gauntlet and he'd picked it up. They'd been squabbling ever since, although he had a sneaking suspicion that on his part, the irritation arose mostly from a desire not to notice any of the other things he felt about her—especially since she'd grown up. She'd been cast in the role of sister, even if she wasn't really, and that meant he had to protect her. Even from himself.

But considering they'd only seen each other a couple of times a year in the past fifteen years, he found it hard to remember that she was supposed to be his sister. He couldn't help noticing that she had a really great figure—not too thin, but just right. Surprisingly long legs for a woman so short. And a bust that . . . well, he had to force himself not to look.

Then she would open her mouth, and he'd remember that she was *indeed* the pesky little sister who'd been forced on him.

Right now, though, all he could see was a tired, frightened young woman. He didn't want to notice that.

Sighing, he pushed the mower out onto the driveway and yanked the cord. The engine turned over on the second pull and came roaring to life. He decided to mow along the street and outside the courtyard first, so he headed toward the gate where Tess was still standing.

When he drew up alongside her, he said, "You need to get out of the sun. I'll run out and get you some sunscreen as soon as I'm done with this."

She amazed him by nodding and walking toward the house. Her head was down and her shoulders slumped.

Hell, he'd been too hard on her. He shouldn't have given her hell over her mother and being an IRS auditor. That hadn't been kind.

Except that he knew damn well that whatever hijinks had gotten this mess under way, Brigitte Wright had been responsible for them. She was dramatic, intensely committed to every idea she had, however minor. It was an attractive trait, her passion and deep involvement in things as inconsequential as the placement of napkins on the dinner table. Brigitte lived every moment of her life fully. But that characteristic could also be troublesome, and more than once Jack's father had nearly torn his hair out trying to find some way to divert her.

So maybe this time he hadn't managed to divert her. Maybe they'd gone off on a vacation to some dangerous place and were stranded. Or worse. He didn't want to think about the worse. He'd seen enough in the Caribbean and South America to know what could happen to travelers who were unfortunate enough to be in the wrong place at the wrong time.

He glanced toward the house again and wondered what Tess was doing. And the thought kept stealing into his mind that they weren't really related. Not in any way that mattered. They were two strangers thrown together in an artificial relationship by their parents' decision to wed. Nothing more. It might have been different if they had grown up together, but they hadn't.

For which, he decided, he should probably be eternally grateful, because that woman had a tongue like an asp. Uncouth? She didn't know the meaning of the word—he'd like to take her into a few bars in the Caribbean and show her uncouth.

Almost in spite of himself, he laughed at his own silliness. Tess wasn't worth all this bother. They'd figure out what happened to their parents and go their separate ways, as they always had. This time next year, he'd hardly remember what she looked like.

He hoped.

The cloud of worry that had been hanging over him ever since Mrs. Niedelmeyer called returned. If Brigitte had gotten his father into trouble, he was going to ... well, he didn't know what he was going to do.

It had always seemed to him that his father's fascination with Brigitte was dangerous. That kind of fascination could lead a man into serious trouble. The only reason it hadn't, Jack was convinced, was because Brigitte seemed to truly love his father. But maybe this time ...

It took him about an hour to mow and trim. Not very long, really, but long enough that he should have come up with a bright idea or two about where they should look next. All that occurred to him, though, was that they should talk to some of the other neighbors.

He put the equipment away, shook the grass clippings off his shoes and ankles, and reentered the house by way of the back door. In the kitchen he stopped for a glass of ice water, then went looking for Tess. She was standing in the foyer, hovering on the edge of the doorway into the study.

"What's up?" he asked.

She jumped as if startled, and glanced at him with that air of disapproval he knew so well. Sometimes he wondered if she looked at everyone that way, or just him.

"I was thinking," she said.

"Obviously. About what?"

She scowled. "Let me finish."

"I'm all ears."

"If they took a trip, they had to buy plane tickets."

"Right. So?"

"So . . ." She pointed to the desk. "It would probably be on one of their credit card bills."

He had to give her credit for brains. "And that will tell us . . . ?"

"That they took a trip. And who the travel agent was. Maybe the agency could tell us where they went."

He nodded. "They might. But I wouldn't bet on it."

"Are you always so pessimistic?"

"Not pessimistic, Shorty, just realistic. I'd be really surprised if a travel agent would give that kind of info out."

"Well . . ." she hesitated. "I have IRS credentials."

Stunned, Jack stared at her, his whole worldview changing. So the Victorian Tess was slipping a lace here and there? The thought absolutely delighted him. "You're willing to commit a crime?"

Her frown deepened even more. "It's not a crime."

"I'm sure it must be. But what the hell—no jury would ever convict you, given the circumstances."

She rolled her eyes and sighed with exasperation.

"So go on," he said. "Look at the stuff."

"It's an invasion of privacy."

He gaped at her, then started laughing, laughing so hard that his sides ached and he gasped for air. "Oh, God, that's good."

She put her hands on her hips and glared at him. "What the hell is so funny?"

"You," he said, wiping his eyes as a few errant chuckles escaped him.

"Me?"

"You. My God, you're an IRS auditor."

"So?"

"So when did you ever have qualms about looking into someone's personal financial records?"

"Cretin! This is different."

"Yeah? How so?"

"I'm not auditing them. I have no right to look at their records."

"Really?" He grew absolutely sober. "I'd think the fact that they're missing gives us a lot of rights. If we have to go to the cops, that's exactly what they're going to start looking at."

"Maybe." Forgetting her anger, she chewed her lip. "But . . . I *am* an auditor, Jack. What if I . . . see something?"

Understanding dawned. "Ahh," he said.

She looked at him, and much as he didn't want to notice, he couldn't help seeing the fear and worry in her huge blue eyes. "Okay," he said. "I'll look. I promise to spare your gaze anything shady—not that there'll be anything. I know my dad better than that."

"I think I do, too. But . . . I would still rather not *know* anything, if you follow me."

"All too well. Although I gotta say I'm a little disappointed you're even having these qualms."

She bristled. "Why? Disappointed that I won't sink to *your* level?"

"No, disappointed that you won't come *up* to mine. Family first, and all that."

She looked as if she were about to give him a lecture, but she closed her mouth and compressed her lips. Well, he didn't need the lecture, anyway. He could have written it himself.

"Let me go take a quick shower," he said. "I'm sweaty and covered with grass and pollen. Back in five."

"Okay."

He left her standing there on the threshold of the study, still looking perturbed. Weird woman. She was willing to use her badge to get information out of a travel agent, but she was afraid of what she might find in her parent's financial records. She drew lines in the oddest places.

Which was probably why they'd never been able to get along.

He showered swiftly and changed into fresh shorts and a clean polo shirt. When he returned to the study, it appeared that Tess hadn't even moved.

"Hey," he said, concerned, "are you okay, Tess?"

She turned and looked up at him with a small nod. "Sure. I'm fine. Just worried."

"Me, too." And he was, though he was doing his damnedest to sit on the feeling. Life had taught him that worrying rarely did any good. You just dealt with things as they came up and did your best. Stewing about it only softened the brain cells.

He passed her and entered the study. It was a room he'd always envied, sort of colonial-tropical, with a heavy teak desk, upholstered wing chairs, and built-in bookshelves. Overhead ceiling fans stirred the air lazily, and wooden blinds covered the windows. Unlike the rest of the house, which was light and airy with a Mediterranean flavor, this room harkened back to the days of British ascendency in the tropics.

He paused to open the blinds, letting in the sunlight and a view of the garden outside. "Okay," he said, eyeing the teak filing cabinets. "Where's a good place to start?"

"How about that stack of envelopes on the desk?"

"Good idea. While I'm at it, why don't you check the mailbox and see if there's anything in it?"

"Okay."

So she *could* be agreeable sometimes. Amazing. Pulling out the chair at the desk, Jack sat down and reached for the envelopes. It looked as if someone had brought in the mail just before they left and had put it here to look at later.

He cast aside the bulk-rate stuff and tugged out a bank statement and two credit card bills. Looking in the drawer, he found his dad's brass letter opener and sliced the envelopes.

"Nothing in the mailbox," Tess announced behind him.

"So they stopped the mail."

"And that means?"

He glanced over at her. "Only that they expected to be gone more than a few days. If nobody's seen them in a week, and they phoned you approximately six days ago saying they were trying to get a flight home . . ."

"Then they ran into some kind of trouble," she said, her voice squeezed tight with controlled emotion.

"That's what I'm thinking." He had a crazy urge to go to her and give her a hug, but she wouldn't welcome the gesture. In fact, she'd probably kick him in the privates and tell him to keep his paws to himself. So, skip the urge to comfort.

He pulled the bank statement out of the envelope and unfolded it. "No good," he said after a minute.

"Why not?"

"No canceled checks. Just check numbers and amounts. And the closing date is more than a week before they left. So if they've been using an ATM somewhere, it's not on this."

"Shoot."

He stuffed it back in the envelope and reached for the credit card statements. "Unless they bought airline tickets well in advance, these aren't going to help, either."

She edged closer to the desk. "But they would have, wouldn't they? Bought tickets in advance, I mean. That's how you get the better fares."

"Maybe. Then again, this whole trip could have been a sudden impulse."

"They could have bought the tickets a couple of months ago, too. Maybe we should look at some of the older credit card statements."

"Maybe. Let me check these first. If there's nothing here, you can put your bloodhound nose to work."

"My what?"

He flashed her a grin. "I figured you auditors must have an unerring instinct for where to look for things. So you could sniff the filing cabinets and find the old statements, right?"

"Oh . . . you beast!"

"I've been called worse." He turned his attention back to the desk and pulled the first statement out of its envelope. He scanned the charges. "Cripes," he said. "Your mother spends a fortune at Saks in Tampa."

She snatched the statement from his hands. "Let me see that."

"Why? Jealous?"

She looked down at him with disgust. "Don't you see? She was probably buying clothes for the trip."

He snatched the paper back from her, ignoring her disapproving look. "Yeah," he said. "Probably. Unfortunately, this doesn't tell us a thing about it. She could have been shopping for a trip to Paris."

"Trust me, if she'd been shopping for Paris, she would have spent a lot more. Or she would have saved her money to shop once she was there."

"So what would she have been buying for this kind of money?"

"Beats me. But it wasn't evening dresses."

He glanced up at her. "You shop at Saks?"

"I wish. But I've been there, and I've seen their prices. This kind of money wouldn't go very far. Play clothes, maybe."

"Play clothes. I thought that was for kids."

"Shows how much *you* know."

"Well, regardless, it's inscrutable." He put the statement back in the envelope and opened the next one. "More inscrutability," he said after a moment. "A car repair, a doctor's visit—nothing major—two trips to the grocery store. Something from the local nursery. . . ." He stopped reading and stuffed it back into its envelope.

"Dead end," he announced. "Unless you can find an earlier statement."

Without a word, she turned to the wooden filing cabinet. Reaching out, she tugged on the top drawer. It wouldn't budge.

"Locked," she announced.

"Great. Stand back." Rising he went to examine the lock. "You wouldn't have a hairpin, would you?"

"I wish." She also wished she had a scrunchy so she could get the damn hair off her neck. "Listen, do you think we could turn on the air-conditioning?"

He glanced her way. "You can't stand a little heat, huh?"

"If it were just warm, it'd be no problem. But

when it's so humid the sweat doesn't dry, it's miserable."

"Sure, go turn it on and close the windows while I figure out how to pick the lock."

"Pick the lock?" She was obviously horrified at the mere idea. "Jack, you can't do that. It's a *crime*."

"No, it's not. I'm in the house. I got in here with a key they gave me. No cop's going to bust me for abusing the rules of courtesy."

She tried another tack. "They locked it for a reason."

"And I'm going to unlock it for a reason. So go deal with the air-conditioning and let me commit my major crime here without a witness, okay?"

She took a step back, then stopped. "I can't let you do it. And where did you learn to pick locks, anyway?"

"While I was lying on the beach with my surfboard. Damn it, Tess, have you forgotten what's at stake here?"

Maybe she had, because she finally nodded, then hurried from the room.

Jack reached for the letter opener and poked it into the keyhole, feeling around. As he had suspected, it was a simple push lock, not designed to withstand even a mildly determined effort to get inside. Whistling, he went to get his suitcase. Wouldn't Tess be horrified when she learned that he carried a set of lockpicks?

The thought filled him with glee.

*   *   *

Tess, meanwhile, raced around the house, closing the windows. Then she turned on the air-conditioning, setting the temperature to seventy-five degrees. She supposed it was wasteful to run it so low, but the heat seemed to be sapping her strength, and it was certainly making her irritable.

Of course, maybe it was Jack and not the heat that was irritating her. She still couldn't believe he was going to pick a lock, though when she thought about it, she wasn't exactly astonished to discover he knew how to do it.

Jack Wright was a big unknown. If he did anything at all useful with himself, she'd never heard about it. Nor did her parents ever talk about him as if he had a legitimate job. In fact, they rarely talked about him at all.

But she could still remember, before she graduated from high school, a conversation she'd overheard between Brigitte and Steve late one night. She'd missed most of it, but had gathered they were concerned about Jack. And she remembered very clearly hearing her mother say, "That boy is going to pay for the risks he takes."

But once, when she had asked her stepfather what Jack had been doing with himself since college, Steve's gaze had slid away and he'd said dismissively, "A little of this and that, I suppose. I don't really know."

The silence on the subject of Jack's career had led her to believe that her stepbrother was on the wrong side of the law. Surely anything else could have been discussed, even if it was just cleaning out restrooms or digging ditches.

On the other hand, their parents had never seemed ashamed of Jack, either.

Cool air finally began to blow out of the vents overhead. Tess stood beneath one for a minute, grateful for the icy blast. Then, refreshed, she went to beard the lion.

Jack had the filing cabinet open. But that didn't catch her interest nearly as much as the small black leather case on the desk, with its assortment of tiny tools.

"Is that . . ." She paused, cleared her throat, and said, "Is that a lockpick set?"

He looked up from the folders he was examining. "Yeah."

"Umm . . . I thought those were illegal."

"Not where I live."

"And where might that be?"

"None of your business." He sighed. "Look, are you going to help me with this, or would you rather cross-examine me?"

Ugly thoughts were beginning to rear themselves in her head. And while she didn't really believe them, she couldn't quite dismiss them. "Umm . . . how come you don't want to go to the police with this?"

He straightened and looked at her. After a moment he shoved the file drawer shut. "Okay," he said. "You've all but come out and said I must be a wanted criminal. I hate to disappoint you, Sherlock, but I've never been sent to jail, I've never been charged with a crime, and there aren't any warrants out for me . . . unless maybe for those parking tickets I forgot to pay in Miami last year. Christ, next thing I know, you'll be accusing me of doing away with the parents."

Her cheeks were hot, more from embarrassment than anger. She wondered about Jack, it was true, but only because he was a mystery. She didn't believe him capable of hurting her mother or Steve. "I never said that."

"But it was probably the next thing that was going to cross your suspicious little Victorian brain."

"I am not Victorian!"

"Yeah, right. Now, look. Either we work together on this, or you get the hell out of my way, go home to Chicago, and I'll let you know when I find them. But I am absolutely not going to put up with your suspicions about me."

"Why wouldn't I be suspicious? I don't even know what you do for a living, and you've got a set of lockpicks."

He stared at her for a number of seconds, his face revealing nothing. Finally he said, "Give me one good reason why I owe you an explanation. Just one good reason this is your business."

"Because I have a right to know who I'm working with?"

"You know who you're working with. Your stepbrother, Jack. The guy you've been driving insane for the last fifteen years. And that damn well ought to be enough."

"My God, I can't believe your arrogance!"

"And I can't believe your nasty little mind. As for why we're not going to the cops . . . Tess, we don't know what cops to go to. We don't know where they went. We're not even sure they didn't just change their minds and decide to stay longer. If I go to the Paradise Beach police, what are they going to do? Pick their noses and scratch their . . . Never mind. No crime, as far as we can tell, has been committed in this town. We don't even know if one's been committed in Florida, let alone the U.S. of A. So who's going to help us?"

She hadn't thought of it that way. She could feel her shoulders slumping, and finally she sat in one of the wing chairs.

"See?" he said. "We've got a neighbor who claims they're missing because they didn't tell *her* they were going away, and we've got a phone call to you saying they were trying to get a flight home." He was covering old ground yet again, but he felt he had to say it for emphasis. "And quite frankly, Shorty, knowing your mother, I wouldn't be the least surprised if she made that call after she and Dad had a tiff, then they got all lovey-dovey an hour later and decided to hang out for another week."

"But she would have *called* me to tell me."

"Maybe. Maybe not. Brigitte can be remarkably scatterbrained."

Lifting her head, she looked straight at him. "If that's what you think is going on, why are we here trying to find out what happened to them?"

He leaned back against the desk and folded his arms. "I'm just telling you how the cops will look at it. I'm worried, too, Shorty. That's why I'm here."

Something inside her softened a little at his willingness to admit his concern. But she didn't want him to know that. "Will you stop calling me Shorty?"

"Sure, as soon as you stop calling me arrogant, uncouth, a beast ... Shall I run through the whole list?"

She didn't answer, mainly because she was guiltily aware of her tendency to call him names when he made her mad. "It's your fault I call you names," she said. "You drive me nuts."

"Well, we're even on that one, then." He sighed and looked up at the ceiling. "This investigation isn't going well."

"No kidding."

"But if it makes you feel better, call the cops. Maybe they'll have some ideas."

She decided he wasn't so awful after all. Rising, she went to the phone on the desk and called the Paradise Beach police.

3

*T*he police officer arrived forty minutes later. Watching from a front window, Tess felt her heart sink as she saw him pause to spit tobacco juice behind a bougainvillea.

"Gross," she said disgustedly.

"Hey, take it easy on the guy. What do you expect? He's a small-town Southern cop."

She turned to frown at Jack, who was lounging in the living room doorway. She wondered if he ever stood up straight or if he spent his life propped against every vertical surface available. "What excuse do you make for ballplayers?"

"Baseball? Hey, that's excuse enough. The game wouldn't be the same without tobacco juice lubricating the baseline."

"Gross," she said again, and looked out the window. The cop, hitching his gun belt up a little higher—a losing proposition, since he had a beer belly to hold it down—was making his way toward the door. "I thought the Paradise Beach police were good."

"They are—at handling drunk drivers and bar brawls. I don't imagine they get much of a chance to do anything else."

"You're just saying that to make me feel silly for calling them."

"The thought never entered my mind."

She knew him better than that. "You were the one who said they might have some ideas."

"True. But I'm rapidly losing hope."

So was she. The doorbell rang, and she went to let the cop in.

"Officer Wentlow," he said by way of introduction. "You made a missing persons report?"

"Yes." Reluctantly, Tess stepped back to let him in. "I'm Tess Morrow and this is my stepbrother, Jack Wright."

The officer stepped inside and let her close the door behind him. "Man," he said, "you need to turn the air down. This place is like an icebox. Waste of energy, you know."

Tess ignored the comment. As far as she was concerned, the place was just beginning to get comfortable. "Let's go into the living room."

Jack obligingly stepped aside to let Tess and the officer pass, then turned to resume his role of holding the doorway up. Tess waved the officer to the couch and settled herself into an armchair. Wentlow took his time leafing through a clipboard, looking for a blank form to fill out.

"Okay, who's missing?"

"Our parents, Steve and Brigitte Wright."

"Spell that, will you?"

"Brigitte?"

"All of it."

So she did, watching impatiently while he wrote down all the information. Finally they got past the insignificant details, such as the address and the ages of Steve and Brigitte.

Then the officer looked up from his pad. "Why do you think they're missing?"

The story poured out of Tess, and as she told it, she noticed he wasn't writing anything down. Finally she interrupted herself to say, "Aren't you going to write anything down?"

He sighed and rubbed his chin. Stubble rasped. "You still haven't given me a reason to believe they're missing."

"They're not here!"

"So? They're adults."

"They called and said they were coming home."

"And maybe they did, then went somewhere else."

She decided she liked this Gomer Pyle even less than she had when she saw him spit. "Have you heard one word I've said?"

"Now, wait one minute," Wentlow said. "Don't you be talking to a peace officer that way."

"Talk to you in what way? I asked you a simple question. Have you heard what I've been telling you? No one has seen or heard from them in a week. They said they were coming home, but no one saw them come home. They've been missing long enough that the *neighbors* were worried enough to call us. What part of that don't you understand?"

Jack spoke from the doorway. "Don't mind her, Officer, she's got a French temper."

Wentlow looked at her, his scowl giving way to a speculative lift of his eyebrows. "French, huh? One of them hysterical types."

"You might say that," Jack drawled.

Tess swung around to face him, mouth opened to tell him exactly what she thought of *him*.

"Tess," Jack said, his voice as even as steel, "shut up."

The tone of his voice, as much as the words themselves, set her back on her heels. She shut up, even though anger was simmering in her stomach like a cauldron about to boil over. Somehow, some way, she was going to find a means to teach Jack Wright a lesson he'd never forget.

"Look, Officer Wentlow," Jack said, coming into the room. "We know it isn't much to go on. But we're really worried. They never go away without telling us they're leaving, and they always call when they get home."

Wentlow, regarding Tess cautiously, nodded. "Okay. I can see why you're worried. But what do you want me to do about it? They probably weren't here when they disappeared, from what you're saying. Do you know where they went? Where they called from? Does *anyone*?"

"No."

The officer stood up. "Then I can't help you."

Something inside Tess snapped. Jumping to her feet, she said, "Then maybe I'll help *you*. I can have your taxes audited—"

"Tess!" Jack barked. Then he turned to the officer. "Ignore her. *I'll* take care of her."

Two minutes later, the officer was out of the house and Tess was in Jack's face. "What do you mean, you'll take care of me, you moth-eaten bum?"

"Moth-eaten?" He started to grin. "Now, now, Tess, you're starting to act like your mother. I thought you were cooler than that."

"Damn you!"

"As for me, all I did was save you from getting arrested. Are you crazy? Threatening a law officer?"

When he put it like that . . . Tess's anger drained from her like the air from a punctured balloon. With the anger gone, there was room for something else—like humiliation. What had gotten into her? She couldn't believe she'd acted that way.

"Oh, my God," she whispered, and covered her face with her hands.

"So tell me," Jack said almost gently, "when was the last you slept?"

He tried to make her take a nap. Not that she could sleep when the bright sun was still pouring through the windows and she was so worried about her mother and Steve. He finally persuaded her to curl up on the couch beneath an afghan—the house was at last cooling down—and he brought her a cup of her mother's chamomile tea.

"When *did* you last sleep?" he asked again.

"Oh, it hasn't been that long. I just didn't get any sleep last night."

"Too worried, hmm?" Surprising her, he reached out to gently brush her hair back from her face. Surprisingly, she didn't mind it. In fact, the touch sent a warm, delicious tingle through her.

"Yes," she admitted, sipping the tea. "I got to thinking of all the places they could have gone, and all the trouble they could have gotten into."

"Yeah, some of that has been crossing my mind, too." He sighed and settled back in the armchair. "But we're casting about in the dark here, Tess. It's a big world out there. They could have gone to India, Southeast Asia, Hawaii, Japan, South Africa . . . They could have gone anywhere. And until we get a hint or a clue of some kind, nobody's going to be able to help us."

"You knew the cop wasn't going to. You said so."

He nodded slowly.

"Then why did you let me call, Jack? You knew you were right."

"But *you* didn't." He shrugged. "I didn't realize you were so on edge, though. Shorty, you came awfully close to spending the night in jail."

"It's not illegal to imply a cop is dumb."

He cracked a half-smile. "Maybe not. But that isn't the reason he'd have put down on the arrest report, if you made him mad enough. He'd have come up with something to keep you for a few hours."

She sighed, reluctant to admit he was right. She really wasn't as stupid as she had been acting. But the combination of too little sleep and too much adrenaline had left her feeling light-headed, and her mind didn't seem to be working well.

Her thoughts turned to her parents, and she felt worry rising like a tidal wave again. Her mother, a young fifty-five, had a lot of good years ahead of her. But Jack was right about her: she was impulsive, passionate—and too quick to shoot off her mouth. The way Tess just had.

Which really embarrassed Tess, since she'd spent her entire adult life trying to be reserved, calm, and reasonable. In short, unlike her mother.

As for Steve . . . well, she had only warm thoughts for her mother's second husband. Steve had always been good to her, right from their very first meeting. And he'd gone out of his way to make her feel she was his daughter, too.

Now the two of them were missing, and she could imagine all kinds of horrible things, including Brigitte mouthing off at some foreign cop the way Tess had just mouthed off—and there were places in the world where that could get you into an awful lot more trouble than it could here.

She sighed. Jack reached out and took her hand, squeezing it gently. "We'll find them, Shorty."

"You can't promise that." But she half hoped he would.

He didn't answer. After a minute, he let go of her hand, and she missed his comforting touch. God deliver her from getting attached to Jack! He was just a wanderer, and as soon as this mess was over, he'd be gone again to surf on some faraway beach, or whatever it was he did to waste his life.

"Okay," he said after a few minutes. "You snooze here for an hour or so. I'm going to talk to some more neighbors. Maybe someone knows something more than Mrs. Niedelmeyer."

The suggestion galvanized Tess. She put her cup and saucer on the coffee table and threw back the afghan. "I'm going with you."

He lifted his brows. "You need some sleep."

"I'll get it later."

He cocked his head. "You don't trust me, huh, Shorty?"

She didn't dignify that with an answer. Because the truth was, she *didn't* trust Jack Wright any further than she could throw him.

The afternoon was waning, and shadows were growing long on the street. Apparently it was exactly the wrong time of day to go knocking on doors, because no one answered.

"Must be napping or out to dinner," Jack remarked, looking back down the street.

"Or maybe they think we're trying to sell something."

He looked at her shorts, then at himself. "Do we look like salespeople?"

"I wouldn't have thought so."

"Do we look like we're passing out religious tracts?"

"I guess that would depend on the religion." She glanced down at herself again. "The Hare Bermudas? I don't think so."

"Me neither. Shit." He sighed and ran his fingers through his hair. "Maybe it's shuffleboard night at the senior center."

"Don't be cruel."

"Cruel? Do you know how many games of shuffleboard I got hornswoggled into last time I visited the folks? I don't even want to remember. That and checkers."

"Not everyone on the street is retired, Jack."

"I know, but I never saw the ones who aren't. They're too busy working to pay the bills." Suddenly he gave a short laugh. "Well, Old Nosy's curtains are twitching. She's probably wondering if we're casing the houses."

A reluctant laugh escaped Tess. "Probably."

Just then, two doors down from the Wright house, a garage door opened. Moments later a gray-haired man emerged pushing a lawn mower.

"Life exists," Jack said, and started hotfooting it in that direction. Tess followed but had trouble keeping up. She *really* had to start jogging again.

"Mr. Castor," Jack called as he approached the

man with the mower. "Mr. Castor, it's me, Jack Wright."

The man looked up from setting the choke on his machine and smiled. "Well, so it is," he said warmly. "Ready for another game of checkers?"

"Not right now," Jack said swiftly, sticking out his hand for a shake. Puffing, Tess caught up with them and saw that Jack wasn't even winded. Now she was *sure* she hated him.

"Hello," Mr. Castor said to her.

"Hi," she replied. "I'm Tess. Brigitte's daughter."

"Oh. Oh! Right! I haven't seen you in so long. Hear you're living up in Chicago now."

"That's right."

"Awful damn cold up there, isn't it?" He shook his head. "This is the place for me."

Tess, who was sweating again, couldn't agree with him, but she managed not to say so. All she ventured was, "It *is* warm."

"She's melting," Jack said, jerking a thumb her way. "Sort of the reverse of a hothouse flower. She can't stand the heat."

She scowled at Jack, but Mr. Castor laughed.

"She's young yet," the older man said. "There'll come a time when the cold will make her bones ache."

Tess already knew the cold could make her bones ache, particularly the ones she had broken falling out of a tree when she was nine. It still wasn't enough to make her want to be hot.

"So how are Brigitte and Steve doing?" Mr. Castor asked. "Haven't seen them in a while."

Jack and Tess exchanged glances. "Well," said Jack, "we were going to ask you about that."

"Me? Look, it's not my fault I haven't seen them."

"I didn't mean to imply it was," Jack said swiftly.

"Damn well better not. They're neighbors, that's all. I'm not *obligated* to see them."

"Of course you're not," Tess said soothingly. "We know that."

"Then what are you accusing me for?"

Jack released a short sigh. "Mr. Castor, honestly, we're not accusing you of anything."

"Then what are you doing going around saying things like that?"

Jack looked at Tess. Tess looked at Jack. Finally she spoke. "Mr. Castor, our parents are missing."

"Missing? Missing what? Me?"

Tess began to wonder if she'd slipped into the *Twilight Zone*.

Jack spoke, spacing his words for clarity. "Mr. Castor, we cannot find our parents."

"Oh. Oh! Well, they'll probably be home soon. The two of them like to spend the occasional day on the beach, you know."

"Actually," Jack said patiently, "they've been missing for nearly a week."

Mr. Castor, who'd been about to pull the starter rope on his lawn mower, paused. "A week. A week, you say? How would you know that? You haven't been here, have you?"

Jack looked at Tess again, his expression speaking volumes. "Actually, Mrs. Niedelmeyer called me to tell me they've been gone for a week."

"Well, people *do* take vacations, you know."

"I know. But there's a slight problem."

"Did they run out of money? Or did they have trouble with their passports? I've had trouble with mine, you know. I sure have. I had a visa for Thailand once, but they refused to honor it when I got there. Wouldn't even let me out of the airport. Then there was the time I took a flight to England, only they canceled my flight and put me on another one. Problem was, the new one wasn't going to England. Landed in France."

"That's terrible," Tess said, "but—"

"Anyway," Mr. Castor continued as if he hadn't heard her, "we landed in De Gaulle. Shouldn't have been a problem. We should have been able to board a flight for Heathrow, right? Only the Frenchies wouldn't let us leave."

Tess blinked. "What?"

"That's right. They wouldn't let us leave the airport to go to Orly airport where we could catch the London flight because we didn't have French visas. After about five hours, I was starting to wonder if I was going to spend the rest of my life in De Gaulle airport."

Tess looked at Jack. He looked at her.

"Do you suppose they wound up in France by accident?" Jack asked.

"Hell, no, it wasn't an accident," Mr. Castor said firmly. "They knew they were flying into De Gaulle. That damn airline . . . beats me why they lied to us and said it was another flight to London."

"It would explain what Mother meant when she said they were trying to catch a flight home."

"Hmm," Jack said, and nodded thoughtfully.

"Of course," Tess added, "we don't know that this happened in France."

"Of course it happened in France," snapped Mr. Castor. "I know where I was. I'm not stupid."

"No, no," Tess hastened to say to him. "We don't think you're stupid, Mr. Castor. We weren't talking about you. We were talking about Steve and Brigitte."

"They got trapped in France, too?"

"We don't know."

"Can't imagine why anybody would buy shorts and sundresses for France at this time of year."

Tess's heart skipped a beat. "Who bought shorts and sundresses?"

"Brigitte, of course," he said irritably. "Who else? Like she didn't already have enough, living here. But she showed them all off to my wife."

"When was that?"

He shrugged. "Three weeks ago? Two? I don't exactly remember. Whole damn wardrobe. My Belle started whining she wanted some new clothes, too. That damn fashion show cost me nearly four hundred dollars. And we weren't even going anywhere."

Jack gave Tess a long-suffering look. "Mr. Castor, did Brigitte say they were taking a trip?"

The older man blinked. "Why else would she buy all those clothes?"

"But did she *tell* you that?"

Mr. Castor frowned thoughtfully. "I don't remember if she exactly said it or if Belle said it."

"Mrs. Niedelmeyer said they didn't tell her they were going away, and that they've been missing for a week now."

"Mrs. Niedelmeyer?" Castor shook his head. "Now she thinks everyone should check in with her before they go somewhere?"

Tess found herself clenching her teeth. Getting information out of Mr. Castor was proving to be extremely frustrating. "Mr. Castor, do you have any idea at all where they might have gone?"

"I thought to the beach. You mean they're not home from their trip yet?"

Tess smothered a sigh. "That's it. They're not home from their trip. Did Belle or Brigitte say where they were going?"

"Belle ain't going nowhere."

Tess couldn't bring herself to ask again, for fear she would bite the man's head off.

"Mr. Castor," said Jack, evidently reading Tess's mood correctly, "can you tell us, please, if Brigitte mentioned where she and Steve might be taking a vacation?"

"Not to me."

Tess felt her heart sink.

"But I'll tell you one thing: I'm sure getting sick of Belle asking me why we can't go to the Caribbean, too."

*   *   *

"Man," said Jack when they got back to the house, "was that a fractured conversation!"

"But we found something out, Jack," Tess said excitedly. "We know where they went."

"Do we?" He headed toward the kitchen.

"We know they went to the Caribbean," she said, trotting after him. "That's good."

"Well, it does eliminate Majorca, South Africa, Australia, Hawaii, and a few other places." He started pulling food items out of the pantry: a jar of Alfredo sauce, a box of fettuccine. "Do you make a good salad?"

"The best." She sighed impatiently. "We've eliminated a whole lot of the world. That's a good thing."

"Sure." He put the jar and box on the kitchen island. "Tess, have you looked at a map lately? Do you have any idea how many islands are in the Caribbean?"

"A few."

"A few? You must be thinking of the ones you see advertised on travel posters. Let me tell you, there's a lot more than a few. Not just St. Croix or Barbados, but little islands, all the way down to Ted's Very Excellent Island and Bob's Best Sandbar."

"Are you always such a pessimist?"

"I'm a realist, plain and simple."

"But this still narrows our search. Besides, they wouldn't have gone to—what did you call it?—Ted's Very Excellent Island. They would have gone someplace really nice. St. Croix. Martinique."

"Martinique is in the process of blowing up. Volcano."

"Oh. Well, you know what I mean."

"I also know my father. Your mother might prefer St. Croix, but my father would prefer Bob's Sandbar. He likes to really get away from it all."

She hadn't thought of that, and she could feel her excitement waning. "You're depressing."

"No," he repeated, "I'm a realist. Saying they're in the Caribbean is about as helpful as saying they're in Europe."

"But at least we know they couldn't be in too much trouble."

He opened his mouth, then sighed and shook his head. Without another word he went to the refrigerator and started pulling out the makings for salad. "This lettuce doesn't look too old," he muttered. "But I'm surprised they left it."

"Why?"

"I never leave fresh vegetables in my refrigerator if I'm planning to be gone more than a couple of days." As soon as he spoke, he straightened up. "Shit."

"What?"

"They were only planning to be gone for a couple of days."

Tess felt her heart hammer. "No. No, Mom's always been sloppy about that. She probably just forgot." She refused to believe otherwise. "And why didn't you answer me when I said they couldn't be in any serious trouble?"

He hesitated, then put the lettuce on the counter and rooted around for a tomato and some green pepper. "Let's just say the Caribbean isn't entirely without its hazards."

"But tourists go there all the time!"

"Right. And when does being a tourist destination make a place immune to crime?"

She flushed, and feeling embarrassed only made her more annoyed with him. "What I mean is, if there was any trouble they would have let someone know. Or the authorities would have."

"Depends."

"Depends on what?"

"What happened to them."

Frustration surged in her like a horse at the starting gate. "Will you please stop being so damn elliptical?"

He paused, a cucumber in his hand. "Do I look like an ellipse?"

She wanted to beat him over the head with that cucumber he was holding. He offered it to her, and that so closely paralleled her thoughts that she stared almost blankly at it.

"This feels soft to me," he said. "What do you think?"

She snatched it from his hand. "It's okay," she said, tossing it on the counter. "Will you just answer me?"

"No need to get bent, Tess."

"I'm not getting bent."

"You look like a pretzel to me." She started to

erupt, but he waved his hand, silencing her. "Spare me—I already know all the names you want to call me. Listen, the Caribbean, like any place, has its set of problems. Depending on where they went, and whether they were staying at some fancy hotel, or whether they were sailing—"

"Sailing?"

"Dad loves to sail. He might have rented a boat."

She hadn't even thought of that. "They could have drowned at sea!"

He sighed and shut the refrigerator door. "Calm down, Tess. Let's not get any more hysterical than we need to."

"What is your father doing, taking my mother out on a boat? She doesn't swim!"

"We don't know they went out on a boat." He snapped his fingers in front of her eyes. "Reality, Tess. Get in touch with it. We don't know anything except that they *may* have gone somewhere in the Caribbean. Considering that covers dozens of islands and the coasts of Venezuela and Colombia, right now we don't know a hell of a lot."

Tess reached out blindly for a dinette chair and pulled it out, plopping down on it. "I think I'm going to be sick."

"Why? Nothing's changed. Nothing's any worse than it was."

"Quit being so reasonable."

He flashed a weary grin. "Buck up, Shorty. Their bodies haven't been found yet."

"Why, you . . ." She spluttered as words failed

her. For an instant he looked as if he were going to laugh, but then he sobered and leaned over so he was looking her directly in the eye.

"I'm psychic," he said.

Startled, she wasn't sure she understood him. "What?"

"I'm psychic. And I can tell you right now, if they were dead I'd know it."

"Well, if you're so damn psychic, Mr. Realist, then how come you don't know where the hell they are?"

Feeling angry, sick, and more frightened than she'd ever been in her life, except when her parents had divorced, Tess got up and stormed out of the kitchen.

Well, he'd certainly blown that, Jack thought. Giving himself a mental kick in the butt, he poured the Alfredo sauce into a glass casserole dish and put it in the microwave. Then he filled the pasta cooker with water and set it on the stove. A little oil, a little salt, and he turned on the burner.

Next he set about chopping the lettuce. He knew you were supposed to tear it—Brigitte had certainly advised him of that enough times—but chopping it on the big cutting board allowed him to vent some of his frustration.

He *was* a realist, but he didn't want to upset Tess needlessly. Besides, if he started talking too much about the Caribbean that he knew, a Caribbean most tourists rarely came in contact with, she'd start asking questions he couldn't answer.

So what now? By saying their bodies hadn't been found yet, he'd intended to get her to avoid catastrophizing, but she hadn't taken it that way. Though when did Tess ever take anything the way he expected her to? They always seemed to come at everything from ninety-degree angles. He didn't know which of them was skewed; maybe they both were. Maybe neither of them was wholly normal.

He could believe that. Normal people didn't do what he did for a living. Normal people didn't become IRS auditors. At least not those *he* would consider normal.

The thought made him smile faintly and he stopped butchering the lettuce. He scraped it into a large salad bowl, then washed and sliced a tomato.

Okay, so the parental units were missing in the Caribbean. Probably. He had to admit, that wasn't so bad, from their current perspective. They at least had a geographical area to look at. And where there was life there was hope, and all that. He'd lived on the edge long enough to know.

But Tess had led a relatively sheltered life, and he needed to keep that in mind. The crimes she was familiar with involved numbers on ledger sheets, not murder and mayhem.

Besides, he was every bit as worried about their parents as she was. Maybe more so, because he knew things she probably didn't. Like there were still pirates in the Caribbean. They weren't hunting Spanish treasure ships these days, but they were hunting boats that could be used to transport drugs. And, of course, there were the more ordinary sorts of criminals, the lowlifes who would kill for the dollars in a man's wallet.

On most of the islands they might have gone to, they'd be relatively sheltered from that. But what if they'd gone to Barranquilla or Cartagena in Colombia? Life could become very uncertain there.

Shit. He dumped the tomato in the salad bowl and began to peel and slice the cucumber. Maybe he needed to get in touch with some of his friends, suggest they put their ears to the ground. A couple of tourists among many other tourists at this time of year might be difficult to locate. Then again, they might not.

When the cucumber was in the salad bowl, he decided to go roust Tess from wherever she'd gone into hiding. This whole situation between them was ridiculous. They were adults, and right now they had a common concern: finding Steve and Brigitte.

At thirty and thirty-six, respectively, they ought to be able to be mature about this. So maybe his humor was unappreciated. Maybe she didn't like him making jokes when they had a reason to be worried. Maybe she needed to know that humor was all that kept your sanity while life was going to hell in a handbasket. But explanations aside, they needed to stop acting like a couple of squabbling kids.

He decided to get the ball rolling. He went down the hall to her bedroom, hammered on her door, and asked, "Shorty? Are you ready to act like a grown-up?"

4

*T*ess virtually levitated off her bed as fury filled her. Was *she* ready to act like a grown-up?

Her feet hit the floor and she stormed across the room, flinging the door open so hard it banged against the stop with a thud. "Am *I* ready to act like a grown-up? Am *I*?"

He looked startled, then held up his hands as if telling her to calm down. "I guess I phrased that rather poorly."

"More than a little poorly, you unemployed waste of humanity."

"Waste of humanity?" He appeared struck by that. "Jeez, Tess."

She flushed, suddenly feeling a little embarrassed despite her anger. "All right, maybe that was too strong. But you're still annoying, impossible, and too full of yourself."

"Well, I can live with that. It's pretty much true." He flashed a grin. "Now listen, I didn't mean to set your dander up. I was talking about both of us. We need to stop fighting and squabbling and start acting like mature adults. You don't have to like me, and I don't have to like you, but we can still behave in a civilized fashion toward each other."

"Civilized?" She looked him over, as if convinced he couldn't have a civilized bone in his body. "That word doesn't have too many syllables for you?"

"Oh, Christ!" He threw up his hands in disgust. "You can't quit for five minutes, can you? Ever since my father stole your mother—"

"Wait a minute! What do you mean, your father stole my mother? From whom?"

He absolutely froze for a second or two. Then he said, "I didn't mean anything. Poor choice of words."

"Was my mother having an affair with your father *before* she left my dad?"

He scowled. "What do I look like? The Oracle at Delphi? Hell, I don't know. The first I heard about anything was when my dad said he was getting married again. And the only thing I remember about that was meeting you two for the first time, and thinking Brigitte was too French and you were too snotty. Anything that came before that isn't in my memory banks."

Tess nodded slowly, her anger forgotten as she

remembered those days. "I always wondered why she left my dad. They never even fought."

"Hey," he said, his voice becoming gentle. "That's a bad sign, them never fighting."

"It is?"

"Sure. It means neither of them felt any passion."

She looked at him, cocking her head at an angle that said she didn't quite believe him but wasn't prepared to argue the point.

"Come on," he said. "Let's go put the pasta in the water before it all boils away. I pretty much made the salad, but I left the seasonings to you."

She followed him, probably because she couldn't think of any reason not to. And she *was* starting to get hungry, as her stomach reminded her that the only thing she'd eaten in the past twenty-four hours was the bag of nuts that the airline doled out.

"Look," he said when they got to the kitchen, "we need to stop disagreeing over every little thing."

"I agree."

"Good."

"We have a basic personality conflict. No reason we can't deal with it."

"Right. We'll work on it."

She looked into the salad bowl. "What did you do to the lettuce? It looks like it was beaten to death."

He looked over her shoulder. "So I cut it instead of tearing it. No big deal. It doesn't change the taste."

"But it's all mangled!"

He muttered an oath under his breath. "You're making it really hard to be civilized and mature."

"Why? I'm just saying the lettuce looks mangled."

"That's insulting."

"It certainly is, to the lettuce."

"It's insulting to *me*. I cut it."

"Chopped it."

"All right, so I chopped it." And he was getting more irritated by the instant, which hadn't been his intention at all.

She lifted a piece of lettuce from the bowl and, much as he hated to, he had to admit that it did indeed look mangled. "Well, okay," he said finally. "It looks a tad bruised."

She arched one eyebrow. "A tad?"

"It's all your fault. You made me mad."

"Mad, huh?" She dropped the lettuce back in the bowl. "That's no excuse to mangle the poor lettuce."

"I didn't mangle it. But if you can't handle it, throw it away. I'll make frozen broccoli."

"That would be wasteful."

"Then enough about the mangling, already!" What had happened to his resolution to be an adult about all this? In two minutes flat, she had him ready to stuff a gag into her mouth.

And her expression said she knew it. She had an almost satisfied look to her, as if she knew she had proved all his talk about being civilized to be a sham.

Well, he'd be damned if he was going to give her that satisfaction. Through his teeth, he said pleasantly, "Really, if you feel I ruined the salad, I'll be happy to make something else."

She blinked, and her expression shifted subtly, to something less satisfied. After a moment she sighed and said quietly, "You didn't really mangle it. I'm sure it's fine."

It seemed to him that she was giving in too easily—and that she was . . . on the edge of tears? Cautiously, he stepped a little closer.

"I was . . ." She paused and drew a deep breath. "I was thinking about Brigitte. That was pretty much what she said to me the first time I made a salad for her."

"I *thought* you sounded like your mother for a minute there." Then he had a thought. "Uh . . . how old were you when you made that salad for her?"

"I'm not sure. Eight, maybe?"

"And she talked to you like *that*?" He suddenly felt a great deal of sympathy for Tess, a feeling that made him very uncomfortable.

"Well, you know Brigitte," she said with a little shrug and a crooked smile. "She's passionate. Extreme. She might accuse me of being the Texas Chainsaw Murderer of lettuce, but she would turn around and tell me how much she loved me with exactly the same amount of passion and extremity. So it kind of balanced."

"Yeah." But somehow he didn't believe it. He didn't know a damn thing about raising kids, but he knew something about people. In his experience, people took negatives so much to heart that you really didn't need to get down on them very hard. The positives, however . . . for some damn reason, the positives were a whole lot harder to believe.

"Anyway," she said, visibly shaking herself, "the salad's fine. Do you have any problem with garlic?"

"I love it."

"Great. I'll make a dressing."

He dumped the fettuccine in the boiling water and turned on the microwave to heat the Alfredo sauce. Then he watched Tess as she made the salad dressing in a measuring cup, mixing herbs and seasonings together in olive oil and wine vinegar. He'd watched Brigitte do this many times and no matter how hard Tess tried not to be like her mother, they had the same way of moving. And the same wide blue eyes.

"Sometimes," Tess remarked suddenly, "I feel as if my mother is taking over my body. I move a certain way, or say a certain thing, and . . . I feel like my mother."

She looked up from the dressing she was mixing, and he saw the shimmer of tears on her lower lashes. He came across the kitchen and around the island in a shot.

"We'll find her, Tess. We'll find both of them. This is probably some kind of cosmic misunderstanding."

She nodded. A silvery tear trembled and fell off her eyelash, rolling down her cheek. He couldn't help himself. Reaching out, he wrapped her in his arms and held her close.

And found himself feeling a lot of things he really didn't want to feel for this annoying woman. He didn't want to feel protective. He didn't want to notice how nicely she fitted against him, or how soft her breasts were. But the feelings got through to him anyway, making him feel guilty but good all at once.

"Look," he said as he stroked her hair, "if anything bad had happened to them, I'm sure we would have heard. I called the State Department yesterday and asked if they had any information about them. They hadn't heard a peep, but they promised to call me if they did. Which means they probably aren't in any kind of serious trouble, Tess. Even if they were kidnapped by guerrillas or something, sooner or later someone would have to demand ransom."

She nodded against his shoulder. "Basically what you're saying is, no news is good news."

"In this instance, yes."

She nodded again. "Okay. I'll try to remember that."

"So will I. It might make me easier to live with."

She gave a shaky little laugh and stepped back. "Yeah. Me, too."

The truce continued through dinner, which wasn't really much of a major accomplishment, because neither of them seemed to have much to say. For that matter, neither of them seemed particularly hungry. They were eating for fuel and nothing else.

After they cleaned up, though, time was heavy on their hands. Tess paced the entire house, up and down the hallway, around the living room, through the kitchen, across the foyer, and into the study.

"Uh, Tess?" Jack said finally.

"Hmm?"

"I'm getting dizzy watching you." She paused to look at him, and he was enchanted to see a blush creep into her cheeks.

"Sorry," she said. "I'm too nervous to hold still."

"If you ask me, you're overtired. Come on, let's take a walk outside. The heat will probably help relax you."

She was of the opinion that the heat would simply irritate her. However, she needed to keep moving, and watching someone pace *was* irritating.

The sun had set while they were eating, but Paradise Beach was well lit. They strolled toward the boulevard and all the brightly lit shops that were still open, catering to tourists.

She thought they would just go past the shops, but Jack had other ideas. "Come on," he said. "I've always wanted to see if these places are as tacky from the inside as they look from out here."

So she followed him into a T-shirt shop. The place was brightly lit, with tubes of neon swirling in every direction, all the better to illuminate rows of garish T-shirts, some of which should have been sold in plain brown wrappers.

"Not exactly a family shop," Jack remarked, eyeing a white T-shirt that displayed a naked female torso.

"No, it's not." Tess kept moving deeper into the shop, wondering if they sold anything else. Behind the T-shirts, she found bathing suits, mostly thong bikinis and Speedos. Some snorkeling equipment, seashells and sand dollars that had been painted garish colors, and, unmistakably . . .

"Bongs," she said.

Jack arched a brow at her. "How is it you're acquainted with bongs? You don't do that stuff, do you?"

"Absolutely not. Unfortunately, I had a college roommate who did. I'm surprised it's legal to sell those things."

"Water pipes can be used for things other than illegal drugs. There are places in this world where tobacco is smoked that way."

Tess headed for the door. "Not my kind of place," she said.

"Somehow I didn't think it was."

"Is it *your* kind of place?" she asked, looking up at him.

"Not exactly."

But something about the way he said it roused her suspicions again. A beach bum probably *did* use illegal substances from time to time. It fit the image.

What a waste. This time the thought held more sadness than accusation.

Suddenly Jack grabbed her hand and yanked her into the dark passageway between two buildings.

"Jack, what—"

"Shhh." He laid his fingers across her lips and pressed her back against the wall until he was leaning into her. She might have thought he had designs on her, except that he was looking back out to the street.

"What—"

His fingers pressed harder on her mouth, silencing her again. Annoyed, she bit him.

"Ow!" He jumped back. "What the hell did you do that for?"

"I don't like being crushed against walls and having a hand over my mouth."

"I didn't have a hand over your mouth!"

"Yes, you did."

"Two fingers. Just two fingers."

"Same thing." She brushed herself off and headed for the street. "I've had enough. Manhandling is not high on my list of pleasurable experiences."

"That's just because you haven't been properly manhandled."

The words froze her in her tracks. Not because they angered her, but because they sent incredibly warm trickles of pleasure running through her until her knees felt weak. This could not possibly be happening, she told herself. She could *not* be getting aroused because he'd said she'd never been properly manhandled. That just wasn't possible.

The strength poured into her legs as suddenly as it had left, and she turned to face him, ready to give him hell.

But he was waving her to silence, and something about the expression on his face caused her to bite back her words.

Lowering her voice, she asked, "What's going on?"

"Somebody I used to know in Miami. Not someone I care to see again."

Curious, she turned to look, but before she could decide which of the passing tourists he was referring to, he caught her hand and tugged her deeper into the shadows. Pressed between him and the wall again, this time she didn't feel quite so annoyed.

"What kind of people do you hang out with?" she asked in a whisper.

"The kind you wouldn't approve of," he replied.

It was amazing, how disappointed you could be to have your worst suspicions confirmed. "You know," she murmured after a few moments, "you can always turn your life around."

His head whipped around and he looked down at her with astonishment. After a few moments, he said, "I can *what*?"

"Turn your life around," she said. "It's never too late."

"Really." He stepped back until there was a foot of space between them, a distance that suddenly felt like miles to Tess. "You really mean that."

"Of course I do."

He nodded slowly, but the expression on his face disturbed her. She had the distinct impression that he wasn't taking what she said in quite the right way.

"I gather from this," he continued deliberately, "that all the insults you've been flinging my way—well, you weren't just saying them to annoy me. You were saying them because you believe they're true."

She could feel a flush stinging her cheeks, and hoped it was too dark for him to see it. "I wouldn't exactly say that."

"Really. Well, you know what, Shorty? I don't especially care to hear what you *would* exactly say. And if it weren't so damn dark, I'd let you walk yourself home."

Suddenly she was flaming mad at him. "What are you talking about, Jack? I was trying to say something nice to you."

"Telling someone they can turn their life around is hardly a compliment. Come on. The sooner I get you home, the sooner I can get out of your hair."

"Don't bother. I'll take myself home."

He was suddenly towering over her, and something in his eyes frightened her. "Look, Tess," he said between his teeth, "whatever kind of scum you may think I am, I am *not* scum enough to allow a woman to walk alone down this boulevard after dark. Got it?"

Then, before she could say a word, he had tucked her arm through his and was hurrying her toward the street and back toward the house.

He was certainly overreacting, Tess thought. The street was crowded with tourists. Other than the possibility of having her purse snatched, she wasn't at any risk at all.

"You know," she remarked as he kept them moving at a breathless pace, "I walk myself home at night in Chicago. I know how to avoid trouble."

He looked down at her. "No, you've just been lucky, Tess."

"What do you mean?"

"You obviously *don't* know how to avoid trouble."

She was about to argue when she realized that would probably only make him angrier. Though what he was angry about to begin with still escaped her. She'd said something well intentioned, and he'd utterly misunderstood her.

Or maybe not. When they reached the house, it was just beginning to dawn on her how her words might have been mistaken. He paused just long enough to see her safely inside the door, then he took off again.

"Where are you going?" she called after him.

"Back to my element," he said scathingly. "Time to go hang out with some lowlifes and scum."

Tess closed the door and locked it, then stood in the foyer for a while trying to figure out what she could do to mend this rift.

Because the simple truth was, it hurt to have Jack mad at her. She'd never felt that way before, and the notion terrified her. She had never cared what Jack thought of her, and she wasn't about to begin caring now. No way.

Pushing such thoughts aside, she forced herself go to the kitchen and prepare a pot of tea for herself.

The important thing, she told herself as the tea steeped, was to focus on Steve and Brigitte's disappearance. She couldn't let concerns about Jack get in the way of that.

Carrying a cup of tea into the study, she got down the big atlas and opened it to the map of the Caribbean. Jack was right: there were an awful lot of islands, many of them too small to be named, at least on this map. And it wouldn't surprise her to discover that there were others too small to even be dots on this map.

But if Steve and Brigitte had gone to the Caribbean, there was certainly no reason to believe they would have gone to some island like that. Jack might believe that his father would go to Bob's Sandbar, but that wasn't Brigitte's style at all.

However, Brigitte's preferences weren't a whole lot of help. Most of the major islands were names she recognized as tourist destinations, from Grand Cayman to St. Kitts. That was hardly any way to narrow the search. And Jack was wrong: it wasn't Martinique that was having the volcano problem, it was Montserrat. Which didn't really help narrow the field much, either.

Closing the atlas, she put her chin in her hand and closed her eyes, focusing every ounce of her attention on the problem.

Her mother had phoned to say they were trying to get a flight home. It was a rather odd message for Brigitte to leave, which was what had given her the first niggles of uneasiness.

She'd called immediately, and when she got her parents' answering machine, she'd left a message for them to call her, figuring they were now home but out for the evening. But they hadn't called her back. And when another twenty-four hours had passed, she'd been forced to conclude that they'd never gotten that flight home that Brigitte had called about. At that point, uneasiness had become full-blown panic.

But going back to the message—it hadn't been a Brigitte-like message. It had been brief. It had been suspiciously lacking in information. Brigitte never told anyone anything without covering every single detail and making at least a dozen digressions—even on an answering machine.

So something had been wrong even when Brigitte called. She had been lying, whether because someone was forcing her or because she wanted to. And either was possible with Brigitte.

She'd been assuming that something was going on, something out of Brigitte's control. But that wasn't necessarily the case, and the more she thought about that brief phone message, the more convinced she became that there was something truly fishy going on here.

But what? What possible reason could her

mother have had to leave that message?

Tess was still wondering when Jack came home.

And he wasn't alone.

5

The man who came into the study on Jack's heels was small, with dark eyes that kept darting around as if seeking escape. He wore a garish palm tree shirt and baggy shorts that came below his knees, and his hairy feet poked out of battered sandals.

"Hey, nice place ya got here," he said to Jack. "Didn't know you could afford this. You on the take?"

"Shut up, Ernesto."

Tess, who had risen, backed away from the two of them. "I'll just excuse myself—" she started to say, but Jack interrupted her.

"Hey, hold your horses," he said, a strange glitter in his eyes. "Don't you want to meet some of my scummy friends?"

"Friends?" Ernesto asked, taking exception.

"Hey, man, you ain't no friend of mine."

Jack shrugged to Tess, as if to say, *What can you do?*

Tess, however, was still easing toward the door. "Have a nice time with your friend," she said.

Jack looked at Ernesto. "Hey, man, *she* thinks I'm your friend."

Ernesto sniffed. "I got better taste than that. This guy's no friend of mine, lady. Wish I'd never met him. So if you don't mind, I'll leave right now."

Jack caught him by the collar of his shirt as he passed by. "Not so fast, Ernesto. We got business to discuss. Tess, quit creeping away and take a seat. Now."

Something in his tone made her scuttle back to her chair, as far as she could get from Ernesto, who reminded her of something she would rather scrape off her shoe.

"What business?" Ernesto said. "I'm clean, man. I did my time, and that was enough for me."

"Yeah, I've heard that before." Jack perched on the edge of the desk and folded his arms. "So why aren't you in Miami?"

"Because I'm on vacation."

"Yeah? You?"

"Yeah, me," Ernesto said, scowling. "What's so hard to believe? I work hard. I got me a job. I get two weeks a year like every other working stiff."

"Yeah?"

"Yeah."

"I don't know," Jack said. He glanced at Tess. "Do you believe him?"

"Me?" Feeling flummoxed, she looked at Ernesto. "Why wouldn't I believe him?"

"See?" Ernesto said. "*She* believes me. Look, man, I'm here to spend some time on the beach. I told you that, plain and simple. You don't believe me, that's *your* problem."

"But I can make it *your* problem."

Tess looked at Jack with surprise. He sounded positively menacing. And Ernesto didn't exactly seem shocked by it, so apparently Jack could be menacing quite often. She wasn't certain how she felt about that.

"Yeah, yeah," said Ernesto, clearly not as impressed as she was by the threat. "What you gonna do, man? You gonna get awful bored watching me build sand castles with the kid."

"That *would* be boring to watch," Tess agreed.

Jack rolled his eyes, but Ernesto turned to her. "Hey, it's boring enough to do. But when you got kids it's what you do. I do a lot of boring things these days. Change diapers. Take long walks so the kid gets enough fresh air. Hell, I even play with blocks."

Tess nodded. "But don't you enjoy it, playing with your child?"

"Well," Ernesto said, "yeah, I guess I do. I mean, it sounds so dumb, but when you're doing it with the kid . . . it's different."

Jack made a disgusted sound. "Could we skip the child study group meeting?"

Tess frowned at him. "Why? You brought this man home with you. Surely we should be sociable."

"Sociable? With *him*?"

"What's wrong with him?"

Ernesto leaned over and confided, "You don't want to know. Besides, he's right. This ain't no social call."

Jack faced him. "Nobody sent you here?"

"Sent me?" Ernest jumped to his feet. "Yeah, man, my *wife* sent me. She'd been whining for years to come here to swim. I tell her she can swim at Miami Beach, but she says this is different. So, yeah, I guess you could say I was sent. But if you asked me, I was dragged. Woulda been a whole lot cheaper to stay in Miami."

"So you don't know anything about Steve and Brigitte Wright?"

"They dealing? I don't have nothing to do with that anymore. You want to nail those two, you gonna have to get somebody else to cooperate. I ain't even on probation anymore, man. I don't gotta do nothing for no one."

Ernesto turned to Tess. "Hey, what you got goin' with this dude? He's trouble, big time. Best advice I can give anybody is don't know Jack."

Suddenly laughing like a braying mule, he started heading toward the door. This time Jack didn't stop him, but he called after him, "You hear anything about Steve and Brigitte, you let me know right away."

"Yeah, yeah, yeah," Ernie said. A moment later the door closed behind him.

Tess looked at Jack. "Who was that and what was that all about?"

"Ernesto? He's one of my old acquaintances. Has kind of a big grudge against me."

Tess let herself absorb that. "You think he might have done something to Brigitte and Steve?"

"I thought there was a remote possibility he might have heard something about it if . . . former enemies of mine were involved in some way."

Tess felt something inside her shrink even more. "You have . . . enemies who would . . . kidnap people?"

"Hell, Shorty, I know people who would kill for a dime. And some of 'em, right now, are looking for our parents."

Tess gasped.

"To *help* them. I'm owed a few favors."

Finding their parents was paramount, of course, but Tess wasn't sure she wanted to deal with people who would kill for a dime.

She looked up at Jack, about to say so, but something in his face silenced her. He wasn't the same Jack she'd been playfully squabbling with a few hours ago. This Jack frightened her. He looked old, and very, very hard. As if a veneer had been stripped away, leaving only his hardness behind.

"See, Shorty?" he said after a moment. "You ought to be careful what you wish for."

A moment later he was gone. Thirty seconds after that, she heard his bedroom door close.

She hadn't wished for this, she thought. She had feared it, but she hadn't wished for this.

And the glimpse of the man behind Jack's lazy, easygoing facade had not only frightened her, it had touched her somewhere deep inside, opening a wellspring of sympathy she didn't want to feel.

Jack Wright was hurting. And Tess would have been a lot happier if she hadn't learned that.

"I hate mornings." Tess muttered the words as she filled the coffeepot and tried not to notice the golden sunshine pouring through the kitchen windows. Back home in Chicago it would have been gray, still nearly dark. Here it was just too damn cheerful to stand.

Another glance out the windows showed her palm trees tossing gently in the early breeze. A glance to her left gave her a view out the sliding doors across the balcony into the morning blue of the Gulf of Mexico. Entirely too pretty, she thought sourly. And the damn coffee couldn't be ready soon enough.

Just then, Jack sauntered into the room. Well, he almost sauntered—he wasn't looking quite as chipper as usual. In fact, there were huge circles under his eyes. He apparently had slept even more poorly than she had.

"Morning," she said, refusing to say *good*. Because it wasn't.

He grunted. "Paper?"

"We're not getting one. They must have stopped it."

"Mm."

"I'll go to the corner and get one from the machine."

He shook his head. "Coffee?"

She glanced at the pot. "Five minutes."

"Mm." He scratched his unshaven cheek and left the kitchen. A minute later she heard the front door close behind him. He must have gone to get the paper.

He seemed to be even less communicative than she was in the morning.

Just about the time the coffeemaker blew its last blast of steam, signifying it was done, Jack strolled back in with the newspaper. He tossed it on the island, giving her a clear view of GET OUT!, a headline she couldn't ignore. A closer look revealed that "Evacuations have been ordered in the bay area as Hurricane Gaspar bears down on . . ."

She looked up and found Jake nursing a mug of coffee and regarding her glumly. She spoke. "That's us."

"Yup."

"We need to evacuate?"

"Not yet. We're not in the zone. But I guess we need to board the windows."

She looked down at the article again. "It's not a really bad hurricane. Category one."

"Bad enough. We need to protect the house for Mom and Dad."

"I know. I'm just trying to put this in as positive a light as I can. Jeez." What she actually wanted to do was sit down and cry. They didn't even know where their parents were, but they were going to board up their house to protect it? What was wrong with this picture?

Suddenly she looked up at Jack. "Where *are* they?"

"I wish I knew." He pulled out a stool and sat facing her at the island. "To tell you the truth, Shorty, I'm starting to get really irritated."

"Irritated?"

"You bet. Where do they get off, taking a trip without telling anyone where they were going?"

She nodded. "They don't usually do that."

"Exactly. I could forgive them if they were usually this thoughtless. But they're usually exactly the opposite. Cripes, I've gotten photocopies of their itineraries over the years, complete with phone numbers at every stop."

"Me, too."

"Which makes this too weird. That's why I was hassling Ernesto last night. Because I'm having a hard time believing those two went off on a scheduled trip without telling anyone."

Tess drew a sharp breath. "You think Ernesto kidnapped them?"

"Not likely—Ernesto is a nobody. He doesn't think that big. But I thought he might have heard something. His being here was just too suspicious for me."

"Because you know him, you mean?"

"Well, I sort of know him. I wouldn't say we

were close. In fact, I think he'd kill me, if he had the guts."

"You know," Tess said after a few moments, "I find myself wondering why I am sharing the same roof with you."

His expression became disgusted. "If you're afraid you'll get corrupted by breathing the same air, maybe you should move to a hotel."

"No, maybe *you* should. Especially if you're going to consort with types like Ernesto."

"I wasn't consorting with him, I was trying to question him. *You* were the one consorting with him, with all that talk about playing with babies. Sounded like a damn tea party."

"I was just being polite."

"Some people you don't have to be polite to. Ernesto is one of them."

"Just what is wrong with the man?"

"He's scum. An ex-con. A former penny-ante drug dealer."

"Oh." She pursed her lips disapprovingly. "Well, that's quite a character recommendation."

He shrugged.

"No, I meant for you."

"Me?"

"Yes, you. It says quite a bit that you know a man like that."

A thunderous look settled on his face. "It also says a lot that I know an uptight Victorian princess like you. And let me remind you, Miss Prim and Proper, that you don't know a damn thing about me."

He rose and stalked toward the door.

"And whose fault is that, may I ask?" she called after him, unwilling to let him have the last word.

He stunned her by turning around and glaring at her. "Yours," he said.

And then, damn him, he disappeared before she could say another word.

There was plywood in the garage. Hardly surprising, Jack thought. Steve had boarded up this house a number of times over the years in just such circumstances. A quick count told him he had all he needed.

Pulling it out piece by piece, he began to match the plywood sheets to the windows they were sized for, laying them on the ground around the house until he was ready to nail them up. Overhead, the sunny morning was giving way to low, racing arcs of clouds that said the storm was near.

As hurricanes went, a category one was nothing to write home about. A little worse than a tropical storm, causing some minor wind damage, some flooding, some power outages. Hardly panic time. Since the house was far enough from the water and high enough on a dune, they wouldn't even have to fear flooding from this storm.

He was laying out the last few pieces of plywood alongside the house when the next-door neighbor, Maudeen Mason, turned up. She was wearing bright orange shorts and a mauve top, and a pair of sunglasses that were encrusted with rhinestones. Jack tried to avoid looking at her for fear he would be blinded.

"Jack!" she said. "I didn't know you were here. Are Steve and Brigitte back yet?"

"Uh, no, they're not." He dropped the last piece of plywood on the grass and wiped his brow. "You wouldn't have any idea when they're due, would you?"

She shook her head. " 'Fraid not. They didn't happen to say. It *does* seem like they've been gone a long time, though."

"Did they say where they were going?"

"You mean they didn't tell you?" Maudeen clucked and shook her head. "What is the world coming to?"

Jack restrained a sudden sense of impatience. "I'm not really worried about the world at the moment. I'm kind of worried about my parents, though."

"Well, wherever they are, at least Gaspar can't be bearing down on them. They're probably worrying about *us*."

Jack restrained a sigh. "They *could* pick up a phone and call."

"Well, yes." Maudeen blinked, as if she didn't entirely understand what they were talking about. Which was hardly surprising, since Jack didn't, either.

"So you don't know anything about this vacation they took?"

Maudeen shook her head. "Didn't even see them leave. But I did get a postcard from them."

Jack was suddenly all ears. "Really? Can I see it?"

Maudeen shook her head. "I threw it away. At my age you find you can't afford to keep such things anymore. You'd be drowning in old letters and postcards."

Forcing himself to remain calm, Jack said, "When did you get it?"

"The postcard? Oh . . . a week ago? I'm not sure. Maybe it was three or four days ago."

Jack ground his teeth. "Where was it from?"

Much to his surprise, Maudeen Mason began to look confused, and even a little frightened. "Umm . . ." She looked away, and even took a step back. "I can't . . . I don't . . . that's it," she said. "I don't remember!" Somehow she looked pleased by that fact.

Odd suspicion began to rise in Jack. "You can't remember anything at all about it?"

She took another step backward. "You should talk to Mary Todd," she said. "Yes, that's it. You need to talk to Mary."

"Why Mary?"

"Because she knows *everything*." At this point, Maudeen Mason was in full flight across her yard. When she reached her front step, however, she peered back around the shrub and said, "Would you mind helping me cover my windows, too?"

"Sure. When I get done with this."

"Thank you!" She disappeared inside, and Jack stood staring after her, wondering what she was up to.

"Something wrong?"

Tess's voice made him spin around. "No, nothing."

"You look so lost in thought."

"I was. Sorry."

She shook her head, and he noticed the way her dark hair trailed across her cheeks and shoulders. An errant thought wandered through his brain. Was her hair as silky as it looked? And was her skin as satiny as it appeared?

"No need to apologize." She gave him an almost shy smile. "I came to see if I can help put up the plywood."

"That would be great." He was willing to accept the olive branch, even if it came without an apology. Wrestling these sheets of plywood into place while he drove screws would be much faster with her help. Without it, he'd still be trying to do it when the hurricane hit.

"Better get yourself some gloves from the garage," he said, looking at her small hands. "You don't want splinters."

And he didn't want to see those soft hands roughened up. Good grief, what was wrong with him? Why was his brain short-circuiting? He didn't want to see Tess this way. Ever. Not now, not next week, not *ever*.

Following her back to the garage, he refused to look at the way her hips swayed in those white shorts she was wearing, refused to notice how smooth and shapely her calves were. Instead he turned his attention to getting the drill and selecting the bit that would fit the bolts that were already screwed into the concrete around the windows. Since Steve generally had to put up plywood at least once a year, he'd left the bolts screwed into the house for handy use every time. Made the job a lot simpler, and it was still cheaper than hurricane shutters.

"Okay," he said to Tess when he'd unscrewed all the bolts from the first window. "Let's levitate."

She smiled faintly and helped lift the first piece of plywood. It was a half-inch thick, and heavy. He could see her discomfort as she tried to hold it in place by herself.

"It'll only be a second, Tess. Just until I get this first screw in."

"Sure. I'm fine."

He drilled the first bolt home as quickly as the drill would let him, then got off the stepladder and drilled in the lower bolt. "You can let go now."

She did so, brushing her gloved hands against her shorts and standing back while he moved the ladder and screwed in the top bolt on the other side of the window.

"One down, thirteen to go," he remarked cheerfully.

"Only thirteen?"

"I'm counting the glass doors as one window, since they're all adjacent."

"Ahh."

He looked down at her. "Next time *you* drill the bolts. It'll be easier than holding the plywood. I should have thought of that."

She looked up at him from the corner of her eye. "Really? I'm flattered."

"Are you being sarcastic?"

She shook her head. "No, I'm being serious. Most men think women can't use power tools."

He thought about that, convinced it wasn't true, but not knowing how to say it without starting a war. "Well . . . not this guy. Power tools are easy to use." Oops. As soon as that came out, he knew he'd made a mistake.

"So I can do it because it's easy?"

He didn't like the glint in her eye. "That isn't what I meant."

"Really?"

"Really."

"Then what did you mean?"

"I meant that anybody, male or female, can use a power tool. That's *all* I meant."

She paused at the next window and looked up at him, a funny smile at the corners of her mouth. "Good recovery, Jack. Are you sweating?"

"I'm not fond of getting into the whole male-female debate thing."

"Why not?"

"Because it's stupid."

"Stupid?"

"Stupid," he repeated emphatically. "People are people. Biology is *not* destiny. I don't believe that X and Y chromosomes determine anything except who's going to be the sperm donor."

Her gaze was suddenly unreadable. "My, my. A very enlightened view."

He shrugged. "Now, do you want to do the

drilling, or do you want to lift the plywood?"

"Well, the Y chromosome *does* determine who has greater upper body strength."

He couldn't help it; he laughed. "Okay. So I get to be the beast of burden."

She climbed the stepladder to unscrew the first bolt. The drill bit skipped over it.

"Um," Jack said, "you need to put the drill on reverse to back the screw out."

"Oh." She flushed. He thought she looked adorable.

Two windows later, he said, "You wouldn't happen to know Mary Todd, would you?"

"Vaguely. I think I met her a couple of times. Isn't she the old lady who drives the lavender golf cart?"

"I don't know. I don't think I've met her."

"Why are you asking, then?" She drove another bolt home and he was able to let go of the plywood.

"Because the next-door neighbor, Maudeen Mason, said we should talk to Mary Todd about Mom and Dad."

She paused in the process of climbing the ladder and looked at him. They were exactly on eye level now. "Why? Did she say why?"

"Because Mary Todd knows everything."

Tess gave a breathy laugh. "Yeah. Right. No one else in town knows where our parents are, but Mary Todd will?"

"That's the thing, though, Tess. There was something odd about the way Maudeen was acting. She said she'd gotten a postcard from the folks, but she couldn't remember exactly when she'd gotten it. She said she'd thrown it away. And when I asked her where it was from, she started to act strange and claimed she couldn't remember."

"Well, she *is* getting on."

"Trust me, she wasn't having a senior moment. Something else was going on. And she fell back on telling me to speak to Mary Todd with something very much like relief."

"Well, I can't imagine what good Mary will do us. From all I've heard, she's the biggest con artist in Paradise Beach."

"Then I can handle her—I'm good at handling cons."

As soon as he spoke, he realized that hadn't been the smartest thing to say. The look she was giving him suggested that she was wondering how he had learned to deal with cons, and was arriving at conclusions that weren't necessarily flattering to him.

He told himself it didn't matter, but that wasn't strictly true. It had always galled him that she thought so poorly of him, and he couldn't exactly remain indifferent to the likelihood that he was busy reinforcing her poor opinion.

And there wasn't a damn thing he could do about it right now. Unhappy with the whole situation, he muttered imprecations at the plywood and stopped conversing with Tess.

Who seemed to be annoyed by his silence. Almost immediately she started trying to drag him into conversation. He responded with monosyllabic grunts—which wasn't all that difficult to do, given his mood and the fact that all her gambits left him utterly indifferent.

He didn't particularly care why Mom and Dad hadn't bothered to have hurricane shutters installed. If pressed to come up with a reason, it would have been that they probably had other things they'd rather spend ten or fifteen thousand dollars on. He figured Tess knew that, so he didn't bother saying it.

She tried to get him to discuss whether he thought they were going to get a direct hit from Gaspar, or whether the storm would edge away farther north before making landfall. He shrugged; he wasn't a weather forecaster.

She speculated on whether the whole island would be evacuated, and he broke his silence long enough to say that it probably would be if they got a direct hit, or if the storm surge increased any.

It seemed to satisfy her that he'd spoken that much, and mercifully she fell silent while they finished boarding the windows.

"Well, what now?" Tess asked when they were done covering the last window.

"I promised to help board Maudeen Mason's windows."

"Oh."

Something about the way she said it alerted him. "What?"

She shrugged. "I thought we were going to see Mary Todd. And if we're really going to get a hurricane, we need to lay in some supplies, don't we?"

"You can go see Mary Todd and do the shopping, if you want. But I made a promise."

For the first time that day, her expression as she looked at him was actually kindly. Would wonders never cease?

"Okay," she said. "I'll help you."

He couldn't refuse her help without being ungracious—and a damn fool besides. "I just hope she has everything we need."

The Masons did indeed have everything that was needed. Joe Mason was apologetic about not being able to take care of it himself, but he'd had a stroke and couldn't get up the ladder anymore. Maudeen insisted on feeding them homemade apple pie and ice cream when they were done.

By then, it was two in the afternoon. An evacuation order still hadn't come down, and other householders on the street were beginning to board their windows as well.

"Might be a good time to visit Mary Todd," Jack remarked.

"Why's that?"

"If we hang around here any longer we'll wind up helping someone else, and I don't think my waistline can stand another dose of ice cream and pie."

She had to laugh, but she noticed as they made their way down the street, walking the two blocks to Mary Todd's house, that Jack paused at nearly every house asking if anyone needed any help.

Okay, so he wasn't a total sleazebag. He could be generous when he wanted to. She kind of liked that, actually, but it still didn't make him a saint.

"Where do we go if we have to evacuate?" Tess asked as they walked along the boulevard. The streets were more deserted than usual for this time of year, and a number of shops were already boarded up.

"Inland. As far as we can."

"Great. I'll bet the roads are already jammed."

"Who knows? It's not the most threatening of hurricanes. I wouldn't be at all surprised if a lot of people decide to ride it out."

"All I have to say is, it's lousy timing. How are we going to find Mom and Dad if we have to evacuate?"

"I told you, I've got some people looking for them."

"People like Ernesto?"

He glanced down at her, and there was suddenly a glimmer of humor dancing in his eyes. "Better than Ernesto. Far smarter. A lot more devious."

"People who would kill for a dime?"

"Depends on the dime, but yes, that's the image."

"I can't believe you know people like that."

"Why not? You probably know some, too."

She was about to argue with him when she realized he might be right. Her work as an auditor sometimes took her to places she was almost positive were fronts for something darker and uglier. "But I don't hang out with these people."

"Sure you do—when your job requires it."

She was still mulling that over when they reached Miss Mary Todd's house. The building was a relic of a more gracious age, three stories tall with white clapboard, dormers, and even a tower at one end. While it wasn't exactly huge, it *was* one of the largest single-family dwellings in the area. Right now, storm shutters had been closed over all the windows.

"I wonder if we should have called first," she said as they stood at the foot of the sidewalk and looked up at the house. "It's kind of presumptuous to drop in."

"Given that our parents are missing, I think we can skip the social niceties."

Which, though Tess, was one of the biggest differences between them. Jack had been brought up in a laid-back American style by his father. Tess had been more strictly raised by a mother who cherished her European roots. Sometimes Tess envied Jack.

Jack strode up the short walk, mounted the porch, which creaked a little beneath his weight, and rang the doorbell. Even from the curb Tess could hear the old-fashioned tinny bell sound, rather than modern chimes.

The clouds grew darker, blotting the last of the sun, and the wind began to gust as if it meant business.

"Maybe we'd better go," Tess said. "Miss Todd has probably evacuated."

"Probably." But he gave the doorbell one more ring anyway.

A few moments later, they were both surprised when the door was opened by an elegant-looking man in his seventies.

"I'm sorry," the man said briskly, "but there's a hurricane coming, don't you know. We really don't have time to listen to a sales call at the moment. Sorry. Come back next week."

He started to close the door, but Jack put out a hand, effectively stopping him. "We're not selling anything. We're looking for Miss Mary Todd."

"Mary's awfully busy right now," the man said. "I don't know why, but she always waits until the last minute to pack all that priceless junk she calls heirlooms. Really, I'm sure she'll be glad to see you in a week or so."

"This can't wait that long," Jack said firmly. "Please. Our parents are missing, and Maudeen Mason said Miss Todd would know about that."

"Oh, God," said the man, and closed the door despite Jack's efforts to hold it open.

A moment later, through the closed door, his voice could be heard bellowing, "Mary, you haven't taken up kidnapping have you?"

6

*T*ess and Jack exchanged looks. "Did you hear that?" Tess asked.

Jack nodded, pursing his lips. "He was just kidding."

"Can you be sure of that?"

"Actually, no. But little old ladies who drive lavender golf carts just don't strike me as the type to commit federal crimes."

"Good point," she admitted. "Until it comes to tax evasion."

"Tax evasion and kidnapping are poles apart."

"Tell that to Al Capone."

He almost laughed. She could see it in the sudden tension around the corners of his mouth, and in the way the corners of his eyes started to crinkle. "Touchée. Damn, I wonder what's taking so long."

"She's hiding the bodies?"

"God!" He looked at her. "Morbid turn of mind there, Tess?"

"Well, give me a better reason why it's taking so long."

"Maybe she's still in her nightclothes and wants to change."

"Hmm." Tess nodded. "Except that it's already two in the afternoon."

"Maybe she was napping."

"Would the guy have shouted for her that way if she was?"

He shook his head slowly. "Reckon not. Okay, what else? She was in the midst of making something on the stove and didn't want to leave it."

"Possible." She was beginning to enjoy this game. "But I've got a better one."

"What's that?"

"She's escaping out the back door."

For an instant, just an instant, she saw genuine consternation cross his face. His body shifted infinitesimally as if he were about to dash away, then he relaxed. "Good, Tess. That was good."

She started to laugh; it felt good to get him in this small way.

Just then the front door opened again, and the older gentleman said, "Please do come in. Miss Todd will see you. By the way, I'm her friend, Ted Wannamaker. And you are . . . ?"

"Jack Wright," Jack said, offering his hand. "Steve Wright's son. And this is Tess Morrow, Brigitte Wright's daughter."

"Ahh, yes. I've met Steve and Brigitte many

times. Lovely people." He shook their hands, then waved them toward the back of the house.

"My dear Mary," he said, "is sitting on the veranda out back. She loves the breeziness before a storm."

They followed him through the darkened house.

"I can see you're all ready for the hurricane," Jack remarked.

"Oh, yes. But Mary and I have been through so many of these. The old house has truly stood the test of time. This is just a little one, though. Hardly more than a tropical storm."

"At least the storm surge isn't supposed to be very high."

"No, indeed. Four feet, didn't they say? And if all goes according to the prediction, it'll hit on low tide and we'll barely get wet."

Tess thought that "barely get wet" was an optimistic view of a hurricane, which, after all, was considerably worse than a tropical storm, and those were bad enough.

The front of the house had the "beach" look, with a couple of palm trees and a rather sandy-looking yard, but out back they stepped into a tropical garden. Mary Todd's veranda was surrounded by lush growth, plants with huge leaves, large ferns, and all kinds of palms.

Mary herself was sitting at a wrought-iron table, sipping from a delicate bone china teacup. A tall, slender woman of approximately eighty, she sported a beautiful crown of white hair. Her eyes, as dark as a bird's, were every bit as sharp, even predatory.

"Sit down, sit down," Mary said when Ted had introduced them, as if delivering a royal command. "Ted tells me you think I kidnapped your parents."

Tess felt her cheeks flush. "Actually, no. Mr. Wannamaker is the one who suggested it. Maudeen Mason said we should come talk to you because our parents are missing and you might know where they've gone."

"Really?" Mary arched a brow and sipped her tea. "Now, where could Maudeen have gotten a notion like that?"

Ted coughed. Tess looked swiftly his way, but found him looking perfectly innocent as he pulled out a handkerchief and dabbed at his lips. "Excuse me," he said. "Allergies."

Mary's dark eyes returned to Tess. "Actually, I think he's allergic to *me*. Which makes it all the more remarkable that he's been dangling after me these past sixty years."

"My dearest Mary," Ted said gallantly, "I could *never* be allergic to *you*."

Mary sniffed, as if she didn't believe his folderol. "He *always* says the right thing. Do you know how unsettling that can be?"

Jack appeared fascinated. "You mean you want him to say the wrong thing?"

"Not exactly. But saints are such boring people." Taking the sting out of the words, she batted her lashes at Ted. "He'll never admit it, but he's actually very glad I've never agreed to marry him. He knows I would have made his life hell."

"Now, Mary—"

Blithely, she interrupted him. "He won't admit it, of course; that would be ungallant. But it's true nonetheless. He's much happier having me in small doses."

She turned to Tess, patting the young woman confidentially on the arm, as if they were old friends. "The secret to happiness, my dear, is knowing the proper limits for each relationship, and never exceeding them."

Tess nodded, although she wasn't quite sure she understood, and was certainly sure that Mary ought not to be giving her advice.

Mary, however, didn't see it that way. "No matter how intimate, how loving, how *close* a relationship is, there are always boundaries that must not be crossed. Places that if one goes, one will rupture the relationship, or make the other party miserable. Those are the boundaries I'm talking about, dear."

Tess nodded again, now understanding. She also wished Mary would get to the point.

"Ted," Mary continued, "is more fortunate than he knows that I recognize his boundaries. Consider: just a few minutes ago he was asking me if I was involved in kidnapping. Now, really, do you think he'd be *happy* being married to a woman he considers capable of kidnapping?"

"Now, wait a minute," Ted said. "I was only teasing you, Mary. I know you didn't kidnap anyone."

"Really?" Mary smiled archly. "Are you absolutely positive?"

She didn't give Ted Wannamaker a chance to answer, which was probably just as well, since Tess had a strong feeling that he might not have been able to answer honestly.

"Anyway," Mary said, returning her attention to Jack and Tess, "I didn't kidnap your parents. No percentage in it."

"We didn't think you had," Jack said. "But as I said, Maudeen thought you might know something about where they've gone."

"Oh. Well, I might. But I thought she'd given you the impression that I knew everything that was going on."

"It wouldn't be the first time," Ted remarked.

"Oh, do hush," Mary said tartly. "You think I'm at the center of every storm in town."

"Aren't you?" Ted asked.

"No, I am not." Mary sniffed. "He has delusions of my grandeur. As to your parents . . . well, I had a postcard from them last week sometime. Let me go try to find it. Maybe that will give you some idea. Although why you think they're missing . . . Didn't they just go on a vacation?"

"Apparently so," Tess said. "That's what everyone thinks."

"Then what is the problem?"

"My mother called me a week ago and said they were trying to get a flight home, only they've never come back. And Mrs. Niedelmeyer called Jack to say they were missing."

"Madge Niedelmeyer?" Mary Todd frowned. "That woman always thinks she knows far more than she does. Well, I'm sorry you've been worried. I'm sure your parents wouldn't want that."

"If they didn't want that, they should have let us know where they were going," Jack said firmly. "That's what they usually do, but they didn't this time. Add that to Brigitte's call to Tess, and we're very worried."

"I can certainly see why." Mary sighed and reached for an ebony cane which was leaning against the table. "Let me go get the postcard for you."

While they waited for Mary's return, Ted offered them beverages, which they both declined. At last Mary hobbled back onto the veranda, carrying a postcard. "Not very informative, I'm afraid."

Jack took it and held it so that Tess could look at it, too. The picture was an anonymous beach with palm trees and aquamarine water. The handwritten message was, "We're off at last! Love, Steve and Brigitte." And the postmark was . . .

"That's a Tampa ZIP code," Tess said. "They mailed this before they left."

He nodded. "Which ZIP code?"

"What do you mean?"

"Well, is it the ZIP for the airport, or the Port of Tampa? Maybe they flew out. Maybe they took a cruise."

"Good thinking. We'll have to check. Maybe

we can connect the date with a departure that will tell us something."

Mary spoke dryly. "Or maybe they dropped it in some letterbox over there as they drove through."

Tess looked at her, feeling a strong surge of irritation, though courtesy prevented her from saying so.

Mary's sharp eyes appeared to take note of that fact, but that didn't prevent *her* from saying something abominable. "Has it occurred to you two that your parents just may not *want* you to know where they are?"

That comment nearly knocked the wind from Tess. She looked quickly at Jack, who stared back at her with a certain hollowness in his gaze that told her he was as unpleasantly shocked by the idea as she was.

"Now, Mary," Ted said chidingly, "you're hurting these young people's feelings and you don't even know if that's the case."

"Maybe not," Mary said tartly. "But *I* received a postcard from Steve and Brigitte. One finds it fascinating that these two haven't."

Jack surprised Tess by rising to his feet and looking down at the woman. "You might remember, Miss Todd, that Tess received a phone call from her mother. Considerably more than a postcard."

"That's true," Mary said. "My apologies, gal. It may just be that they decided to have Thanksgiving elsewhere this year. After all, there's no reason to stay home."

Five minutes later, they were out on the street, walking home in the strengthening breeze. The rain bands from the approaching storm nearly blotted the sky now.

"What is wrong with this picture?" Jack said.

"Wrong?"

"Yeah, wrong." He kicked at a dead palm frond on the sidewalk, getting it out of their way. "We need to stop by the grocery on the way home. Get some food and a tube of caulking."

"What do we need caulking for?"

"To seal the bathtubs so we can fill them with drinking water."

"Oh."

"Anyway, this whole thing is beginning to stink to high heaven."

Tess nodded. "It is. The problem is, I'm not sure what's stinking, if you get my drift."

"I'm starting to feel pretty sure the two of them aren't in any trouble."

"Yeah. Me, too." She sighed. "I guess I should just go home and get back to work. They'll turn up when they're good and ready."

"Are you kidding? Are you going to give in to this?"

"Give in to what?"

"This manipulation."

Tess stopped walking and turned to face him. "What manipulation? I got one stupid phone call."

"One stupid phone call that told you absolutely nothing, and that was enough to get you hotfooting it down here to find out what happened to them."

"Well, yes. Jack, are you sure you aren't getting . . . paranoid?"

His eyebrows rose. "Me, paranoid? Of course I'm paranoid. So are you, if you're honest. Come on, Tess, use that brain of yours for something besides numbers, and think about this. Isn't this whole thing beginning to sound smoky?"

It was, even to her. But Jack was the last person on earth she wanted to admit that to, especially now that she was beginning to feel silly about taking time off from her job to come racing down here, all because her mother didn't answer the phone.

"I don't know," she said to him. "They *are* missing."

"Probably because they want to be. And you know what tipped me off?"

"What?"

"What Mary Todd said about Thanksgiving. Think about it, Tess: we're being punished."

"For what?" Although she knew. When he put it like that, it made entirely too much sense.

"We're being punished because we haven't been coming home for the holidays. Which is stupid, because they both as good as said they were sick of us squabbling and ruining the holidays."

Tess looked down at her feet and felt a painful squeezing of her heart. "We weren't that bad," she said.

"Well, I didn't think so, either. We both spent a lot of time biting our tongues."

"Yes, we did. There were a lot of nasty things I could have said to you."

"Same here."

She looked up at him and had the wildest urge to laugh. "I can't believe we're saying these things."

He shrugged. "Why not? They're true. So we get along like cats and dogs—can't help it. We have a mutual antipathy."

She didn't like the sound of that, even if it was true. It was like admitting there was something intrinsically wrong with her. "I don't know if I'd call it antipathy," she said. "We just don't get along."

"We don't get along because you can't stand my guts."

Her temper flared, just a little. "You can't stand my guts, either."

"Okay. So we feel this *antipathy*."

From the way he emphasized the word, she knew he was rubbing it in. "Do you want to say 'I told you so'?"

"Thanks, but I'll pass." He flashed a grin. "It was clearly implied."

"It certainly was."

"Thank you."

She sighed. "Can we get back to the issue at hand, please?"

"Sure. But let's keep walking, okay? I'd like to do the grocery store *before* the hurricane hits."

They resumed their stroll up the boulevard,

past their street, toward the supermarket. The wind pressed on their backs, hurrying them along.

"Okay," Tess said finally, unable to stand the suspense any longer. "What do you think is going on here?"

"Thanksgiving is five days away, right?"

"Right."

"I think they set this up so we'd have to come home for Thanksgiving."

She looked away. She looked up at the gray, racing clouds. She looked down at the pavement before her feet. "Really?" she managed to say finally.

"Okay, you don't agree. Why not?"

"Don't you think this is just a little bit elaborate to get us home for Thanksgiving? Either one of them could have picked up the phone and told us to be here or they'd never forgive us, and we both would have come, right?"

"Maybe."

"There's no maybe about it," she snapped. "I'd have come."

"Sure. The way you've come the last three years."

"That wasn't the same. They didn't insist, they just asked if I was coming."

"Admit it: when your parents ask a question like that, it's not the same as if a casual acquaintance is asking your plans. No way."

She glared up at him. "Are you ever wrong?"

"It's been known to happen."

"Do me a favor?"

"Sure."

"Let me know next time it does. I want to mark it on my calendar."

"Ooh, low blow," he said, but there was a laugh in his eyes. "Are we going to have a knock-down, drag-out fight right here?"

"I wouldn't give you the satisfaction."

"Aw, gee." But he let the subject go and returned to their real concern. "I'm convinced Thanksgiving has something to do with this mess."

"Well, we'll see on Thursday morning, won't we? If they don't jump out of the laundry hamper like jack-in-the-boxes, we're in trouble. In the meantime, I'll just try to forget that *they* might be in trouble."

"Leaping to conclusions again?"

"What in the world do you mean?"

He sighed. "Tess, you leap to conclusions the way a jackrabbit leaps away from a fox. Just because I suspect they might be up to something doesn't mean I'm going to quit looking for them."

"Oh. But I still don't see why you think this is all some kind of huge plot."

They were at the store now, and he paused before entering, causing her to do the same. The automatic door whooshed open and stayed that way.

"Brigitte."

Then he turned and entered the store. Reluctantly, Tess trotted right after him. She hated to admit it, but he might be right.

"It's simple, Shorty," he said when she caught up to him. "Where Brigitte is involved, all bets are off."

"Will you slow down?" she demanded.

"Get longer legs." But he grabbed a cart and slowed down so that she didn't have to trot to keep up.

"And stop calling me Shorty."

"I don't think so. Calling you Shorty gives me an emotional distance, one I'd like to hang on to," he said frankly.

What in the world did he mean by that? She was afraid to ask. When it came to Jack, there were some things she was better off not knowing. And among those, she was quite convinced, were Jack's thoughts about her.

She helped him pick out enough nonperishable foods to get through four or five days if they lost power that long. Their selection was pretty limited, though, because the shelves were already nearly bare. They did manage to get a bag of charcoal, though. The last one remaining.

When they were done, they had too much to carry.

"So we'll take the shopping cart," Jack said. "I'll bring it back."

"That's stealing!"

"The store doesn't think so."

"Of course they do!"

"Not around here, sweetie. There are so many senior citizens who do exactly this that they have cart drops at the condos and apartment houses."

Tess couldn't believe it. "You're kidding, right?"

"Swear I'm not. I'll show you one, if you want. Anyway, the store just sends employees out every couple of days to pick up the carts. Trust me, they won't mind as long as I bring it back."

Which was how Tess came to be walking down a public street in broad daylight pushing a shopping cart—something she would never have believed she would do. Something which, she was sure, would classify as theft if the store chose to get sticky about it. Either way, she was pretty sure it wasn't appropriate behavior for a government employee.

But despite her uneasiness, no officer accosted them on the way home.

"See?" said Jack, his grin just a little wicked. "Thunderbolts didn't strike and your picture isn't going to be in the post office next to Ma Barker's."

"I wasn't thinking any such thing."

"No? I could have sworn you had that 'dead man walking' look to your face."

"Cut it out, Jack."

"Tell you what: you put the groceries away while I ease your conscience by returning the purloined cart. And you might want to turn on the Weather Channel, too. Maybe somebody will give us some good news for a change."

Tess switched on the TV in the kitchen and listened while she put the groceries away, but the Weather Channel wasn't in the good news business today. It seemed Hurricane Gaspar was strengthening and it might become a category two before landfall.

The news was delivered by a pleasant-looking woman with a pleasant-looking smile as she warned that the storm surge would now be greater than previously anticipated.

At least it made a great distraction from the things Tess didn't want to think about—such as where her parents were, and whether Jack's suspicion was correct.

Correct or not, though, it was certainly possible. Brigitte was capable of nearly anything in order to get what she wanted. Steve was very different, calm and staid and very upright, like the eye at the center of Brigitte's hurricane. But not even Steve could always get Brigitte to behave.

Tess was still thinking about her mother when Jack popped back into the house. "What's the weather say?"

"Predictions are getting worse. They're talking a possible category two now."

"Would you rather head inland? I'll take you if you want."

Earlier that day, Tess probably would have leaped at the chance. But now she couldn't bring herself to go. It would feel too much like running. "No, thanks. I'm sticking this one out."

"Yeah, me, too." He surprised her by reaching out and squeezing her shoulder. "I'd better warn you, Shorty. I'm getting pissed. And when I get pissed I don't always do the smart thing."

She looked up at him, wondering why she'd

never before noticed just how comforting his large hand could be. "Pissed about what?"

"Them. The parental units. The people I'm beginning to think planned this whole thing to teach us a lesson."

She sighed. "I don't know, Jack. It seems kind of extreme, doesn't it? But on the other hand . . . well, they may have planned this, but they didn't plan the hurricane. So maybe the tables are turning on them."

He cracked a smile at that. "You might be right, cutie. I can just see them sitting on some tropical island at this very moment, watching the weather and wondering if we're still here or if we're getting out."

"Yeah." She had a sudden image of Steve and Brigitte sitting on a beach, holding frosty, fruity drinks in their hands, worrying about their children and the hurricane. "Nah," she said after a minute. "It doesn't work."

"No. It doesn't." He sighed. "Hell. Let's go caulk the bathtubs."

"I need to clean them first."

The tubs were already spotless—hardly surprising in a house that had a separate shower in every bathroom. Still, Tess wiped them down with bleach and rinsed them thoroughly. Then Jack dried around the drain and applied the caulk.

Watching him bend over the tub to apply the caulk had a surprising effect on Tess's libido. She couldn't help but notice just how great his backside was. Embarrassed by her own reaction, she quickly looked away, then snuck another peek.

And found Jack watching her in the mirror. When their gazes met, he gave her a knowing grin. That was bad enough, but then he said, "You like the view, huh?"

She wanted to bean him, but had to settle for grabbing a bath towel and throwing it over his head. His laughter followed her down the hallway.

She would have liked to leave right then. Except that there was a hurricane coming and she didn't particularly want to spend the next ten or twelve hours in a cab stuck in evacuation traffic going nowhere. By now they were probably closing the airport to outbound as well as inbound flights.

So she was stuck here with Jack. Jack, whom she had cordially disliked since the moment he had asked her where she got a stupid name like Tess. Jack, who was the bane of her existence when she let him come within ten feet of her.

So what was she going to do? They'd gotten through the last twenty-four hours in a reasonably civilized fashion, but she wasn't willing to bet they could get through the next twenty-four as well, especially now that the worry about their parents was giving way to a suspicion that this whole thing had been staged.

Well, she could just stay in her room. Barricade the door if necessary.

With the windows covered in plywood, the house was dark inside and for some reason the lamplight didn't seem to be doing enough to counteract it. Lighting that felt cozy at ten o'clock at night right now felt gloomy. Maybe it was because her internal clock knew it was still daytime.

She felt a sudden need to step outside and see the daylight, however gray. Tess stepped out of the steel front door into the wind, and felt relief run through her at the sight of the racing gray clouds, and the feeling of air whipping over her skin.

Wanting to see the water, she walked around the back of the house. From the patio above the seawall, she looked across the wide expanse of white beach at the choppy, dark gray waters of the Gulf of Mexico. The storm surge would cover the entire beach tonight and would batter against the seawall. Come morning, they'd probably have no beach left at all.

The wind and the surf were so loud that she was startled when a hand touched her arm. Whirling around, she saw Jack.

"Sorry," he said, raising his voice to be heard. "I didn't mean to scare you. I also didn't mean to drive you out of the house."

"I was just getting claustrophobic."

"I do have a tendency to make large rooms feel small."

She didn't know whether to laugh or to make a snotty remark. She decided on the latter because it was safer. "Your ego doesn't leave room for lesser mortals."

"At least you realize your proper position in life."

She tried to be indignant, but a sputtering laugh escaped her.

"Come on, Shorty, get your butt inside. I don't want to have to explain to Steve and Brigitte that you blew away because my ego was too big. Brigitte might forgive me, but Dad never would."

"Sure he would. You're his fair-haired child."

"Nope. He dotes on *you*."

Tess heard something in his tone that gave her the niggling feeling he wasn't entirely jesting. She wanted to ask him about that, but she couldn't imagine how to do it, not after all these years of antipathy, as he called it. But for the first time, it occurred to her that the marriage of their parents might have been as difficult for Jack as it had been for her.

All along, she had assumed it was different because his mother had died years before, while her parents had divorced, and she'd been cherishing hopes they would get back together again. Jack had had no such hopes to be dashed when Steve married Brigitte. But maybe something else had been going on.

She reluctantly followed him back into the house. The wind was strengthening, and at some point very soon it was going to become dangerous.

But inside, as silence and stillness closed around them, she wondered if she was going to be able to stand it.

"What about our parents, Jack?" she heard herself ask. "What do we do about them?"

He shrugged. "I don't know. Play out this

hand and see where it leads. If they're up to something, we'll find out soon enough. If they're missing . . . well, I don't know what else we can do about it right now."

"So what do we do? Sit around and twiddle our thumbs until the storm passes?"

"Actually," he said with the devil's own grin, "I thought we could play strip poker."

7

TEMPTING THE WRIGHT 126

"*T*ess, I was only kidding!"

Her response was muffled by her bedroom door. "Yeah, right."

Jack stood staring at the closed door, wondering what in hell he had done to deserve such an uptight, prudish, pain-in-the-butt stepsister. For the last twenty-four hours he'd actually been warming a little toward her, convincing himself that she really wasn't all that bad. Now one stupid joke and she was barricaded in her bedroom.

"You're crazy, you know that?" he yelled.

"Crazy to have ever believed you could be civilized."

"Just what exactly do you consider civilized? Wearing a muzzle?"

"If you're a mad dog, yes!"

Cripes. He closed his eyes and wondered what

the hell he was doing. Did it really matter if Tess stayed locked in her bedroom until the hurricane passed? Was he really concerned that he might have to spend the next twelve or sixteen hours *without* her acidic little tongue and all her hang-ups? Why didn't he just walk away right now and leave her to stew in her own juices?

Because . . . because. Because he was feeling guilty about the way he'd treated her over the years. Because he had a sneaking suspicion that this whole mess had been orchestrated to punish him and Tess for all the times they'd made their parents miserable with their squabbling. Because he was afraid that if he and Tess didn't manage to hammer out some kind of truce in the next couple of days, their parents were going to be irrevocably disappointed in them.

"Tess?"

"Go away!"

"I can't. There's a hurricane out there."

"So blow away."

"I just wanted to tell you that you don't have to hide in your room. Frankly, my dear, I wouldn't play strip poker with you if you were the last woman on earth."

As he'd hoped, the lock turned and the door flew open.

"I wouldn't play strip poker with you if you were the last man on earth!" she spat at him.

"Color me wounded to the core." He shrugged, making sure she saw his indifference, and sauntered away toward the living room.

He'd accomplished his purpose; she'd opened her door.

It would have been great if it had stopped there, but of course it didn't. She followed him down the hallway into the living room.

"You're impossible," she told him.

"No, just improbable. The impossible doesn't exist."

"Well, you're an exception."

"I usually am." Much as he didn't want to, he found himself enjoying their silly sparring. "In fact, a great many people take exception to me."

"I can well believe it. Do you work at being obnoxious or do you come by it naturally?"

"Oh, it's perfectly natural. Just like breathing." He was on the verge of laughter and could tell she saw it and was annoyed by it. "Come off it, Tess. Are you always so sober and crabby?"

"Crabby?" The word didn't settle well in her craw, he could tell. "*You* were the one who made an obscene suggestion."

"*Obscene?* I was joking, for crying out loud. When did you have your sense of humor amputated?"

"About the time I realized men don't have a right to talk to me that way."

"Talk to you what way?"

She put her hands on her hips and glowered at him. "Don't you see, you big jerk? We're staying here alone together."

"So?"

Then he got it. Later he realized that his reaction wasn't the wisest, but it escaped him before he was aware of what was coming. He began to roar with laughter.

"What is so funny?" she demanded.

He couldn't answer immediately because he was laughing too hard to get his breath. He expected her to storm away and lock herself in her room again, but Tess was no longer the girl he remembered. She'd apparently gotten better at standing her ground.

"So," she said again, her voice dripping irritation, "what is so funny?"

"You," he said. "Your attitudes. My God, Tess, you're a hundred years out of date."

Her face darkened. "I assure you I'm not."

"No?" He felt a wicked grin stretch his face. He tried to bite back his next words, but Tess could drive him past caution merely by breathing. "So, what's wrong? Are you afraid I *won't* take advantage of you?"

She gasped. Then color flooded her cheeks and rose upward to her hairline.

"I didn't know you could get so red," he remarked. "Calm down, Tess. I was only teasing. Don't have a heart attack, okay?"

"You rude, insufferable, uncouth, disgusting . . ." She spluttered, apparently unable to think of anything else nasty to call him.

He nodded. "You're right. And for the life of me, I can't figure out why I can't resist teasing you."

Much to his relief, her color was returning to something more normal and less explosive.

"Teasing," she said stiffly, "is a socially acceptable expression of hostility."

"Really?" He didn't like the sound of that. "Only hostility? Because I really don't feel hostile toward you. Sometimes I think you want to excise my gizzard, but I don't feel the least desire to amputate any part of you—or even tape your mouth shut."

"Excise your gizzard?"

"Metaphorically speaking. But honestly, Tess, I don't feel at all hostile toward you. So I couldn't possibly be teasing you for that reason."

"You don't?" She looked uncertain.

"Not a bit of it. But I do find it irresistible to tease you. Are you sure it can't be something besides hostility?"

Her posture was relaxing, he noted. She was letting go of the last of her anger and resentment, which was a good thing. "It can be an expression of tension," she said finally. "A sign of strain."

"Well, we certainly do have a tense and strained relationship. Tell you what. We haven't eaten all day and that certainly makes people crabby. So how about I go make us some dinner while we've still got power and running water? Which reminds me—that caulking is probably dry enough now to fill the tubs with water. Do you want to do that?"

"Sure."

"Thanks. I'll go cook."

It embarrassed Tess to admit to herself that she had overreacted. Going from bathroom to bathroom to fill the three tubs gave her plenty of time to consider her own conduct, unfortunately.

She *had* overreacted to Jack's remark about playing strip poker. It wasn't the kind of thing anyone suggested seriously to someone with whom he wasn't a lover—unless he was drunk, which Jack wasn't. Off color, yes, but hardly a transgression of the size she had turned it into.

Sitting on the toilet lid while she waited for one of the tubs to fill, she fought a sense of humiliation. Why did she *always* overreact that way to Jack? If anyone else on the planet had made that remark to her, she would have uttered some kind of retort, not acted like an offended maiden. Unfortunately, she was living down to Jack's expectations of her.

And she was a better woman than that. She *wasn't* the uptight prude he seemed to think her. She was just . . . reserved. She had to be, given her calling in life. An IRS auditor who couldn't remain absolutely controlled regardless of provocation wouldn't have a job for long. She had been called names that would make a marine blush.

But the instant she got anywhere within shouting range of Jack, all that self-control went up in smoke. She even started acting like a spoiled brat, which only irritated her more and made her act worse. It was a vicious cycle.

But she couldn't figure out how to break it. When all was said and done, over the years she hadn't seen all that much of Jack. Pretty soon after their parents had married, he'd graduated from college and then had disappeared, showing his face at home only on holidays.

And each and every time she had vowed that she was going to behave better the next time he came home, she wound up behaving just as badly as ever.

The tub was full. Leaning over, she turned off the water and moved on to the next bathroom. It seemed like an awful lot of water, but if things got really bad this water might have to last for the next two weeks or so. Not that she was planning to stay that long.

She started the next tub running and leaned against the vanity, watching the water get deeper. Basically, she decided, being around Jack made her despise herself because of the way she acted. And no resolution was proof against the way the mere sight of him got under her skin.

But imagine him having the gall to suggest that she actually wanted his sexual advances. Hah! Not in *this* lifetime.

Of course, if she was to be honest with herself, he'd only said that to get her goat. He hadn't really meant it. Had he? No! She'd let him get her goat the way she always did, and found the whole thing all the more irritating because he hadn't meant what he said.

Listening to her own thoughts was beginning to convince Tess that she must have a loose cog somewhere. She wasn't exactly making sense. Of course, feelings were always illogical, which was one of the reasons she tried to avoid dealing with them. Unfortunately, with Jack, she couldn't seem to do anything *except* feel.

And now he was telling her she was crabby. Really, she wasn't. By nature she was very even-tempered. Maybe what she needed to do was avoid Jack. He had a very bad effect on her.

Jack had dinner nearly ready by the time she finished filling the tubs. When he asked her to set the table, she was happy to oblige. It gave her an excuse to do something pleasant in his presence . . . which she had to admit she hadn't done much of in the last fifteen years.

They sat down to a meal of meatball sandwiches, which wasn't something that was usually on Tess's menu. After one taste, she wondered why. "These are great! How'd you make them so fast?"

He grinned. "Frozen meatballs, jarred spaghetti sauce, and a package of provalone cheese. No big deal."

"Frozen meatballs? I'm glad to know that. I've never figured out how to make a decent meatball."

"I don't know anybody who can."

"Mom can."

Jack shook his head, assuming a sorrowful expression, and put his hand over his heart. "Tess, sweetie, I hate to disabuse you of a cherished illusion, but . . . Brigitte uses frozen meatballs. These frozen meatballs. The ones I pulled out of her freezer."

"Really?" She was amazed. "She never told me that."

"Of course not. Why would she give away a secret?" He cocked his head to one side. "You know, now that I think about it, maybe I ought to check out her freezer more carefully. Think of all the other secrets I could unearth."

Tess laughed.

"Like that Alfredo sauce we had yesterday. That's the stuff she always serves, and it was out of a jar."

"But really, she's a great cook!"

"Did I say she wasn't? As far as I'm concerned, the proof is on the table, and I don't care where it came from, jar or box or garden out back."

"Very pragmatic attitude."

"Pragmatic?" He lowered his brow. "Is that an insult?"

But he was teasing her; this time she could see it in the twinkle in his dark eyes. "Nope. It's a compliment."

"Oh, Shorty, I feel sorry for you if you think pragmatism is a good trait."

"I'm very proud of my pragmatism."

"A hopeless case, hmm?"

Before she could reply, a strong gust of wind hit the house, causing it to creak a little. It was followed by the hammer of heavy rain on the tile roof.

"Gaspar's here," Jack remarked, looking upward. "Maybe we ought to turn on the tube and see if there's any more news."

He was crossing the kitchen when they heard a loud hammering on the front door.

"Don't tell me we're being evacuated," Jack

muttered. "The storm's not strong enough for that."

Tess followed him, not wanting to miss anything, particularly when it might affect her survival.

What they found standing at the door was a plump man who appeared to be in his mid-sixties. In his teeth he clenched a pipe which was probably as drowned as he was. He was dressed in a bright but soaked Hawaiian shirt, shorts, and sandals with black socks.

"I beg your pardon," he said, removing the pipe from between his teeth. "I'm Hadley Philpott. Professor Philpott. Miss Mary Todd sent me to see you."

Jack and Tess exchanged glances. "In a hurricane?" Jack asked.

Philpott sighed. "You don't know Mary. Something or other about your parents?"

"Come in." Tess reached out to take the man's arm and urge him into the house. "Can we make you some coffee?"

"I'd appreciate a towel, frankly. And yes, coffee or tea would be divine."

"I'll get the towel." Jack disappeared down the hallway.

Tess ushered Hadley Philpott into the living room, but before she went to get him some coffee, she asked, "Have you heard from our parents?"

"Oh, heavens, no. I wish I had."

Her heart, which had been lifting ever since he had said Mary had sent him about their parents, took a nosedive. Presumably he knew *something* that Mary thought was important, but after their discussion with Mary earlier, Tess wasn't so sure about that.

There was hot coffee on the warmer, so she poured a cup, got out some cream and sugar, put everything on a small tray, and carried it back into the living room. Jack had returned with a towel, and Hadley Philpott was turning his thinning hair into a woodpecker's crest by drying it vigorously.

"It was stupid of me to come out in this without an umbrella," Philpott said. "One of those occasions that calls for that particularly obnoxious expression everyone is using these days: duh."

The corners of Tess's mouth quirked with amusement and Jack chuckled. Tess placed the tray on the coffee table. "Here, Professor, help yourself to some coffee."

"Thank you, dear," he said in the avuncular way of older men. It grated on Tess, who wasn't used to being talked to that way anymore, but she forced herself to ignore it. It wasn't as if she was going to have to deal with this man on a regular basis, and besides, she wanted to hear what he had to say.

"Ah, delicious," he said, once he had fixed his coffee and sipped it. "A premium Costa Rican blend."

"I wouldn't know," Jack said with amusement. "Brigitte keeps it in a clear glass jar that reveals no secrets."

"Well, I must make certain to ask her where she gets this. It's quite delightful."

"Do you know her well?" Tess asked.

"We're acquainted." Philpott favored her with a smile. "Mary and I are old and dear friends, and Mary knows just about everyone in Paradise Beach. So, if one knows Mary well enough to spend any time with her, sooner or later one gets to know a great many people hereabouts."

"So you met Steve and Brigitte through Mary?"

"I suppose you could say that."

Tess felt the first niggles of frustration and she glanced at Jack. He looked as if he were enjoying himself.

Tess turned back to Philpott. "You said Mary sent you here? Something about our parents?"

"Oh, yes. She said you were afraid they were kidnapped or something?"

"It crossed our minds," Jack said. "They've . . . disappeared, if you will."

"But whatever makes you think that?"

So Tess and Jack explained once again.

"Well," said Hadley Philpott, "I can certainly see why you would leap to such a conclusion. If they've always made it a rule to tell you where they were going and for how long . . ."

"Always," Tess said. "Always."

He nodded. "But are you sure of that?"

"Of course I'm sure."

"Really. How can you be absolutely positive that they haven't done something like this before, and that they simply didn't tell you and you never heard about it?"

Tess opened her mouth to disagree, then snapped it shut and looked at Jack. He shrugged.

"Not that I'm saying you're wrong," Philpott said. "You'll have to pardon me. I used to teach philosophy, and I tend to get rather involved in pursuing various avenues of possibility."

"But why," Jack said, "did Mary want you to come see us? Did she learn something?"

"No, I don't believe so."

Jack sighed. He didn't even bother to conceal his impatience. "Professor, we're enjoying your visit immensely, but there had to have been a reason you ventured out here on a stormy night with a hurricane just offshore to see us."

"Well, of course there was."

"Would you mind sharing it?"

"That was the whole reason I came here, wasn't it?"

"We certainly thought so."

Philpott nodded. "Mary thought you would want to know something that Brigitte said to me a few weeks ago. I don't see that it's all that significant, but Mary insists." He sighed. "That woman can be remarkably difficult sometimes. But then, she's a remarkable joy, too."

Tess was about to leap up from her chair, cast basic civility to the winds, and *demand* to know what Brigitte had said to him. But before she could do so, there was a pounding at the front door.

"Excuse me," Jack said. "I need to go see who's beating the door down."

"That *is* rather loud, isn't it?" Philpott said as he sipped his coffee. "Sounds a bit harried."

"I wonder if we're getting evacuated."

"If we are, I'd be very surprised. They're not expecting that much flooding, and at last call, the evacuations were voluntary." Philpott put his cup down.

Tess spoke. "I always thought everyone had to be evacuated when a hurricane is coming."

"It depends on the anticipated storm surge. We're going to be on the north side of the eye, which means we shouldn't get much of a surge at all."

Tess supposed there was a reason for that, but she quite frankly wasn't all that interested in the mechanics of hurricanes right now. Primarily she wanted to know what her mother had said.

Voices were coming from the foyer, along with the sound of a crying baby. Curiosity overwhelmed her, and Tess excused herself. Out in the foyer, she found Jack facing Ernesto, a young, dark-haired woman, and a squalling infant.

"I'm telling you, man," Ernesto said, "we got no place to go. The bridges are closed because of the storm, so we can't get out of here. How was I supposed to know our motel was gonna throw us out?"

"What about another motel?" Jack asked.

"They aren't letting anybody in. I called every one of them. So what am I supposed to do? Sit in the streets with my baby?"

"I don't believe this," Jack muttered.

"Me neither," Ernesto agreed. "I mean, this place doesn't even have a storm shelter!"

"They're all on the mainland." Jack looked at Tess.

"Well, of course they can stay here," she said, hoping her uncertainty didn't come through in her voice. It wasn't her house, after all, and while she believed that Steve and Brigitte would do the very same thing, she didn't like doing it without asking them.

But while she didn't at all care for the looks of Ernesto, his wife and child were a different matter. The woman's dark eyes were full of fear. She was so delicate that the child she held looked large in her arms, though it couldn't have been more than six months old.

"Where will we put them?" Jack asked.

"They can have my bedroom."

"What about you?"

"I'll sleep on the couch."

"Yeah, right." He sighed. "Cripes, I never thought I'd be giving my bed to somebody I'd put behind bars. Come on, Ernesto. You guys get *my* bedroom."

Tess stared after them, questions racing around in her head. *Somebody he'd put behind bars?* Jack put people behind bars? That was hard to believe. If he was a cop, he wouldn't make such a secret of what he did.

So maybe he was some kind of informer?

What kind of people had she just invited into this house?

Not that it mattered, she told herself. She couldn't abandon *anyone* to the mercies of a storm. But still . . .

Informant? The word filled her stomach with lead. It wasn't the way she wanted to think of Jack—as someone who might sneak around behind peoples' backs, getting them into trouble. Like a schoolyard tattletale.

She supposed informants were very important to police work, and that informing on people who committed crimes wasn't anywhere near the same thing as being a tattletale, but . . .

It was so sneaky. Underhanded. Not at all the way she wanted to think of Jack.

Which was stupid, because she didn't want to think of Jack in any way at all.

A few minutes later, he came down the hall carrying his suitcase. He dropped it in the foyer.

"Why did the motel owner throw them out?" she asked.

"They were staying at one of those cheap cottage things right on the beach. No protection from the storm surge."

"Mary," said Hadley Philpott from the doorway of the living room, "would like to see those beachfront cottages removed."

Tess started and turned around. "Oh! I'm sorry! I forgot you were there."

"Me, too," said Jack. "Sorry."

"No problem," said Philpott, settling the stem of his pipe between his teeth. "There's hardly any reason to hurry, since it appears I'll be here for the night myself."

"You will?" Tess looked blankly at him.

"You might take another look outside."

Jack turned and reached for the doorknob. The gust of wind that blew in nearly bowled him over, and a large palm frond blew in with it, skittering across the floor toward Philpott.

Jack leaned back with all his strength and pulled it closed, then set the two deadbolts. Straightening, he smoothed back his hair and looked at Philpott. "It appears you're right," he said. "We're all here for the duration."

8

*T*hen the lights went out. Jack was still standing by the door, Hadley Philpott was still on the threshold of the living room, and Tess was ... Tess was wherever she was. She couldn't stand the total darkness. Her skin began to crawl and she could almost feel things reaching out for her from the shadows.

"Jack?" Her voice betrayed more than she would have liked. "Jack?"

"I'm here, honey," he said. "I'm right here." A hand touched her arm and she jumped. "It's just me, Tess. It's okay."

She turned blindly toward him and came up hard against the wall of his chest. A moment later his arms closed around her, holding her snugly.

Outside, the storm moaned. It wasn't Tess's

first hurricane, but she had forgotten how a storm could sound like a beast at bay, so loud as it clawed at the house, making the roof creak and the plywood over the windows rattle.

"You know," Jack said quietly in her ear, "I could enjoy holding you like this for a long time."

A surprisingly pleasurable shiver ran through her and the storm seemed to move far away.

"However," Jack said, ruthlessly dashing the moment, "it would better serve us all if I found some lights."

She stepped back and said with cold formality, "By all means."

"Ooh, the ice queen," he remarked, but quietly so only she could hear it.

She considered bringing her heel down on his instep, but abandoned the notion when she realized she wouldn't be able to find it in the dark.

Hadley Philpott cleared his throat. "Uh, yes, some light would be very welcome right now."

From down the hallway, a door banged open. "Hey," Ernesto shouted, "anybody got a flashlight?"

"Give me a minute," Jack shouted back.

"Well, don't dick around, man. It's dark back here."

"Do I kill him now or later?" Jack mused aloud.

"Oh, very definitely later," Philpott remarked. "You want to be absolutely certain that the satisfaction his murder gives you will be sufficient to balance the consequences. That requires some thinking."

"If I think about it, it becomes a cold-blooded act," Jack pointed out. "I don't see myself becoming a cold-blooded murderer."

"Precisely!" said Philpott, sounding very much like a professor who was proud of a student.

"Hey, hurry with the light, okay?" Ernesto shouted. Then the baby started squalling.

Jack swore. The sound came from farther away, and Tess sensed that he was making his way across the foyer.

Then she was alone in the dark again. It was the deepest darkness she could ever remember. There was no light from anywhere to alleviate it, not starlight, not streetlights, not even the red or green glow from a digital clock. There was nothing.

Her skin began crawling in earnest, and she had the disorienting sensation that she might be falling.

There was a thud, and a quiet curse as Jack bumped into something. The baby shrieked more loudly, an ear-piercing, high-pitched tone that Tess was amazed to discover could come from human vocal chords.

"Damn it," Ernesto shouted. "Where's a light?"

"Hold your horses," Jack shouted back. "I'm trying to get to them without killing myself."

"Patience is an admirable trait," Philpott intoned.

"Too bad I don't have more of it," Tess remarked tartly. "And what *did* Mary send you here to tell us?"

"Mary? Oh, yes . . ." His voice trailed off as Jack cursed again, but then Tess heard the sound of the kitchen door flapping. The flashlights and lanterns were all in the pantry, which at this moment didn't seem like the brightest place to stash them.

"Professor? What were you going to tell me?"

"About what?"

"About my parents!"

"Oh. Why would I have anything to say about your parents?"

"That's why you came here. You said that Mary told you to come tell us what you know."

"Oh, yes. Right. Well, I don't actually *know* anything, you see."

"No?"

"Yes, *know*. As in touch, taste, feel, have actual experience of. That sense of knowing. You are familiar with the word?"

Tess wondered if she'd missed an essential connection somewhere, because what he was saying didn't seem to follow on what she had said. "Of course I know the word."

"Then why did you ask?"

"Ask you what?"

"You said, 'Know?' "

She really was losing her mind. "I said, 'No.' As in N-O."

"Oh."

"Exactly."

"I beg your pardon."

At that moment another gust of wind grabbed the house and seemed to shake it, even though Tess knew that wasn't possible, since the house was built of cinder block. But if that was the roof . . . Instinctively, she looked upward and realized she couldn't see a thing. If the storm blew the roof off, she'd know it by the wind, rain, and debris hailing down on her.

"So what is it that you don't know that you came over here to tell me?" she asked.

"Oh, yes. Sorry I keep getting distracted. It comes from too much solitude, my dear. My mind is accustomed to wandering its own paths without regard to anyone else. I need to learn to control it more effectively."

Tess felt ready to explode from impatience. Or maybe she felt ready to explode because she was discovering a pathological dislike of total darkness. She said rather sharply, "Will you *please* just tell me?"

"Tell you what?"

She was going to kill him. She was really going to cross the pitch-black foyer and wrap her hands around his throat and squeeze until . . . Shock ended that train of thought. She really couldn't be thinking such things. "About Steve and Brigitte," she said.

"What about them? Oh, yes. Yes! I'm so sorry. My mind was wandering off on a tangent again. I was thinking how very much you sounded like my late wife."

Tess wondered if his late wife had ever considered killing him. Most likely. It was probably that edge in her voice that was reminding him of his departed spouse.

"Anyway," he continued, "Steve and Brigitte. I met them a couple of times at Mary's house."

"Yes, so you said."

Ernesto chose that moment to bellow out again demanding a light.

Tess, who'd had quite enough, snapped, "Shut up, Ernesto. You'll get a light when you get a damn light."

Jack's voice unexpectedly joined the discussion. "It would help," he said, "if any of the flashlights actually had batteries in them."

"What about the oil lamps?"

"I can't find the matches to light them without a flashlight. Do you remember where they kept the batteries, Tess?"

She had to think about it. "Umm, the drawer on the left side of the breakfast bar, I think. That's where they used to be."

"I'll look. Don't anybody move. I've almost broken my neck twice and I don't want anybody else getting hurt. I doubt we could get any medical attention right now."

Philpott spoke. "Perhaps you should take your own advice."

"If I do that, we'll never have light."

There was a thud on the roof as the wind blew something against it. "Please, Jack," Tess heard herself say, "let's get light. Any light. This is terrifying."

"I'm working on it, Shorty. Honest, I am."

Down the hall, the baby hiccuped into silence,

which was something of a relief. At least Tess could hear the violence of the wind unimpeded now and be certain that the roof wasn't blowing off yet.

Moments later, the first ray of a flashlight came around the corner and into the foyer. "Here we go," Jack said. "Flashlights for everybody. Then I'll get the oil lamps."

He pressed a flashlight into Tess's hand and she immediately turned it on, grateful for the way it drove the darkness back. Now she could see Hadley Philpott still standing in the living room doorway, and could make out Jack's back as he went down the hall to give Ernesto one of the lights.

"Thanks, man," Ernesto said, displaying considerably more politeness than he had earlier.

Jack came back down the hall. "Let's not burn these things too much. The batteries won't last that long. The oil lamps will do a lot better."

Ten minutes later, there were three lamps burning in the living room, and Ernesto had one back in the bedroom for his wife and baby. Hadley Philpott resumed his position on the sofa and sipped the last of his cooling coffee.

"I might point out," he said, "that this coffee is still warm. It may be the last hot coffee you get for days, so if there's any left . . ."

"I'll freshen your cup," Tess offered. "Jack? You want some?"

"I may as well, since something tells me no one is going to get much sleep tonight."

Probably not, she thought, as she turned on

her flashlight once again and went to the kitchen. Carrying a couple of mugs and the pot, she returned to the living room and poured for them all.

Another buffet of wind seemed to shake the house, as if a freight train were roaring by. Tess almost thought she could see the pictures on the wall shuddering.

"Now," she said, sitting across from Hadley, "can we get to what it was you came to tell us about Steve and Brigitte?"

"Ah, yes!" He sipped his coffee and put his cup down. "It isn't much, and I really can't think why Mary thought it was so imperative to tell you. But basically all it is was something your mother said a few weeks ago. She said—and I'm not a hundred percent sure of the exact wording—that if she had her way she'd lock the two of you up in a small room until you sorted yourselves out. Is that any help?"

Jack and Tess exchanged looks.

"Uh . . ." Jack hesitated, then said, "It might be."

"Well," Hadley said, "I thought it was singularly uninformative, but Mary would have her way. As she always does."

Tess looked at Jack again and heard herself say, "She can't make hurricanes."

"No. Of course not." But something strange was happening at the corner of his mouth, almost like a grin that couldn't quite be born. "She can, however, make herself disappear."

She certainly could. And terribly unfilial

though it might be, Tess had no trouble imagining her mother scheming such a thing. Sometimes it could be appalling to be related to Brigitte.

"Yeah," said Jake, as if he read her mind. "I wonder how she coopted Dad into it."

"Your father's no saint," Tess said tartly. "Keep in mind that he's remained with her for fifteen years, despite all these hijinks you hold in such disapproval."

"Did I say I disapproved? Because actually, Tess, I don't disapprove at all. And I think your mother has gone a long way to lightening up my father's life. Still . . . he's not usually willing to engage in something underhanded."

"What's underhanded?" Tess demanded, feeling a strong urge to defend her mother against these implied insults. "There's been nothing underhanded at all. They've simply disappeared."

"There *was* the phone call to you."

"All they said was that they were waiting to catch a flight."

Jack stood up and looked down at her. "Wait a minute. You said she said that they were waiting for a flight *home*."

"Well, I may have misunderstood that part. That was the impression I got, but I couldn't swear to it in a court of law."

"Convenient memory, hmm?" He grinned through his teeth.

"Why, you—"

Hadley Philpott cleared his throat loudly. "Excuse me," he said in booming tones. "But this is getting you nowhere."

Tess bit her tongue, but it required a great deal of effort, like holding stormwater behind a dam.

Jack turned to Hadley. "Look, we don't need a referee. We've been squabbling for a long time, and I can take anything she dishes out."

The professor harrumphed into his chest and chewed on the stem of his pipe. "I don't know that I'd be bragging about that."

"Why not?" Jack asked. "We're good at what we do."

"Jeeeeeez," Tess groaned. "Do you have to make it sound like a career choice?"

Jack looked at her, an odd gleam in his eye. "Isn't it?"

She opened her mouth to retort, then snapped it shut. Then opened it again. Then gave up.

"She's speechless," Jack remarked to no one in particular. "I never thought I'd see the day."

"Oh, just shut up," Tess said irritably.

"No, I won't. Because we've got more important considerations: namely, finding our wayward parents."

"Why should we bother?" Tess demanded. "The way I see it is, why give them the satisfaction? As soon as this storm is over, I'm heading home. They can come out of hiding whenever they get bored enough."

"Tess, Tess, Tess," Jack said, shaking his head. He perched on the coffee table facing her, and reached out to take her hand.

Tess snatched it back. "Don't touch me, you jerk."

"Okay. But listen. Are you really going to let those two get away with this? They scared us half to death. We've been worried sick for days now. All so they could get us to stay here for a few days and get past our differences?"

"Pretty crummy, huh?"

"Yeah," he said emphatically. "In fact, it stinks. So what we're going to do is find out where they are, so we can go give them what for. We're going to make sure they never pull another lame-brained stunt like this again."

That sounded good to Tess. In fact, the more she thought about it, the better it sounded. "So how do we find them?"

"They're in the Caribbean, right?"

"Maybe. That's kind of an assumption."

"It's the best assumption we've got."

She sighed. "I'm just reminding you of all the difficulties you were so determined to remind me of earlier. When did *you* become such an optimist?"

"Along about the time you decided to become a pessimist."

She looked at him, realizing that was the statement of a very basic truth between them. "Are you saying that you're basically contrary?"

"Only with *you*." The grin he flashed looked positively diabolical. She really *didn't* like him at all.

"I suppose I should be flattered," she said archly.

"Oh, absolutely," said Hadley Philpott, appearing rather amused. He held the bowl of his pipe in the palm of his left hand, and managed somehow to look professorial despite the Hawaiian shirt and the bony knees poking out above his black socks.

"Absolutely?" Jack asked, looking annoyed at the mere idea.

"Definitely," Philpott repeated. "It requires an immense amount of effort to be deliberately contrary. Most of us don't bother unless we consider it to be important."

"Hah!" said Tess, beginning to enjoy herself. "Exactly what I suspected."

Philpott sat back in his chair looking pleased with himself. Jack, on the other hand, looked as if he'd swallowed something unpalatable. "Actually," he said, "I disagree with Tess because she's usually wrong."

"Yeah, right," Tess said, unruffled. Philpott wisely maintained a silence.

"Anyway," Jack said, emphasizing the word, "we need to devise a plan of action for locating the parents as soon as this storm blows over."

"Sure," said Tess, suddenly feeling flippant. "We'll rent a sailboat and go island to island until we find them."

He frowned at her.

"It would be a great vacation," Hadley said. "Wouldn't mind taking a trip like that myself."

"I'm sure my bosses will give me the next two or three months off," Tess continued blithely. "I can't imagine why they should have a problem with it."

"Look," Jack said, "what is with you? We need to discuss this seriously."

"Discuss what seriously?" she demanded. "We've been discussing this seriously since we put our heads together yesterday, and all we've managed to come up with is that they're probably in the Caribbean, and oh, it looks like this was all a plot to throw the two of us together. And while I'd really like to give the two of them a sharp piece of my mind for putting us through this scare, it seems to me the likelihood that we could find them in any reasonable amount of time is nil. Now, maybe you don't have to work for a living, but *I* do, and I can't afford to devote months to trying to find them."

"Are you saying we're utterly stymied?"

"That's exactly what I'm saying."

Jack shook his head. "I'm ashamed of you, Tess."

"What in the world do you have to be ashamed of me about?"

"Your lack of perspicacity."

"My lack of *what*?" Her temper was beginning to flare again.

"Think, Tess. If they set this up to teach us a lesson, don't you think they'd make sure we could find enough clues to locate them?"

She snorted. A delicate, ladylike snort, but a snort nonetheless. "You're assuming a whole lot there, Jack. Maybe they don't want us to find them. Maybe they're planning to pop back in here in a few days and see if there are any survivors."

"Nah."

"Nah?"

"Nah. Thanksgiving is in five days."

"So? *So?*"

Jack shook his head. "I realize your mother has never considered it *the* most important holiday, seeing as how she's Canadian, and French Canadian, to boot—"

"Wait a minute," Tess interrupted. "She's always celebrated it."

"Yes, but she's said things that indicate to me she doesn't consider it all that important."

Tess stood. "You know, Jack, one of your biggest problems is the way you slander people."

"I'm not slandering anyone."

"Yes, you are. My mother is a dear, sweet woman who has been cooking Thanksgiving turkeys every year for at least thirty years. You're implying that she's somehow un-American."

"Well, she is. She's French Canadian. Did I say that was a crime?"

Hadley cleared his throat noisily. "Is this *relevant*?"

Tess felt herself flush. Jack had the grace to look mildly embarrassed.

"Not at all," Jack said.

"Certainly not," Tess admitted in a stifled voice. How did Jack do this to her? Why did she feel bound to take exception to nearly everything he said? And once again, he'd managed to make her feel utterly juvenile.

"Frankly," Jack said after a moment, "I can't even remember why this came up."

Tess wracked her brain, trying to remember what had led up to this.

Hadley spoke. "Something about how Thanksgiving is in five days and even though Brigitte doesn't consider it the most important holiday—"

"Yes!" said Jack. "Thank you, Hadley."

"No problem." The professor waved his pipe, dismissing the gratitude.

"The point I was trying to make," Jack said, turning back to Tess, "was that even though your mother doesn't consider it to be the most important of holidays, she's always been sure to observe Thanksgiving."

"Oh." Tess felt embarrassed that she'd leapt so swiftly to a conclusion that she'd been arguing with Jack about something he hadn't even said. "You're right."

"Of course," he said with male arrogance. "You should let me finish what I'm saying before you start arguing with me."

"Maybe you should be a little more careful about how you phrase things!"

Philpott sighed loudly. Jack and Tess glanced his way, then looked at one another.

"Sorry," Jack said.

"Me, too."

"Okay." Jack paused a moment. "Given that Brigitte has never missed at least the attempt to have a family Thanksgiving, it seems to me that she's not about to take a miss on it this year. In fact, the timing of all of this would seem to indicate that she's determined to have us all together this year for the holiday, unlike the last several years."

Tess flushed again, well aware that she'd been the person who had refused to come for the holidays. "So, she'll just show up here."

Jack shook his head. "Somehow I don't think so."

"Why not?"

"Not nearly dramatic enough for Brigitte."

Hadley Philpott nodded. "I would tend to agree with that."

Tess looked at the professor, wondering why he was inserting himself into the conversation.

"It would be *my* guess," Jack continued, "that we are supposed to find them."

The instinctive urge to argue with Jack rose again, but Tess quelled it, forcing herself to seriously consider what he was saying. Forced herself to consider her mother in an objective light, rather than defensively as she was accustomed to doing.

"You're right," she said finally. "You're absolutely right. It would delight her. She's probably laughing her damn fool head off right now, thinking of the mess she's made for us to sort out."

Jack suddenly laughed. "I know. God, I love that woman. Never a dull moment when she's around."

Tess, who could have used a few dull moments in her childhood, decided not to say so.

She was getting rather tired of squabbling with Jack, anyway.

"Okay," he said, "it's a treasure hunt."

"Probably," Tess agreed glumly. "That *would* be just like Brigitte."

"Now all we have to do is figure out where to look for the clues."

Before anyone could speak another word, however, Ernesto showed up in the living room doorway. "We're hungry," he announced. "Ya got any food in this place?"

"I can't believe I'm standing in a dark kitchen in the middle of a hurricane trying to make a meal for a total stranger by the light of an oil lamp."

Jack nodded agreement. "That pretty much sums it up, hon."

"I'm not your hon."

"Guess not," he said meekly enough, but even in the dim light cast by the oil lamp, she could see a gleam in his eye. "But to come back to the problem at hand . . ."

"Yes, by all means. Let's consider the problem at hand, a man who happens to be *your* friend."

"He's not my friend," Jack said, holding up his hands as if to push the mere thought away. "Not my friend at all."

"I thought you knew him from Miami."

"I know a lot of people, Shorty. Most of them are *not* my friends."

"Then why did I invite him to stay here?"

"Because you have a soft heart?" he suggested. "Although, I gotta admit, the idea of an IRS auditor with a soft heart kind of boggles the mind."

"Will you please lay off my career choice?"

"It was a choice?" He looked appalled. "I though a job like that had to be a sentence."

She wanted to bean him, but in the dim light there was nothing she could see that looked safe enough to throw at him. "Cut it out, Jack."

"Yes, Tess."

She looked suspiciously at him, but he had assumed a cherubic pose. "None of this explains why I invited that man to stay."

Jack shrugged. "Why do you suddenly need an explanation? You weren't going to let that slimeball, his wife, and baby be caught in the storm without shelter. Good Samaritan, that's you. It's only a minor problem, Tess. I'm sure a good whirl with an IRS-approved shrink will cure you of these humanitarian impulses."

She was just pulling a bag of fresh snap peas from the refrigerator, and she turned and threw it at Jack.

He caught it. "Hey, great pitch!"

She ignored him and turned her attention back to the contents of the fridge. The smartest way to use their food was to go first for the perishables that they could eat without cooking.

In relatively short order, she came up with

cold cuts, cheese, lettuce, and other sandwich fixings. "Will this do?"

"He'll be happy with whatever he gets," Jack said firmly.

"I have to admit, it seems odd to be making a meal for a man you were just yesterday accusing of kidnapping our parents."

He looked sheepish. "I think I went overboard. It gets to be an instinct, you know."

"What does?"

"The assumption that when you see someone familiar in the wrong place, they must be following you."

Tess put down the tomato she was holding and faced him. "Why would anybody follow you, Jack?"

He went suddenly very still, and his face grew distant. Then, as if somebody were flipping a switch, he shrugged, slouched, and grinned at her. "Told you, I'm just paranoid."

But Tess didn't believe that, and she found her gaze following Jack as he began to make sandwiches, thinking about all the things that statement could have meant. One thing that came through loud and clear, though, was that he was used to being followed. Either that or he was used to *fearing* that he was followed.

Either one could mean some pretty nasty things.

As she stood there passing him slices of salami and ham, she found herself seeing him in an entirely different light. Instead of pegging him automatically as the older stepbrother who had hated her on sight, she found herself looking at him as if they had no history together.

And what she saw made her heart squeeze in her chest.

Jack, she realized, was alone. Utterly and completely alone. But he'd always been a loner—all the way back to when they first met.

Maybe it had something to do with his mother's death when he was twelve. By the time Tess had met him nearly ten years later, Jack seemed to have developed the habit of always being by himself. He lived at home with his dad—although that had changed almost the instant that Brigitte and Steve had married—and attended college. He never brought home any friends. He never went out with any friends. Back then she'd dismissed him as a stupid geek.

But looking back, she could see that she had done some of the same things herself, as if trying to make up for her mother's sorrow over the divorce. Maybe that was what Jack had been doing: trying to fill the aching hole in his father's life after the death of his mother.

In retrospect, it hadn't been the wisest thing to do, she had to admit. Neither Brigitte nor Steve had found the solution to the holes in their lives until they had met each other.

But maybe that, and that alone, was why Jack had been so antisocial. And maybe, once cultivated, the habit had stayed with him. She'd kind of developed some of that habit herself.

"Do you have a life?" she asked him bluntly.

He looked up from the sandwiches. "What kind of question is that?"

"An honest one, Jack. Do you have friends? People you hang out with and have a good time with?"

"Sure. Don't you?"

"Well, yes."

"Then what makes you think I don't?"

"Did I say that?"

He sighed and started placing lettuce leaves on the sandwiches. "Somehow we always seem to be at cross purposes. Shall we try this again?"

"I just wanted to know if you have friends," she said, feeling defensive. "I thought maybe we could chat about life apart from the parents and this fiasco."

He looked up again, and this time a smile began to slide across his face. She didn't know if she liked it, because there was something about that smile that was almost . . . predatory. It was certainly masculine. "Aw, Tess," he said. "Are you trying to get to know me?"

All she had done was feel a surge of empathy for a man who struck her as very lonely, so she had asked about his life, hoping to discover he wasn't lonely at all. Now he was treating it as if she had made some kind of sexual advance. That was a man for you.

"No," she said icily. "I can't think of any reason on earth why I would want to get to know you. I merely wondered if you were the isolated misfit you appear to be."

"Wow!" His eyes grew huge, but there was

something mocking in the way they did it. "Isolated misfit. That's a creative epithet. Where did you pick that one up? In some pop psychology book?"

She cemented her teeth together, refusing to give in to the urge to hammer him with the roll of salami. "I was merely expressing an interest in your life. Being friendly. Surely, at some time over the years, you've actually had occasion to learn the rules of *friendliness*?"

"Well, yes," he said agreeably enough. "I haven't had much cause to apply them around *you*, though."

"And here I've been excusing you by thinking you simply didn't know any better."

"Uh-uh," he said, "*I* know better. You're the one who doesn't seem to. Of course, with Brigitte for a mother—"

"Leave my mother out of this."

"I would, except I have a strong feeling she's the entire reason you and I are housebound together in the middle of a hurricane. And I take back what I said earlier, about how she couldn't have caused this storm. I'm firmly convinced she went to the islands and found some witch doctor to summon this damn storm just so I couldn't get on a plane out of here."

Instead of snapping back at him, Tess felt her heart squeeze. Just a little. But a little too much to ignore. Good heavens, she couldn't possibly be feeling hurt because Jack Wright wanted to get the hell away from her? Not possible. Because if someone had offered her a trip out of here right now, she would have jumped on it.

Wouldn't she?

"What's the matter?" Jack asked. "Cat got your tongue? Or are you too angry to speak to me—not that it would be a novelty if you are, but inquiring minds want to know."

She looked down swiftly at the salami. "I'm not angry," she said, her voice muffled. What was the matter with her? Surely she couldn't be developing a fondness for her maddening, possibly reprehensible stepbrother?

"Hey, Tess," Jack said, his voice unusually gentle. "What's wrong? I didn't mean to hurt your feelings with what I said about Brigitte."

Tess managed a smile and an uncertain shrug. "Hey, she might have summoned the storm herself," she said with forced lightness. "Did you check to see if she took her broom with her?"

"Her broom . . . ?" Then Jack caught the allusion, and he laughed. "Nah."

She forced herself to be brisk, although all she really wanted to do was crawl into her bed and bury her head under her pillow, away from everything. "Come on, let's get these sandwiches made. And where's Hadley going to sleep?"

"Yeah, I guess we can't send him home in this." Jack sighed and slapped mayo on the last sandwich. "The sofa is a bed, isn't it?"

"I think so. But if he uses that, what are you going to do? Sleep in our parents' room?"

Jack shrugged. "I'll think of something."

She noticed he didn't say he'd sleep in Steve and Brigitte's room. Funny, but when she thought about it she felt the same way. Maybe because Steve wasn't a blood relative.

They passed out sandwiches at the dining room table, and Tess gave Ernesto's wife, Julia, a chance to eat by holding the baby for her.

The child's name was Guadalupe, a big name for a baby with a shock of black hair and big dark eyes, and who couldn't have weighed much more than twenty-five pounds. Whatever had been disturbing Guadalupe earlier had apparently passed because the child was looking around alertly and waving her little hands.

"She's beautiful," Tess told Julia, who beamed proudly.

"Yeah," Ernesto agreed, looking almost as proud.

"So what do you do, Ernesto?" Tess asked him. It was a casual enough question, but she was hoping he would say something that would give her more information about Jack.

Jack tensed, as if he were nervous about Ernesto's response, but the man merely said, "I'm a mechanic."

"He works on Mercedes," Julia said proudly. "We're going to buy a house soon."

Ernesto beamed. "Yeah. We already got it picked out. Nice little bungalow. Two bedrooms. Even got a bit of a backyard for the kid to play in."

"Sounds nice," Philpott remarked, a bread crumb clinging to his chin. "Very nice."

And it didn't tell Tess a thing about Jack, or

about why he'd tensed before Ernesto answered her.

The problem was that Jack raised too many questions and didn't offer many answers. That and that alone was an excellent reason not to grow fond of him—if she needed another reason, other than his being a pain in the neck.

Over the last hour, she'd grown so accustomed to the wind keening around the house that it came as a shock when it suddenly stopped.

Everyone at the table froze. Slowly they began looking around, certain that something must be wrong.

Jack spoke. "Could we have come through the eye wall already?"

"It sounds like it," Hadley replied. "Rather quickly, though. I thought it wasn't supposed to be here until two or three in the morning."

"Maybe the storm speeded up," Tess suggested.

"Maybe."

The silence was eerie. Uncomfortable. Oppressive, somehow. Tess, who hadn't been very hungry to begin with, now pushed her half sandwich aside untouched. The baby stirred in her arm. "I don't like this," she admitted frankly.

"Me neither," said Julia. Ernesto immediately slid closer to her and put an arm around her. She reached out and took her child back from Tess, who found she missed the child's warmth and weight against her.

"It won't last long," Philpott remarked, reaching for another half-sandwich. "The eye wasn't very well formed. We'll get a gust before long."

Almost as soon as he finished speaking, the wind's fist hammered at the side of the house again.

"See?" said Philpott, looking almost proud.

Tess and Jack exchanged glances, and Jack rolled his eyes.

"Well," Jack said after a moment, "you all go on eating. Tess and I have something we need to take care of."

She almost demanded to know what he was talking about, but caught herself in the nick of time. Restraining her curiosity, she managed to murmur, "Excuse me," and leave the table.

She followed Jack down the hall into their parents' bedroom, where he closed the door.

"That was rude," she said to him.

"Rude? They're not houseguests. We don't have to entertain them. They're flotsam tossed up by the storm."

"Flotsam?" She didn't know whether to laugh or be offended. Although in a way he was right. "Still—"

"Still nothing. Ernesto practically invited himself to stay here. For that matter, so did Philpott."

"Which is strange," Tess said after a moment of thought. "Don't you think so?"

He raised a quizzical brow. "What's strange?"

"Hadley Philpott showing up. Not the fact that he showed up, but that he showed up at the time he did—right on the edge of the storm. Ten minutes later and he wouldn't have been able to get here. Ten minutes earlier we could have sent him on his way."

He sighed. "Now *you're* being paranoid. It was just happenstance."

"You think so?" She frowned and shook her head. "We'll see."

"Come on, you don't think he's part of the master plot, do you?"

"Master plot?" It was her turn to look quizzical. "It's a bit much to assume everyone else in Paradise Beach is involved, isn't it?"

"I don't know. This place is crazy even without your mother. Name one other town where half the residents wore dog collars as part of a political protest."

"True," she admitted, smiling faintly as she remembered the event.

"And where else do you have the police chief dating a fortune-teller?"

"Oh, that's long over," Tess hastened to tell him. "They've both married someone else."

"Really? When?"

"Well, I think he married around the time of the dog collar thing, but I'm not sure. Rainbow might have married later."

"Rainbow. God, what a name." He sighed and went to sit on the edge of the bed.

True to Brigitte's taste, this room had nothing of the tropics about it. In fact, Tess had often thought it looked like a French whorehouse, with all the pink satin and black lace. But that was Brigitte. "This room gives me the willies," she said.

"Yeah, me, too," Jack said. He looked around. "I wonder if she has any idea what it looks like."

"I'm sure she does."

He looked at her with interest. "Why? Did she tell you?"

"No, I told *her*."

Jack's eyes widened, then he burst into laughter. "Oh, man, I wish I could have seen that."

"It wasn't all that exciting," Tess admitted, sitting on one of the pink upholstered Louis XV chairs. "She just looked at me as if I were incredibly slow and said, 'But of course, *cherie*.' "

Jack's laughter redoubled.

"Shh," Tess said. "You'll have all the rest of them down here wanting to know what's going on."

He promptly covered his mouth, but his eyes kept right on dancing. Too bad that he was so charming when he smiled.

"Anyway," she said when he'd quieted, "what *are* we doing in here?"

"I thought we'd search the place for clues."

"Search?" The thought made Tess quail. This was her mother's bedroom, and the trespass seemed too enormous to contemplate. "I don't know about that, Jack."

"Why not? What did they think we were going to do when they turned up missing? Sit around down here with our thumbs up our ... er ... noses?"

Tess flushed faintly, because she'd heard the expression he'd narrowly avoided using, and she'd always found it distasteful. Hardly surprising, however, that Jack would use it. "Maybe not. But this is . . . Look, we already searched the desk. That was trespass enough. Maybe we just didn't see what we were supposed to find. Or maybe we're really not supposed to find anything. Jack, it's entirely possible they're planning to come home on Thursday for Thanksgiving."

"Possible, but not very likely, and you know it as well as I do, Tess. Quit changing your mind. We agreed Brigitte would prefer that we have to find them."

It was true. In her heart of hearts, Tess knew it was true. Brigitte wouldn't have gone to these lengths just to make a dramatic reappearance on the holiday.

"Besides," Jack said, "if the whole purpose of this was to get the two of us to stop squabbling long enough to work together, then she can't just be planning to pop back home. It wouldn't work. We wouldn't have to cooperate at all."

She reluctantly had to admit he was right. "Still, searching their bedroom . . ."

He arched a sardonic brow. "What's the problem, Ms. Auditor? A sudden discovery of hitherto unrecognized ethics?"

"This is different from what I do, and you damn well know it. But I'm beginning to wonder about *you*. Don't *you* have any qualms about invading their privacy?"

"Well, of course. But I'm not overly concerned about it when they're the ones who set up the situation that demands it."

"We can just do nothing until they turn up! And they will, eventually."

"Assuming this is some plot on their part . . . yes, eventually they'll turn up. I agree. Six weeks, six months, whenever. But there are two problems with sitting around and doing nothing, Tess."

"What are they?"

"First of all, I can't have the sheer joy of getting even. And second, what if they really *are* missing?"

"Oh, God, we agreed they're probably not!" She couldn't believe he was doing this to her. "Will you just make up your mind?"

"I pretty much have. They're going to get what they deserve for this little scheme, and that includes having me go through their bedroom looking for clues."

She could have left. She didn't. Instead she remained sitting on the chair, watching as Jack began to open drawers and paw through them, beginning with the nightstands.

After a bit, something struck her. "You're awfully good at that," she said.

He looked up from a dresser drawer. "Thanks. I guess."

"So how often do you search people's rooms?"

Something in her tone must have disturbed him, because he suddenly straightened and looked straight at her. "What do you mean by that?"

"Just that you're awfully good at looking through things without disturbing them. I bet when you get done, no one will ever notice you were in those drawers."

His face darkened. "Where are you going with this, Tess?"

"Oh, just wondering if you're a jewel thief or something."

He looked thunderstruck. Then he laughed. "My God, what an imagination. Shorty, if I were a jewel thief, I'd be living the high life in the south of France."

She nodded, smiling wryly. "I guess I would be, too."

"You? Really? I'd have thought you would have preferred the more straitlaced climate of England."

"Shows how well you know me." Because somewhere deep inside, she cherished dreams of someday being able to burst out of the gray-suit class into something considerably more relaxed. But it wasn't a dream she ever mentioned out loud because there was no point in it. "I'm really not straitlaced, you know."

"Really? You could fool me. I have a permanent mental image of you as a severe Victorian headmistress, laced up so tight in your corset that you can hardly breathe."

"Hmm." A devil grabbed her mouth then, because she said, "So that's the way you lean?"

"Wouldn't you like to know."

She realized with surprise that she *would* like to know. In fact, there was a whole lot about Jack she would have liked to know. Starting with what he did for a living. That thought brought her sharply back down to earth.

Jack opened the bottom drawer on the dresser and froze. He let out a low whistle.

"What?" Tess asked.

He whistled again. Then he picked up something and turned, holding it out to her.

Tess stared. Then a hot blush rose from her throat to her hairline. "Oh, my God," she said in a muffled voice. "Are those . . . ?"

"Handcuffs," he said. "Well, actually, slave bracelets. Soft leather, wide enough not to cut off circulation—"

Tess couldn't stand it. "Oh, please, stop! I don't want all the details." Her heart was pounding uncomfortably, and it was suddenly difficult to breathe.

"Really?" He flashed a wicked grin. "You were the one who asked."

"That's enough. I really don't want to know this."

"Don't you have even a little healthy prurient interest?"

"No!"

"Why? Because these belong to your mother? Or because you really are a straitlaced prude?"

Now how in the world was she supposed to answer? Finally she said, "We have no business prying into their personal business. Particularly this. It has nothing to do with their having vanished."

"Maybe, maybe not." He dropped the cuffs back in the drawer and pawed around a little more, giving another whistle. "My, my, my. It's appalling to realize my dad has more fun than I do."

Tess felt the blush burning her cheeks again. "Jack, please."

"Please what?" He shoved the drawer closed and turned toward her. He was only eighteen inches away now, and his voice dropped seductively. "Please don't talk about what it might be like? Haven't you ever wondered what it would feel like to be totally at your lover's mercy, Tess? To be unable to do anything except accept whatever pleasure he chooses to give you?"

"Jack!" But her voice sounded smothered, and she couldn't even look at him. Her heart was pounding too hard, and she was feeling a yearning ache in places she usually did her best to ignore.

His voice was low, sinuous. "Has a lover ever done that for you, Tess?"

"I don't take lovers." The words burst out of her, born of a desperate need to shut him up before he managed to turn her into a puddle on the floor.

He stiffened, then dropped to the floor, sitting cross-legged facing her. "My God," he said, his voice hushed. "You're exaggerating."

She hunched a shoulder, refusing to argue. She wasn't going to admit to *him* of all people that she was utterly inexperienced. Well, except for that "almost" time with her first boyfriend, where she'd recovered her senses in the nick of time.

"You aren't exaggerating," he said after a moment. "Tess . . . Tess . . . are you a virgin?"

"It's none of your business," she said weakly.

"You're right, it isn't. And that's all the answer I need anyway."

After a moment, he shoved himself back to his feet. "I'll check out the closet. And we'll pretend we never had this discussion."

Which, she supposed, was a very generous thing for him to say. Jack could have taken this little bit of knowledge and turned it into several months of torture, if he'd chosen to.

He disappeared into the walk-in closet, giving her a chance to persuade her respiration and pulse to return to normal. Unfortunately, it also gave her time to think. Time to think about the soft, hungry feeling that had blossomed inside of her and that wouldn't let go. About the way his voice had seemed to stroke her nerve endings when he lowered it to intimacy. About what he had said about being able to do nothing but accept pleasure from her lover. . . .

Her heart was thudding heavily, and there was a throbbing between her legs that made her wish Jack would just come out of that closet and touch her.

But he didn't come out of the closet, and that was a good thing. Because just as soon as her body returned to normal, she wasn't going to want him that close.

She hated him, she reminded herself. She'd hated him for years. And it was going to take more than a momentary sexual urge to overcome that.

She hoped.

10

"**Y**ou're not going to sleep in my room!" Tess stood in the doorway, staring at Jack with utter disbelief.

"Well, what else am I supposed to do? You've at least got a couch in there that I can stretch out on."

"Sleep in Steve and Brigitte's bed!"

He shook his head. "I wouldn't be able to think about anything except what I found in that drawer."

She wished he hadn't reminded her of that. She really wished it. Because the instant he did, she felt that heavy, internal melting again.

"Sleep on the living room floor," she forced herself to say sternly.

"Hadley Philpott snores. He's louder than the hurricane."

Which had quieted down some. Apparently the worst was over. None of which was going to get rid of their houseguests—not before morning, anyway.

"Fine," she said. "I'll sleep on the living room floor."

"Be my guest." He stood back and waved an arm grandly, inviting her to go. She snatched the pillow, blanket, and flashlight out of his hands and marched down the hall and into the living room.

Unfortunately, he was right about Hadley's snoring. Tess stood there a minute, listening to a roar that ought to shake the roof, and considered going to sleep in her mother's bed.

Except she knew Jack was right. She couldn't do that. Especially *now*. She wouldn't sleep a wink. Groaning, she turned on her heel, deciding to just go back to her room and put up with Jack . . . all of which she could have done a whole lot more easily if he hadn't followed her.

He was standing just inside the living room, leaning against the doorjamb with his arms folded, looking at her with one of those hateful *I told you so* smiles that he seemed to hold the patent on.

"Too noisy, Tess?" he asked.

"Don't rub it in," she snapped, wishing she could wipe that obnoxious look off his face.

"Why not? It's one of life's greatest pleasures."

She pushed past him, stuffing the pillow and blanket back into his arms but keeping the flashlight. "Sleep wherever. Just don't keep me awake."

"I wouldn't dream of it," he said, too sincerely. She sniffed loudly, but refused to rise to the bait.

Back in her room, she climbed under the covers fully clothed, because she was damned if she was going to change into a nightie to share a room with a man. Especially Jack.

He made a big deal out of spreading the blanket out on the couch, and of punching the pillow into comfortable shape. Then he blew out the oil lamp that was burning on the night table and lay down. She heard the couch creak a little beneath his weight.

She tried to pay attention to the sounds from outside, because they seemed safer than the sounds within the room—sounds like the heavy beating of her own heart.

The wind seemed to have lightened; it no longer sounded like a banshee. It was a quieter moan now, and the house wasn't creaking as much. It would be mostly over by morning, a thought which comforted her.

But after a while, the quieting storm couldn't hold her attention any longer. She fancied she could hear Jack breathing, and found herself unable to ignore the sound.

She wasn't used to sleeping in the same room with someone else. All her life she'd had her own bedroom, even at college where she'd rented an apartment off campus with two other girls.

Yes, she was sure she could hear Jack's breathing, and now that she thought about it, it didn't sound as if he were sleeping, either. Every now and then an impatient sigh escaped him. Moments later it would be followed by the sound of him tossing on the couch. Finally he confirmed her suspicion.

"Damn it," he said.

"What's wrong?"

"The couch supports are catching me right in the kidneys."

"Nasty." What was she supposed to do—offer him her bed?

Instead of the thought being sarcastic or even irritated, it unexpectedly turned into something else altogether. *Not fair*, wailed a voice in her mind as she found her thoughts straying down paths they rarely followed. Paths she didn't want to tread while thinking of Jack.

But as if someone had thrown a switch, changing her mood entirely, she suddenly felt languorous . . . heavy, warm, and deliciously weak. She knew what the feeling was—she wasn't *that* inexperienced—but it wasn't a feeling she wanted.

Wanted or not, it flooded her, infusing first her body and then her brain with longings whose strength terrified her.

She didn't want to have the hots for anybody, but Jack least of all. Stupid as it sounded, Jack was a symbol of a very bad time in her life, the time when her mother had left her father, then married another man. That marriage had meant one thing and one thing only to her: that her father and mother would never get back together again.

She had hated her mother for that, at least for a time. And by extension she had hated both Jack and his father for being a party to her mother's defection. Steve had made it really hard to be angry with him for long, though. He had welcomed Tess into his life as if she were his own long-lost daughter, treating her with such affection and kindness that before long she was won over.

But Jack . . . Jack had made it easy to stay angry with him. At twenty-one, he'd been just old enough and just young enough to make her absolutely miserable with his sniping and sideways remarks.

In all fairness, though, she had to admit she'd been responsible for a lot of that. Her own mouth had been going all the time, too, spilling the anger she felt toward the whole world back then. So she had deserved at least some of what she got in kind from Jack.

In retrospect, she must have been about as welcome to Jack as he to her. He clearly hadn't been any happier about the marriage than she had. But at least he'd had a way out. A few weeks after the wedding, he'd packed his bags and had ridden off into the metaphorical sunset, returning only for holidays.

Holidays which had grown increasingly uncomfortable. Because as the two of them had grown older, their animosity had metamorphosed from angry, childish rantings into something that ran much deeper and created far worse tensions. Yes, they still squabbled, but the tension underlying those squabbles had become profound.

She wondered why that was. But before she could pursue this uncomfortable line of thought much further, Jack stirred and cursed.

"I'm going to throw this damn couch out the window," he groused.

"Hey, *some* people are trying to sleep."

"Really? I thought you were wrestling with the bedcovers."

For the first time she realized that all the while she'd been thinking, she been tossing and turning, too, trying to find a comfortable place on the mattress. "This bed is too hot," she finally said. "And my pillow has hard lumps."

"Sounds exactly like this blankety-blank couch. This room is a torture chamber."

She was inclined to agree, but not for the same reason. The irritation that was riding along her nerve endings, making her as sensitive as the Princess and the Pea, was not being caused by the bed. Or the temperature. Or the pillow.

"You know," she said acidly, "I could probably get comfortable a lot faster if I didn't have to listen to *you* tossing and cursing."

"I wasn't tossing and cursing. I was forcing myself to lie perfectly still."

"Yeah, right."

"I was. Until I got fed up with *you* tossing and turning, and decided I didn't have to get a bruised kidney from holding still if you were going to thrash around."

"I was *not* thrashing."

"No? Mud wrestling, maybe? Scrambling for first down in the football game? Rock climbing a horizontal slope?"

"Oh, just hush up!"

He did. But now she could hear him breathing. The raging of the storm had given way to quiet, and she could actually hear him breathing. Or maybe he was breathing heavily?

The thought of what might have him doing that made her grow languorous and heavy all over again. She found herself wishing he'd breathe like that right in her ear. Close. Really close.

A shiver trickled through her, a rare sensation of sensual pleasure. And all because of the thought of Jack Wright actually breathing in her ear. Oh, God, this was appalling.

But however disgustingly weak she might be, she couldn't corral her thoughts. They strayed, reconsidering the way Jack looked in a polo shirt and shorts. His broad shoulders. Really *nice* broad shoulders. Tanned, powerful arms. And those narrow hips. . . .

She was hardly aware that she sucked in air as she thought about Jack's hips. What was wrong with her? All of a sudden the only thing she could think about was putting her hands on Jack's hips. Feeling how hard and flat they were. Drawing them closer to her own. . . .

Grabbing the pillow, she pulled it over her face

and pressed it hard against her mouth. She couldn't be thinking these things. She couldn't be thinking about those slave bracelets in her mother's bedroom, and wondering what it would be like to wear them. Wondering what it would be like to make *Jack* wear them.

She was afraid to move a muscle. The drumming need in her body was reaching a fever pitch, and she knew with absolute certainty that if she moved a muscle she'd be flying across the room and throwing herself on Jack like some kind of wanton.

She tried to chide herself out of the mood, but nothing was working. It was as if her body had decided to betray her, and her mind was joining the conspiracy against her wishes. To think she'd used to laugh at people who said they couldn't help themselves.

Jack was only a few feet away. All that kept her from calling out to him was an awareness at the back of her mind that when this mood passed she would feel utterly humiliated.

The bed dipped beside her and she jumped, flinging the pillow off her face. The flashlight was on now, lending a shadowy yellow glow to the room, making it possible for her to see Jack sitting beside her on the bed.

"Thank God," he said. "I was beginning to wonder if you'd suffocated."

Oh, no, he was too close.

"Sorry I bothered you," he continued. "I got up to go to the bathroom and saw you with the pillow on your head. You weren't trying to commit *hara-kiri*, were you?"

Was he crazy? She couldn't seem to find her voice. Or her breath, for that matter. She was breathing so heavily it would have embarrassed her, if she hadn't been aching so badly between her legs. If she hadn't felt so helpless in the thrall of this unwanted desire.

"I didn't think so."

His voice had grown husky and even a little thick. He sounded just like she felt. The warning bell that sounded in the distant outback of her mind was faint, easy to ignore.

"You're a pain in the butt," he said, but the breathiness of his voice took all the sting from the words.

"You, too," she managed to say around a tongue that had grown disobedient.

"At least we agree on something." He leaned closer—too close?—and looked directly into her eyes. The light from the flashlight was dim and growing dimmer, but she could still see the heat in his gaze. Could feel the touch of his eyes like the lick of fire.

"It occurs to me," he whispered, and the sound seemed to brush sensuously against her nerve endings, "that there might be something else we can agree on."

She had a feeling his thoughts were running in the same direction as hers. A soft gasp escaped her and her brain went into total meltdown. She couldn't move a muscle. She could only wait. And hope. And need.

His face came closer, his breath feathered her cheeks . . . then, wonder of wonders, his mouth settled on hers, a warm, firm pressure that was the answer to her every wish.

Oh, he smelled so good. Felt so good. The prickle of his beard stubble against her cheek was surely the most exciting thing she had ever felt. His mouth gently touching hers, as if seeking but never demanding, the scent of him, the exquisite sensation when his chest brushed against her breasts as he leaned closer. . . .

She was lost, needing more and yet more. Yearning to the deepest parts of her soul. She forgot who he was. Forgot who *she* was. Didn't care how many hatchets they needed to bury. All she knew was she wanted this perfect moment to go on forever.

But all too soon he lifted his head. The flashlight was dying, and she could barely make out his face. He touched her cheek, brushed a strand of her hair back.

"I vote," he said huskily, "that we explore the possibility of détente."

Then, before she could gather enough of her brain to form a word or two, he rose and returned to the couch.

Tess lay without moving, listening to him toss around until finally he fell asleep. She didn't join him in sleep for a long, long time.

Because she had just realized that she was in very deep trouble.

* * *

Morning brought watery light and steady drizzle. Jack rose before everyone else and went to check on the world. He felt grungier than he could say, and wished he'd had the presence of mind last night to retrieve his clothes from the room he'd turned over to Ernesto and family. Right now a close encounter with some hot water and a toothbrush would be welcome.

But there was no hot water, because the power still wasn't on. Using his finger, he made an attempt to clean his teeth at the kitchen sink and felt marginally better. Then he went to the front door and stepped outside.

The world had been changed. The neat yard, which he had mowed only yesterday, was covered with debris: scraps of paper and plastic, tree branches, and palm fronds. Nothing too serious; just a mess.

He stepped through the gate and looked up and down the street. Other than the windblown debris and standing water wherever there was a dip or depression, the street didn't look too bad. All the roofs seemed intact, and everyone had boarded up or closed their shutters.

Down near the corner an oak had been uprooted, but the wind had tossed it across the street, not against anyone's house. By and large, Bluebird Lane had come off pretty well. He wondered how it was down on the beach.

He also wondered how he was going to get rid of Ernesto, now that the danger was past. Philpott he wasn't too concerned about; the man would probably be eager to get back home. But

Ernesto was another problem altogether.

Pausing at the sidewalk to look back at the house and check the roof, it suddenly struck Jack that he might be wrong about things. Ernesto's appearance here in Paradise Beach was just too damn coincidental. What's more, it was a little hard to swallow, now that he thought about it, that Ernesto had been thrown out of his motel *after* the drawbridge had been closed.

Ugly suspicions had been put away in the belief that Brigitte had planned this entire escapade. But what if . . . ?

No, he told himself firmly. Too many other things indicated that Brigitte and Steve were off on some vacation and had set this whole thing up. Besides, Ernesto was a penny-ante drug dealer, with none of the connections that would make what Jack was contemplating possible. If he'd been dealing with the Colombian cartel, that would have been a different matter. But Ernesto? Ernesto, the dime-a-bag corner dealer who bought his inventory from a slightly bigger dealer who sold out of a 1987 bright green Cadillac Seville? Ernest was so far removed from people who might be interested in using a kidnapping to make a point that the whole idea was laughable.

Okay, what if Tess was right when she accused him of being too paranoid? Maybe his lifestyle had affected his brain. Maybe he needed to reconsider whether he wanted to spend the rest of his life looking over his shoulder.

Or maybe he was just losing it. That was entirely possible, given that he'd kissed Tess last night. If that wasn't a stroke of insanity, he didn't know what was.

Getting a trash can from the garage, he started picking up the debris. It was a great excuse not to face Tess.

Who, after that kiss last night, was probably going to be looking to boil him in oil or flay him alive. He didn't figure she was the kind of woman who would take his insolence lying down.

Insolence? Good God, he never used words like that. It did, however, sound exactly like the epithets she loved to fling his way. Had she ever called him that in the past? He couldn't remember. But it was definitely a Tess-type insult.

He'd filled two cans with debris and was thinking about trying to sneak inside for some garbage bags when the front door popped open and Tess came out.

She had changed into clean clothes and brushed her hair, but she didn't look as if she felt any better than he did.

"It's so humid," she said irritably as she came to stand beside him. "It's humid in the house, too. Did you notice? It's starting to feel like the inside of a tent."

"Maybe the power will come back on soon."

"I just hope the sun doesn't come out. We're going to roast if it does."

"Yeah."

She looked at him finally. "You *do* know you're getting wet from the rain?"

"Yeah. So are you."

"Well . . ." She hesitated, then folded her arms and looked down at the ground. "I was wondering if you're okay. I mean, when I realized you weren't in the house, I came out here, and I find you standing here in the drizzle getting soaked. . . ." She trailed off, as if realizing she might be saying too much.

He couldn't help it. He really wanted to be sober, serious, gentle, all those modern guy types of things, but instead all he could feel was a quiver of genuine delight that slapped a broad grin across his face. "You were looking for me!"

She glanced up at him, and a frown appeared between her brows—a deep crease that he was sure must intimidate taxpayers all the time. "I wasn't looking for you!"

"No?"

"No! I just wanted to find out what you think we should do about breakfast for the mob."

"Breakfast? You wanted to ask me about *breakfast*? I'm crushed."

For the merest instant, he almost thought he saw a smile twinkle in her eye. Despite himself, he was enchanted.

"Exactly," she said primly. "I have a whole bunch of people to feed, and no power. I wanted a suggestion."

"I've got a suggestion," he said, brushing his hands together to get some of the dirt off. "Follow me."

She hesitated, as if she were thinking about balking, and he half hoped she would, because her contrariness would remind him of all the reasons he shouldn't allow himself to feel anything at all about her. But with an almost imperceptible shrug, she followed him back into the house.

Ernesto and his wife were sitting in the dining room with an oil lamp burning on the table, looking as if they were waiting for something.

"We're hungry," Ernesto said.

"Where's the baby?" Jack asked.

"Asleep."

"Good. Get your shoes on."

"My shoes?"

"You wanna eat, you gotta help."

"Now, wait a minute, man—"

Jack turned sharply and looked straight at Ernesto, an expression that would freeze fire. "This isn't a hotel, Ernesto. Accommodations don't come with room service. If you want to eat here, you're going to help."

"Absolutely," said Hadley Philpott from behind them, startling them all because they hadn't heard him come from the living room. "What do you need done?"

Jack, who hadn't been thinking of asking Hadley for any help at all, given his age, couldn't think of a graceful way to refuse the offer. "We need to take down the boarding over the windows so we can see in here. Then we'll get around to breakfast."

"Sounds like slave labor to me," Ernesto grumbled.

"Not at all," Philpott said bracingly to him. "It's barter. Work for food. A very old tradition."

Jack led his partly reluctant crew outside. Tess followed to lend a hand, but he sent her back inside and suggested she have Julia strip the bed she and Ernesto had slept in, and maybe clean the bathroom they'd used.

Apparently Tess got the idea, because she grinned and disappeared inside.

The neighbors were soon out doing much the same thing, and Jack had no qualms about volunteering his crew to help them as soon as the Wright house was done.

"But what about breakfast?" Ernesto whined.

"We're working up a wonderful appetite for it," Hadley said bracingly.

"Actually," said Jack, "I just want to know anything you two might know about my parents."

By this time they'd moved along to the Mason household and were helping to take down the last of the boarding. The rest of the street was nearly done, too.

"Are we back to that?" Ernesto demanded, stomping his foot. "I can't believe you, man! I told you I don't know *nothing* about no kidnapping."

"Kidnapping?" Philpott suddenly looked concerned. "Have they been kidnapped? I thought they'd taken a vacation to St. Kitts or Aruba or something."

Jack turned to him. "Where? Where did you say?"

Philpott blinked, taken aback. "Well, that's just it. I'm not *sure* exactly where they said they were going. I have it in mind that they're down there somewhere, but there are so many islands, and I'm not really all that interested in the Caribbean. It's too much like home. So I generally take my vacations in Europe. Brigitte quite agreed with me on that, you know. She loved Paris, but Steve preferred Britain."

"Then why did they go to the Caribbean?" Jack demanded.

Pillpott looked regretful. "That I really couldn't say. I *was* rather surprised that Brigitte seemed delighted at the idea, though."

"Why didn't you tell us this last night?"

Philpott shrugged. "Mary wanted me to be sure to tell you that one thing. Apparently she thought it was significant."

And it might have been, Jack admitted. "Did my folks talk to Mary about this trip?"

"Now, that I wouldn't know."

"But you're sure they said St. Kitts or Aruba?"

"No, no, that's just it. For all I know, it could have been St. Croix. They're all the same to me." Philpott sighed. "I'm truly sorry to disappoint you, Jack. But at this point, I'm not even sure that they *did* mention any particular island."

Jack felt deflated.

They finished removing the boarding from Maudeen Mason's house, stashing it in her garage. Then they escaped her gratitude as quickly as possible and headed back to the Wright house.

There Julia was pouting because she'd been forced to help make beds with fresh sheets. Looking at the two of them, Jack figured Ernesto and his family would be leaving right now if there were any place to go.

Which was the way he wanted it. He hadn't minded taking them in when they had nowhere to go, but they were rather demanding for uninvited guests. And he wanted to be sure they didn't impose any longer than necessary.

But with the windows and doors unboarded, life got considerably easier. There was gas in the gas grill, so he moved it onto the patio and fired it up. Brigitte, bless her, still preferred pressed coffee, so it was easy enough to boil a saucepan of water and make the coffee in the press. Everyone had a cup, and tempers seemed to calm a little, even though a hot drink wasn't exactly the most comfortable choice on such a warm, muggy day.

"It's awfully late in the year for a storm like this," Philpott remarked.

"Yes, but remember the No Name Storm?" Jack asked.

"That's true. Very true. Basically a hurricane in March. Disrupted the entire East Coast."

Tess left her coffee on the patio table and disappeared into the house. A few minutes later she came out carrying a large frying pan, which she set on the grill. "I don't know about anyone else, but I'm starved. Will someone help?"

There was no shortage of hands. Even Ernesto was willing to help when there was food involved.

An hour later they were eating eggs, sausage, and pan-fried toast. Not a bad meal. Everyone was feeling all sociable and pleasant.

Then Ernesto had to open his mouth. "So," he said, around a mouthful of toast, "you two must be really something to make your parents run away from you."

"**H**e was right, you know," Tess said glumly a short while later. She and Jack were in the kitchen, washing dishes. Philpott had gone home, now that the weather had improved. Ernesto and his family had set out to see if they could get back into their motel.

"Who was right?"

"Ernesto. What he said about how we had to really be something to make our parents run away."

"Our parents ran away from home." Jack said it out loud, testing it. "Sounds pretty bad, I do confess."

"It sounds *awful*."

"So maybe that's not what happened."

She looked over her shoulder at him. He was

standing at one of the cupboards, dish towel in hand, drying a cup.

"You know," he said, "cold water sucks for washing dishes. They're impossible to dry."

"I'm not going to let the egg harden on them."

"Of course not."

"So," she said, still looking at him, "what do you mean, maybe that's not what happened?"

"I don't know. This whole thing is driving me nuts." He shook his head and reached for another plate. "First we think they've disappeared. Maybe gotten into trouble somewhere. But if that were the case, we'd have heard something about it."

"Are you sure of that?"

"As sure as I can be of anything. By now they would have contacted someone for help. And how much trouble could they get into, anyway?"

Thinking of her mother, Tess shuddered. "Don't ask."

"Okay, but Steve is there, too. And to be honest, Tess, he *can* put a damper on your mother when he wants to."

She acknowledged it, though she wasn't one hundred percent certain.

"What I *am* sick of," he said, "is spinning my wheels. We're going 'round and 'round and getting nowhere. Okay, we know they flew because that's what your mother said. So we don't have to worry that their boat sank and no one knows it. We know they went to the Caribbean because two independent sources have confirmed it."

"If you can call what we were told confirmation."

He shrugged. "It's what we've got. We go with it."

"Okay."

"They were taking a Caribbean holiday. The weird thing is that they took a vacation without giving both of us a copy of their itinerary."

"True."

"Which means, for some reason, they didn't want us to know. And that leads me directly back to Hadley Philpott's rendition of what your mother said."

Tess finished the last dish and set it in the drain. She shook her hands off and reached for a towel to dry them on. "It sounds like a plot," she said finally. It sounded *so* much like Brigitte.

"Right. And my guess would be that either we haven't found all the clues we're supposed to yet, or Brigitte screwed something up."

Tess bristled. "You're assuming this was all my mother's idea."

Jack grinned. "Hey, I love my father, Shorty, but he couldn't be this original if his life depended on it. The man has spent his entire life coloring inside the lines."

"And my mother hasn't," she admitted unhappily. When she was safely all the way up in Chicago, she could appreciate her mother's appeal a whole lot better than when she was on the receiving end of one of Brigitte's schemes.

"Besides," said Jack simply, "this is all we've got to go on. What's making me crazy is that there isn't something more. Hadley mentioned Aruba and St. Kitts. But that's too damn easy."

Tess pulled out a chair at the kitchen table and sat, resting her chin on her hand. "Why? Just how difficult should they make it?"

"Difficult enough that we get tired of our own company and stop sniping."

"We already have."

He arched a brow. "You think so?"

Well, no. But she was tired of being cooped up in this house with no air-conditioning—good heavens, it was a wonder she wasn't growing mildew!—with no lights, no hot water, no television, and wondering what in the world she had done to deserve this.

"I'm going to kill her," she announced.

"I may join you." Finished drying the dishes, he pulled out the chair next to her and sat. "I don't think we were *that* bad."

"Me neither."

"A little bit of sniping is healthy."

"Absolutely. Keeps the blood moving. Damn it," she burst out, "they've ruined my Thanksgiving!"

"Did you have plans?" he asked with patent surprise.

"Yes, as a matter of fact, I did," she snapped. "A group of us from work had rented some cottages on a lake up in Wisconsin. We were going to have a great time cross-country skiing, sitting by a fire, cooking a big Thanksgiving meal.... And now I'm going to miss it."

"You can still go," he suggested. "I'll keep

looking for them, but there's no reason *both* of us have to."

She was appalled. "You're joking, right?"

"Uh, no, I don't think so."

"Are you crazy? I can't go run off to have fun when I don't know what's happened to them!"

"But we're pretty sure this is a hoax."

"And what if it isn't? Give me some credit, Jack."

"I do," he hastened to assure her. "It's just that you're redundant."

"Redundant?" She stared at him in astonishment. She thought, but couldn't be sure, she saw a gleam in his eye.

"Well, yes," he said. "The two of us are doing exactly the same thing. One of us could do it just as well."

"Oh, my God." She groaned the words. "Are you sure you don't work for the IRS?"

He paused. "It's my understanding that I *do* work four or five months every year for the IRS. Doesn't everyone?"

"Oh, stop it. That's irrelevant. Just quit talking like a bean counter."

"Bean counter!" His eyes were dancing merrily. "Hey, what happened to my life of crime? Or my beach bumming?"

She scowled at him. "Why don't you just tell me what you do for a living, and put me out of my misery."

"That's just it," he said, leaning close. "Telling you would take all the fun out of it."

That was bait she ordinarily would have been

unable to resist, but this time the instinctive response didn't rise in her. It couldn't. He was so close she could feel the whisper of his breath against her cheek, and all of a sudden she was in the bed last night again, feeling him close, feeling his lips on hers.

Something in his expression changed. She saw it happen, knew that he was reading her mind as surely as if she had a neon ticker running across her forehead. A flare of panic rose in her, but it wasn't strong enough to free her from the paralysis that had gripped her.

The heat, the traitorous heat, was rising in her again, filling her with needs that had nothing to do with beaning Jack Wright. And everything to do with the fact that he was a man and she was a woman, and how could she have missed noticing that all these years?

"Tess," he said. His voice seemed to have lowered an octave, and was soft. Sinuous. Enticing. "We'll find them, Tess. I don't care what it takes. I promise."

She nodded slowly. And she was enthralled enough that she didn't even question his ability to make such a promise. Instead, she just sat there gazing at him like a rapturous ninny.

The thought struck her just as he blinked and moved quickly back, as if he, too, had come to his senses.

"Um . . ." He went to stand by the stove. "Détente," he said almost desperately. "Let's shoot for détente, at least temporarily."

"Okay." She couldn't seem to say more than that.

"As for our parental units..." He shook his head. "They must have left clues somewhere. Otherwise this entire exercise is pointless."

"We've said that before, Jack, and we searched their bedroom." The memory of that still made her blush. "Nothing. Zip. Zero. The big goose egg."

"All that means is that we're not looking in the right place. Remember those treasure hunt parties Brigitte used to throw? The woman took diabolical delight in hiding the clues in ridiculous places."

"True. My favorite was the exhaust pipe on the car."

"I kinda liked the one in the rain gutters, myself."

Tess shook her head. "I always thought that was a bad choice. Somebody could have gotten hurt on the ladder."

"Are you sure you aren't an insurance actuary?"

Irritation caused her cheeks to flush. "Can we get back to the point here?"

"I thought we *were* on point. Brigitte is unpredictable. Well, predictably unpredictable."

She looked askance at him. "Okay, so what do you want to do? Check out the gutters? The attic? The garage?"

"All of the above."

She wanted to groan. She wanted to flee. She didn't want to do any of this. But she wasn't going to be able to rest easy until the two of them had been found, even if it *was* nothing but a stupid treasure hunt.

And if Brigitte *had* planned all of this, Tess was never going to forgive her. Never.

"It's not that bad," Jack said soothingly. "I'll do all the dirty stuff."

"I'm not afraid to get dirty!"

"No?" He glanced over her pristine white shorts and bright yellow top. "Well, okay. Then what's the problem?"

"I just resent the hell out of having to do this."

"You and me both, Shorty. You and me both."

First they checked all the toilet tanks in the house.

"I never would have thought of that," Tess said as they looked in the first one.

"Great hiding place," Jack said. "People stash drugs in the tanks all the time. Course, now that everyone knows about it, it doesn't work as well."

She didn't ask how he knew about that. She didn't want to know.

She did, however, think he was going too far when he wanted to dismantle the pipes under the sink to check the traps.

"Come on, Jack," she said impatiently. "Can you see Brigitte taking apart the plumbing? It'd ruin her nails."

"Yeah, but it wouldn't ruin Steve's and I can see her making him do it."

Tess shook her head impatiently. "I think that's going way too far. The sinks would back up."

He looked disappointed, almost as if he had been looking forward to tearing apart the plumbing. "All right. I'll save it for a last resort."

They checked under the sofa cushions, then, with a great deal of effort, they turned the sofa over.

"Too hard," Tess said as they struggled to tip the sofa bed. "They didn't do this."

"Maybe not." He wiped his brow with the back of his arm and muttered, "Damn, I wish the power would come back on."

"Me, too." Ardently. Devoutly. Her clothes were plastered to her from sweat.

Nothing under the couch. Tess gave Jack an *I told you so* glance that made him shrug.

They checked the undersides of drawers in the kitchen, shook magazines until loose mailers covered the floor. They looked at the undersides of the dining room chairs, pawed through the drawers in the potting bench on the patio, and even scanned the shrubbery and trees for some sign of a clue.

Finally, all that was left was the garage. By now they were both tired, frustrated, and hungry.

"I don't care if we ever find them," Tess muttered, collapsing on a lawn chair.

"How unfilial."

"How unparental of *them*."

He sank into the chair beside her. "My kingdom for some ice."

"Maybe some of the stuff in the fridge hasn't completely melted."

He gave her a look that said, *Yeah, right.*

Just then, careening around the corner of the house in a lavender golf cart came Mary Todd. She braked to an abrupt halt in front of them, leaving a skid marks on the patio. "Good afternoon," she said, her dark eyes gleaming inquisitively. "Did you ever find them?"

Jack and Tess exchanged looks. "Hi, Mary," Jack said.

"Hi," Tess echoed.

"Hi yourselves," Mary said tartly. "Now what about your missing relatives? Did you locate them?"

"Not yet."

"Hmm." Mary frowned in perplexity. "Imagine that. I was sure you'd have it all sorted out by now."

"Well, we haven't," Tess said.

"No, we haven't," Jack agreed pleasantly.

"Hmm," Mary said again. Reaching for her ebony cane, she used it to steady herself as she climbed out of her golf cart and came to sit near them on a lawn chair. "Hadley *did* give you the message, didn't he?"

Tess was beginning to feel a strong prickle of suspicion. Mary's interest in the matter was too ... intense. "Yes, he did. In fact, he spent the night here because of the storm."

"Tsk," Mary said. "I told him not to dawdle

on his way over here, or he'd get caught by the storm. The damage from it isn't that bad, by the way. I just drove along the boulevard. Some beach erosion, of course, but I don't think anyone on the beach was flooded." She gave a chuckle. "The dang storm can't have been a hurricane by the time it hit us. If it had been, that seedy motel I keep trying to find an excuse to evict off my property would be gone. Damn it."

A surprised laugh escaped Tess. "I wonder if that was the place where Ernesto was staying."

"Who's Ernesto?" Mary asked, her eyes sharp.

"Some friend of Jack's."

"Whoa, there," Jack said swiftly. "No friend of mine. Someone I met through . . . work. Unfortunately."

"Well, what about him?" Mary asked, ignoring Jack. "What about Ernesto?"

"Nothing, really," Tess said. "Just that he stayed here last night with his wife and baby because they were tossed out of the motel where they were staying. Apparently the motel was worried about getting flooded. The problem was, the bridge was closed so they had nowhere else to go."

"Hmm." Mary cocked her head. "That's exactly what Dave Carr would do. Get the willies at the last minute, when it was too late, and throw somebody out. Just one of the multitude of reasons I want that motel off my property. The man gives a bad name to the business. In fact, he gives a bad name to the whole town."

"Can't you just throw him off?" Jack asked. "Refuse to renew his lease?"

"Unfortunately," Mary said with a harrumph, "I was foolish in my younger days. I liked the man, so I gave him a fifty-year lease. It's only been thirty years now."

"Well," said Jack with a grin, "chances are, a hurricane will take him out before then."

"That's what I've been saying for the last thirty years. Damned if he isn't still there." Her sharp gaze fixed on Tess. "So, gal, I hear you can't stop fighting with this young stud."

The color that rose in Tess's cheeks was probably bright enough to light the darkest night. It certainly felt hot enough to cook an egg on. "I beg your pardon?" she said stiffly.

"Hah!" Mary's eyes grew even more intense, if that was possible. "Don't go all Victorian on me, gal. It doesn't impress me."

Jack snickered. "So she strikes you as Victorian, too?"

Tess glared at Jack, wondering why he didn't burst into flames. He simply smiled back at her. It wasn't fair that he could be enjoying her discomfiture so much.

But now Mary's gaze fixed on Jack. His turn. "So you think she's Victorian, do you?"

"I was merely agreeing with you."

"Really?" Mary arched one heavily penciled eyebrow at him. "In my experience, when a young stud claims a woman is Victorian, it's usually because she won't put out for him."

Now Tess's cheeks were so hot that she was

sure they were going to melt off her face. It was worth it, though, to watch the ruddiness creep into Jack's cheeks for the first time in memory. He'd met his match in Mary Todd.

"And don't tell me your thoughts haven't run that way, boy," Mary said sternly. "I know men. I swear they think with their gonads."

Tess felt like she was going to strangle, but whether from suppressed laughter or annoyance, she didn't know.

"I think," said Jack, spacing his words evenly, "that I've long since outgrown that stage."

"Really? Then why do you think Tess is Victorian?"

Jack looked at Tess. "I'll get killed if I say another word, Mary."

Mary laughed, a dry cackle of delight. "Good. You understand the power of a woman."

"Damn straight I do," said Jack. "It's the power to lead a man around by the nose. So how many men are you leading around that way?"

Mary blinked, evidently taken aback by someone who was every bit as outspoken as she. "You'll do," she said after a moment.

"Answer my question . . . unless you're afraid to."

"Oh, heavens no," Mary said, smiling broadly. "The question doesn't frighten me. I lead poor Ted on a merry dance, and have been these sixty years. But he loves it."

"Or he pretends to," Jack said. "I don't know many people who really *like* being led on a dance."

Her smile grew knowing. "My dear young stud, I'd have thought you were one yourself."

Tess watched in amazement as Jack started to laugh. And why, she wondered, did Mary keep referring to him as a stud? He might be—Tess didn't consider herself to be a judge of such things—but she didn't think it was very polite.

Mary's intense black eyes suddenly focused on Tess again, and she wished she could disappear before Mary said something else outrageous to make her blush. She spoke quickly.

"Have you thought of anything else that might help us find our parents?"

Mary sat back a little in her chair, as if taking a moment to decide if she was going to allow herself to be diverted from making the two of them miserable. After a few seconds she said, "You know, attraction often takes the form of hostility."

Tess bristled. Jack merely got a strange smile on his mouth.

"Who made *you* an authority?" Tess demanded.

Mary ignored her. "Yes, I've gotten hostile a few times in my life because I was attracted to someone. I just don't like that out-of-control feeling."

Jack looked at Tess. She could feel his gaze boring into her as if he were considering what Mary said.

She blew a frustrated sigh. "You know, Mary, sometimes people just don't like each other. At all. Jack loathes me, and I detest him."

"Wait a minute," Jack said. "Speak for yourself there, Tess. I don't *loathe* you."

"You could fool me. From the first time you set eyes on me you've been picking on me about everything. My name. My height."

"Well, you kind of rile me when you call me a useless beach bum. Uncouth, arrogant . . . well, I don't have to remind you of all the descriptions."

"Only because you told me I had an awful name! And because you keep making fun of my height."

"Ooh," said Mary with obvious delight. "The truth comes out. Now, Jack, why in the world would you pick on the child's height?"

"I'm not a child!" Tess said through her teeth.

Mary lifted both her eyebrows but said nothing. After a few moments, Tess began to shrink— because, though it was lowering to admit it, she *was* acting like a child.

"Of course," said Mary presently, "given that you're Brigitte's child . . ." She sighed. "The gallic temperament, you know."

"Hey," said Jack, "let's not insult entire races of people, Mary. Brigitte, yes, the entire population of France, no."

Tess sent him a smoldering look.

"I'm not insulting anyone," Mary snapped back, rapping her cane on the patio for emphasis. "The French are a passionate people. That's not a criticism."

"Let's just leave my mother out of this," Tess said, glaring at Jack.

"Oh, that's rich," he said. "Considering she's the cause of this entire mess. The Machiavelli behind our misery. The Richelieu who's pulling the strings."

Mary laughed delightedly. Tess sighed pointedly. "Let's not get carried away," she said.

"Why not?" Mary demanded. "Brigitte's always been a schemer. It's one of her most charming attributes. I could *always* count on her to come up with an outrageous plan. Rarely, of course, since I don't have any trouble coming up with them myself. But on those few occasions . . . Brigitte was always there with her peculiar form of brilliance."

Tess looked at Mary, trying to decide how to take this fulsome compliment.

Jack regarded her as if she were a curiosity. "You're proud of being an outrageous schemer?"

"Of course I am! How dull the world would be if everyone behaved themselves."

That, thought Tess, was certainly an original view.

"So," Jack said flatly, "what exactly do you know that you haven't told us about Brigitte's latest scheme?"

Tess had the dubious pleasure, for the first time in memory, of seeing Mary Todd at a loss for words.

"What makes you think I know anything?" Mary asked finally.

"Come on," Jack said. "You're involved in this."

"Where in the world did you get such a cock-amamie idea?"

"From listening to you."

"Well, I never!" Mary said, but her indignation was ruined by the sparkle in her dark eyes and that cackle of laughter that followed.

"Look," Jack said, "it's kind of ridiculous to keep us in limbo like this. We've both had to leave our jobs . . ."

Jack had a job? Tess marveled. He really had a *job*? That was the first time she'd ever heard him admit it. Unfortunately, now she had to revise her estimate of him upward. But only a little—she didn't want to give him too much of the benefit of the doubt.

". . . leave our homes," Jack was continuing, "to come down here on a wild goose chase. We've been frightened to death that something bad had befallen them—"

"Bad?" Mary interrupted. "Did you really think that?"

Tess spoke. "We thought they might have been kidnapped. Or maybe arrested in some foreign country."

Mary started laughing again, clearly enjoying herself immensely. "I pity anyone who tried to kidnap Brigitte!"

So did Tess, now that she thought about it.

"That's neither here nor there," Jack said sternly. "If you know something, you should tell us. We need to put this matter to rest before we both lose our jobs."

Mary cocked her head, studying each of them

in turn. "No," she said finally. "You're still squabbling."

Then, laughing to herself, she mounted her lavender golf cart and drove away.

12

"You know," Tess said, "if anyone but my mother were involved in this, I wouldn't believe what I just heard."

They were still sitting on the patio, soaking up the humidity as low clouds continued to hang overhead.

"Yeah," he said. "But I gotta say one thing."

"What's that?"

"This alleviates my last, lingering concern that they might actually be in trouble."

"There is that." But it didn't make her feel a whole lot better. Uncertainly, she glanced at Jack. "Are we really *that* bad?" As soon as she spoke, she wished she could recall the words. They revealed entirely too much insecurity, and if there was one thing she'd learned not to reveal, that was it.

But Jack didn't seem to notice anything spectacular in what she had said. "I don't know. I guess maybe we were. At least from Brigitte's perspective. And to be fair, probably from my dad's as well, since he evidently went along with this."

She glumly agreed. "I guess so. Considering I didn't come home the last few years because I didn't want to spend my time arguing with you. . . ."

It wasn't a pretty picture. She didn't want to believe she could be that obnoxious. On the other hand, Jack just brought it out in her. It was like a reflex, something over which she had no control.

"You made fun of my name." The words surprised her, even as they emerged. That was so long ago, and it sounded so petty now.

"What?" He was confused.

"You made fun of my name the first time we met."

"You made fun of me for living at home."

They exchanged looks, and something of understanding passed between them.

"Okay," Jack said after a moment. "Why *are* you called Tess, instead of Terry or Theresa?"

"It was my dad's nickname for me." It was hard to reach back that far now, but in fairness to both of them, she tried to reconstruct what she'd been feeling on that awful day. "I guess I was still hoping my mom and dad would get back together. Even though we hadn't seen my dad once in the whole two years since the divorce. Anyway, I even made my mom call me Tess after they separated. And I was really, *really* frosted that my mom was getting married again. Because it meant she and my dad would never reconcile. Childish thinking."

"Natural thinking."

"Maybe. I don't know." She sighed. "I think I should have been a little more mature at fifteen."

"Don't be so hard on yourself."

"Why not? I deserve it. Especially when you consider it was your dad I wanted to be mad at, but he was just too nice to me. So I guess I turned it all on you."

"I can understand that."

She looked at him. "You can?"

"Sure." He looked almost sheepish. "I hated you because of the way my dad was doting on you. I felt like you were pushing me out of the family."

"Oh, God, really? Do you still feel that way?"

"Hell, no. I've growed up some, lady." He said it humorously, using faulty English to get a faint smile out of her. "But at the time . . . well, I'd been trying for nearly ten years to replace my mother in my dad's life. I lived at home when I went to college, I did all the cooking and cleaning, made sure we got out to the movies and stuff, sent him off to parties he might otherwise have skipped. . . . Crazy, huh? I was trying to fill the hole—not that I could. Then you came along and suddenly I wasn't the only kid in the family, and your mother was doing the other stuff. . . ." He shook his head and laughed quietly. "Would you believe it took me a year or so to figure all that out? It wasn't intuitively obvious to me why I was feeling the way I was feeling."

"Me neither. I just hated you."

"Yeah." He glanced her way, and a smile creased the corners of his eyes. "But we're older and wiser now, right?"

She had to laugh. "I'm not so sure about that. We're still sniping all the time."

"Yeah, but it's so much *fun!*"

She laughed again, shaking her head. Jack *could* be a lot of fun when he wanted to be. The thought made her uneasy, so she shoved it aside and moved on to more important matters. "But this still doesn't answer what we do about *them*. Maybe we should just go home. Why give Brigitte the satisfaction of playing this out any further?"

"You *are* hard-hearted," he said. "You couldn't possibly want to disappoint your mother that way."

"Oh, yes, I could."

"Well, I can't. I'm not going to let her get away with this."

"Jack . . . Jack, she only gets away with this if we keep on this wild goose chase looking for them. She gets away with nothing if we go home."

But there was a hard gleam in his eye, one that worried her a little. "No," he said, "she gets away with this if we quit. And I am not a quitter."

That was an odd statement coming from someone she had always assumed was a dropout. And why did he feel quitting would be letting Brigitte get away with this?

The thought continued to trouble her, but she didn't know quite how to bring it up, especially later when Jack was crawling around in the attic with a flashlight, swearing noisily and bumping into things.

Suddenly he stuck his head down through the trapdoor. "I am going to have some serious words with your mother when I find her."

"Be my guest."

"She is going to have sore ears when I get done with her."

"Good. And I'm going to add a choice few for your father."

"Damn straight." He disappeared again and moments later she heard a thud and he swore again. "Shit!"

"You know, Jack, she really wouldn't have hidden anything up there."

Another curse, followed by Jack's head peering down at her again. "You can't know that."

"Yes, I can. Do you really see Brigitte climbing up there, doing what *you*'re doing?"

"No, but I can see my dad doing it, under threat of being nagged to death."

"Maybe you have a point."

"I always have a point." He disappeared again. More thuds. An occasional bang. Another oath.

When he reappeared, he was covered with wisps of pink insulation.

"Oh, Lord," Tess said, "you've got fiberglass all over you."

"No kidding. It itches like hell."

"Maybe you'd better take a shower."

He lowered himself to the ladder, then closed the trap. "A cold one. Unfortunately, there's still no hot water."

Tess was unsympathetic. "The water's never that cold here. It won't be any cooler than going swimming."

Now that she thought about it, that actually sounded pretty good. After being in the heat and humidity all day, she was beginning to feel as if she were sticking to herself and as if her clothes were glued in place.

"Agh," he said disgustedly. "Can you help get this stuff off of me?"

The thought was intriguing, and in a way that made Tess want to blush. She managed a nod and began to pluck the little pink wisps from him. The fiberglass clung, which gave her little choice but to touch him as she pulled each strand away. Through his shirt she felt a muscle twitch as her fingers sought purchase.

"Relax," she said, trying to imbue her voice with a polite distance her heart did not feel. "It's sticky."

"Damn stuff," he replied.

She heard the almost imperceptible waver in his voice and forced herself not to guess at what it might mean. Trying to focus her attention on the task at hand, and not on the stirring within her at the touch of powerful muscle and sinew, she worked his way from his shoulders down to the small of his back. Now it was her turn to flinch.

"Umm . . . there's more down here. I don't know if you can reach it."

"You're doing fine," he said evenly.

It was maddening. Maddening to feel what she was feeling. Maddening not to know if he was feeling it, too. Maddening to feel trapped in this intimate contact and not have the measure of its intimacy. Maddening that her body seemed determined to adopt a measure all its own.

His bottom was as firm as his back, she noted as she pulled a wisp away. Another clung beneath that, in exactly the right place to inspire an almost overwhelming urge to pinch playfully. Her hand reached closer, fingertips almost in contact, her mind undecided as to what would happen when they reached their destination. The struggle became a delicious tease for her, reminding her of the cartoons with a little angel on one shoulder and a little devil on the other. Closer, and now she felt the merest touch of the fabric stretched tight across his flesh. Would the angel groom, or the devil pinch? Not even she was sure.

"Youch!" he said. But he hadn't moved away.

"That one was . . . really clingy."

"Not a problem."

Now she heard the smile in his voice, or thought she did. A flush came to her cheeks and she chided herself silently for the direction her thoughts were taking. But they kept heading that way. The devil was winning.

Nice back, nice hips, nice buns, nice legs. In fact . . . yummy. Mary Todd hadn't been far from the mark when she'd called him a stud.

Except that he didn't act like a stud. Without realizing that she was speaking out loud, she continued her train of thought. "Was it embarrassing when Mary called you a stud?"

He turned suddenly to face her. Considering that she was bent over, examining the seat of his shorts for the last strands of pink fiberglass, she suddenly found herself face-to-face with a part of the male anatomy she wasn't used to being this close to. She straightened up so fast that she became light-headed.

"You okay?" He reached out and steadied her with a hand on her arm.

"Umm, yeah . . . I just stood up too fast."

"Oh." The grin he gave her was suddenly evil, as if he knew exactly why she'd straightened that quickly.

Desperate to keep him from saying anything about it, she said, "You haven't answered my question."

He shrugged and shook his head, but for some reason kept his gaze cemented to hers in a way that left her feeling as if she were doing a high-wire balancing act, trying not to fall. Fall where? Into what?

"Nah," he said dissmisively, but his voice had taken on that honeyed, husky note again, as if his thoughts were straying elsewhere. "*Stud* is just a word, but not even remotely does it describe me."

"Really?" She was breathing a little heavier, and had the feeling that if she could just look away from him, life would get a whole lot safer.

"Just a word," he repeated. "How would you react if someone called you a Delilah?"

"Me?" If she hadn't been so mesmerized, she would have laughed. But laughter was far beyond her now. "I'm no Delilah."

"That's how I reacted," he said. And somehow he seemed to move closer without moving at all. "But you *are* a Delilah, you know."

"Me? No way." When had somebody pumped all the air out of the room?

"Yes, you," he murmured. And now she wasn't imagining that he stepped closer, because he did. Almost close enough for them to touch. "You're a temptress."

Just like that the mood was shattered. "Temptress? Me?" Laughter rolled up from deep inside her, spilling over. "Me?" she asked gasping.

He'd almost had her, but then he'd gone too far, to a point so ridiculous that she couldn't even be offended.

"Get real," she said, wiping her eyes. She looked at Jack, expecting sheepishness, or disappointment, or something, anything but what she found.

He looked hurt. "Fine," he said stiffly. "Have it your way."

Pivoting sharply, he walked out of the room, wisps of insulation still clinging to his hair.

Hurt? Amazed, all she could do was stare after him.

Jack was overreacting and he knew it. He hated it when he knew he was being stupid but couldn't stop himself. This was one of those banner times.

Telling Tess she was a Delilah was a stupid move. Grossly dumb. You didn't say things like that to a woman who gave you the feeling she'd like to roast your gonads over the fire.

There was something seriously off-kilter in his brain.

But that was nothing new. Anytime he was around Tess something went off-kilter. Sometimes he likened his brain to a magnetic tape or a floppy disk . . . and Tess to a powerful magnet. She walked by and all the carefully ordered iron filings that were the repositories of his intelligence got scrambled hopelessly.

Why was that?

Now that he'd asked himself that question, he realized he really didn't want the answer. In fact, he had a strong suspicion that he'd be happy if it remained a mystery for the rest of his days.

But Tess was preying on his mind entirely too much for him to ignore the issue.

He didn't hate Tess—not exactly. He wouldn't even say that he wasn't fond of her, because he was. It was just that . . . being around her started to rub him the wrong way. Set him on edge somehow. And it wasn't the same kind of edginess he got being around somebody he loathed.

No, it was more like the edginess . . . when he was afraid of someone.

Cripes! He jerked his head up. Afraid of *Tess*?

Over the years he'd known people he was afraid of, and Tess didn't even fall into the ballpark. Not even close. Hell, not even on the same continent.

But, said a quiet little voice of reason somewhere within the confines of his aching skull, *she's not that kind of threat.*

And, much as he hated to admit it, he was a little ashamed to feel that way about her. She was, after all, just a pint-sized, pain-in-the-butt stepsister. A relative who wasn't really a relative. An accident of his father's love for Brigitte. Except for that, he and Tess probably would have gone their separate ways fifteen years ago, happy never to see one another again.

But Brigitte and Steve, bless their little souls, insisted that they all ought to be one happy family, at least at the holidays. Hah.

Maybe the problem he and Tess had was caused less by conflicting personalities than it was by the roles that had been forced on them. Maybe if they'd been allowed to go their separate ways, instead of having Steve and Brigitte try to hammer them into the "family" mold, they wouldn't feel this great antipathy toward each other. Maybe they were both just reacting to being bent out of shape.

Because Shorty really wasn't so bad. Oh, she was a little straitlaced, and he kept having this vision of her in Victorian black, laced up so tight she could hardly breathe, with one of those prim little white caps on her head. The untouchable.

Yet he had called her a Delilah. Bright, Jack. Really bright.

He squeezed his eyes shut, remembering what it had been like when he kissed her last night. Remembering the almost smoky miasma of desire that was beginning to fill the atmosphere whenever she was around. Found himself wondering why all he could think about was unlacing those stays of hers and finding out what the real Tess Morrow was like.

He was, however, old enough to know what sexual attraction could do to common sense. And that was all that was going on here. Just because he hadn't felt this overpowering desire for a woman in years didn't mean he wasn't still capable of it. And here he thought maturity had freed him from the goad of his gonads.

Another *hah.*

Yet why had he never felt that attraction to her before? What was different about this time?

Then he realized: Steve and Brigitte weren't around this time to remind him of his role in this misbegotten family. This time there was no one to pressure him to be a "brother."

Without their parents around, he and Tess were simply a man and woman who didn't know each other that well. It wasn't surprising that an attraction had arisen.

For Tess *was* attractive. Especially those waif-like blue eyes. They had a way of sucking him in, if he wasn't careful. Maybe that's why he always felt as if he had to be on guard around her.

What he'd been feeling around her for the last twenty-four hours was a powder keg, and he needed to be careful. Very careful.

He heard her come up behind him, and he cursed his luck. What he needed was to get the hell out of this house for a couple of hours. Some space would help him get himself back on kilter so he could deal with her more rationally.

But here he was, standing at the window as if he didn't have the sense God gave a gnat, and she was coming up behind him, bringing all the temptations right along with her.

"Jack?"

She sounded tentative, which for Tess was something akin to a palm tree growing in Antarctica. It didn't happen.

Which, naturally, affected him in a totally unexpected way. He felt a twinge of concern, which was not what he wanted to be feeling right now.

"What?" he asked, then winced inwardly at how short the word sounded.

"I'm sorry," she said.

The unexpectedness of it made him turn right around and look at her.

"For what?" he asked.

"For laughing. I didn't mean to hurt you."

Hurt him? He started to deny it, but then two things dawned on him. The first was that he *had* been hurt by her reaction, and the second was that he actually liked seeing her look so concerned about him.

"It's okay," he said, managing to sound more generous than convinced.

"No, it's not. I guess," she continued hesitantly, "that you didn't understand why I was laughing. I wasn't laughing at *you*."

"Then what was so funny?"

"The mere idea that I was some kind of temptress."

Lights went on in the dank caverns of his mind. "Oh."

She flushed. "You *know* it's ludicrous," she said. "Way over the top. So I laughed. But honestly, Jack, I wasn't laughing at you for saying it. It's nice that you wanted to make me feel good."

He hadn't thought of it as wanting to make her feel good. From his perspective he'd merely been telling the truth.

He looked at her now and found himself thinking how very different she was when she was honestly concerned for someone. Those blue eyes of hers were soft, liquid, warm. And her whole face seemed to have grown gentler. He *liked* this version of Tess.

And that scared him even more. He could handle lusting after her, but liking her was another matter altogether.

"That's okay," he said. "I was only trying to get you to admit you're attracted to me."

It was the most asinine thing he could think of to say. Heck, he would have given himself honors for the title of Male Chauvinist Pig of the year for being jerk enough to say such a thing. And it worked like a charm.

"Why, you disgusting, loathsome slug! You belly-crawling slime mold."

"Pretty good," he said, fixing a grin on his face. "You're getting more creative all the time."

"Oh, just shut up!" Turning, she stormed away, leaving him alone with his thoughts ... and a deep-rooted sense of loneliness.

Men! thought Tess as she marched to the farthest end of the house. Disgusting, loathsome creatures that ought to crawl back into the primordial ooze. Sooner or later they all revealed themselves to be utter jerks.

Although that shouldn't come as a major surprise from Jack. But something about what he had just said surpassed his former jerkitude by a country mile.

Trying to get her to admit that she was attracted to him? She'd walk barefoot on hot coals first. She'd dig a tunnel to China, cross the Sahara on foot, and swim the Atlantic Ocean solo before she would ever admit such a thing.

And how very, terribly lowering it was to know that he was right. Because she *was* attracted to him.

Which clearly meant that she had bats in her belfry. How could she *possibly* be attracted to a man who personified all the worst of his gender? How could she be attracted to a man who apparently had a job he was embarrassed to discuss and who could say things like that?

Didn't she have better taste?

She certainly thought so. Over the years she had dated a number of men, but after a few dates had stopped seeing them, usually because they became too pushy about having sex, and always because they sooner or later revealed they were no better than the rest of their ilk. Life was difficult enough without marrying additional problems.

She was self-aware enough to admit that this view had probably come about because of her father, who hadn't visited her even once since her mother left him. Oh, he'd sent her birthday and Christmas gifts, but he hadn't made any attempt to see her.

So Tess didn't really trust men. She freely admitted it, was even willing to acknowledge that she probably wasn't being fair to the majority of men on the planet. Which was the only reason she dated at all.

But sooner or later, every male lived down to her expectations. And since Jack had been doing it all along, there was really no reason to feel so suddenly disappointed in him.

But she did.

God, how she wished she were back in Chicago, away from all of this. The sky was clearing from the storm, and the garish green was beginning to dominate the world outside again. Looking out the kitchen window, Tess found herself hating that vibrance. Gray—she wanted gray. Drizzle. Snow. Anything but bright sunshine and a green, summery world.

Squaring her shoulders, she turned around to

go tell Jack they needed to quit fighting and resume their search for clues.

He was right behind her and she bumped into him, her nose dragging across one of the buttons on his polo shirt.

"You need a shower," she said, as his aromas filled her nostrils. They were good aromas, scents that called powerfully to her.

"Really?" He lifted his arm and sniffed. "I don't smell anything."

"You'd be the last to know. Look, Mary Todd knows where they are."

"I realize that. I came to apologize."

"For what? How do we get the information out of her?"

"I haven't a foggy. I wanted to apologize for acting like a Neanderthal. The mood comes over me sometimes."

"No kidding. We could roast her over hot coals."

"Hang her by her thumbs?" There was a twinkle in his dark eyes that she found herself responding to helplessly.

She quickly backed up, realizing that if she didn't put about six feet between them right now, she was probably going to disgrace herself by reaching out for him. "Okay," she said. "Mary knows the story. Therefore they *are* safe."

"I thought we'd already come to that conclusion. Are you sure you don't find me just the *tiniest* bit attractive?" His tone was almost wheedling.

She wanted to shake her head in denial, realizing it was the safest thing to do, but innate honesty wouldn't let her get away with a blatant lie. So she hedged. "You're . . . okay, I guess."

"Okay? Just okay? I tell you you're Delilah, and you tell me I'm *okay*?"

Oh, no—she was beginning to enjoy the exchange. "It's better in the long run to be honest."

"Just okay?" He shook his head. "I'm better than that."

"I'm sure you left a string a broken hearts dotting every beach in the world."

"Now I'm a globe-trotting beach bum, huh?" He shook his head. "I'm glad to know I get around."

"I'm sure you do."

He wiggled his eyebrows at her. "I've gotten to a few places here and there. But I couldn't possibly leave a string of broken hearts in my wake if I'm merely *okay*."

He had her, and there was a gleam in his eyes that told her he was as aware of it as she.

"Cornered?" he asked almost kindly.

"Give me a minute."

He started humming the *Jeopardy* music.

"Oh, knock it off." She *did* feel cornered, and she didn't like it. Nor did she want to keep playing this verbal version of chicken with him, because sooner or later she was going to put her foot in it and let him know just how much she had been thinking about him since last night.

"Can't stand the heat, huh?" He was grinning at her. "Okay. I'll be nice."

"Thank you," she said with as much dignity as she could muster. It was better than giving in to an urge to stomp her foot. "Now, what are we going to do about Mary?"

He shrugged. "I don't know about you, but going one-on-one with that woman strikes me as foolhardy."

"You're kidding, right?"

He shook his head. "No, I'm not. She's cagey, canny, and a natural schemer. If you think anything we could do short of murder or mayhem would get one thing out of her that she didn't choose to share, you're wrong. What's more, if we tried to twist her arm, she'd take great delight in misleading us."

Tess sighed. "I'm going to kill Brigitte."

"I'll help you. But first we have to find her. And unfortunately, Shorty, I think we're stuck playing it out Brigitte's way. Which, I gather, means waiting for the clues to turn up."

"Well, the clues had better not take too long because I have to be back at my desk on Monday morning, no matter what."

"Yeah. Me, too."

That got her attention. They were so close she had to tip her head back to look up at him. "You have a *desk*?"

His answer was impatient. "Of course I have a desk."

"You *work* at a desk?"

The impatience in his expression was replaced by unholy glee. "No."

"Then . . ." She trailed off. "You said you have to be back at your desk."

"I do."

"But you don't work at it?"

"Well . . . as little as I can. Which is to say almost never."

Now impatience surged in her, propelling words upward and outward. "Just what exactly do you *do* for a living, Jack?"

"What difference does it make?"

She put her hands on her hips. She knew he was doing this just to irritate her, and it made her even madder that she still couldn't resist getting irritated. "To satisfy my curiosity."

He shrugged. "Not important enough."

"Oh, you . . ." She caught herself. "So . . . the only possible reason you could be so shy about telling me what you do for a living is that you're doing something you're ashamed of."

The creases at the corners of his eyes deepened. "Really? I'm ashamed of you, Tess. You have a better brain than that."

"Oh, for . . . cut it out, Jack! Come clean. What do you do? Sell drugs?"

Something about him went utterly still. "You really don't know anything at all about me, do you?" Then he turned and walked out of the room.

And Tess was left to wonder why she kept putting her foot in it so royally.

13

She was going to have to apologize, Tess realized. That accusation had flown out of her mouth in an attempt to say something so horrendous that he would automatically defend himself, not because she believed he was capable of such a thing. Whatever nasty thoughts she'd had about Jack over the years, she'd long since realized that he was a basically decent guy.

But she couldn't find him. She hadn't heard him leave the house—there wasn't a door in this place that didn't make enough noise on opening or closing to be heard throughout the house—but he wasn't to be found anywhere. Moving from room to room, she began to wonder if she'd slipped a reality cog somewhere.

"Jack?"

No answer. The house remained silent.

"Jack, I apologize! I didn't really mean it. Where are you?"

Still no Jack. He must have gotten out somehow without betraying himself with a squeaky hinge or that inescapable thud as the front door closed. Even the sliding glass doors made a sound that could be heard everywhere. But somehow Jack had managed it.

Tess finally flopped on the living room couch and stared up at the ceiling unhappily. She'd been carrying this whole antipathy-with-Jack thing too far. It may have been remotely excusable when she was fifteen, but she was thirty now and there was no excuse for some of the things she said.

Calling him a doofus wouldn't even dent his armor. Calling him uncouth and arrogant only made him laugh. But calling him a drug dealer went way beyond that. It went past the realm of harmless insults. At least for Jack.

She started wondering about that, because she was certain that most people she knew would have found such an accusation so outrageous that it wouldn't have affected them. They'd either have laughed outright or just heaped withering scorn all over her. Jack hadn't reacted that way. Why not?

Then there was that thing he'd let slip in passing about how he'd put Ernesto in jail. Maybe she'd hit the nail on the head?

The thought locked her breath in her throat, but the instant she had it, she knew it was wrong. Not Jack, no way. If he'd put Ernesto in jail, it was because Jack had caught the guy doing something wrong and had reported it. Not because Jack was in any way involved.

She couldn't accept any other possibility.

And from this moment forward, she resolved, she would treat Jack with exactly the same courtesy she would show a stranger no more or less. No matter how he goaded her, she would remain civil or silent. No more insults. Absolutely none.

Feeling better about her resolution, she was just sitting up to go hunt for Jack again when the power came on. She heard a thunk and the refrigerator compressor switched on—which reminded her she needed to get rid of most of the food in there, and any frozen items that had thawed. She'd better check that now before everything refroze.

Moments later she felt a blast of warm sticky air as the air-conditioning began to stir the air in the house. She wondered how long it would take for the unit to cool this place down to a livable temperature again.

She was just starting to pull potentially spoiled food from the fridge and dump it into a trash bag when she heard Jack swear.

"Jack?"

She was answered by a thud, but she couldn't tell where it was coming from.

"Jack?"

No answer. Just a distant rumble of some kind. Shrugging, she went back to clearing out the fridge.

She had about half the perishables taken care

of when she heard Jack again. She wasn't sure if he cursed, but he sounded frustrated.

Growing annoyed, she went out into the foyer and called him again. "Jack? What in the world is going on?"

This time she got an answer of sorts from the depths of the house, a mumble—or grumble—that seemed to come from far away and was utterly incomprehensible.

"Where are you?"

An oath was her answer. Irritated, she considered her alternatives. She could just go back to emptying the refrigerator before all that food started to stink. She could ignore the man and his maddening behavior.

But she *had* promised herself that she was going to try to treat him more courteously. The way she would treat a perfect stranger.

Funny, she thought as she started moving toward the back of the house, how it was easier to be civil to a total stranger than to a family member. What was it about relatives that brought out the worst in people? Somebody ought to do a doctoral dissertation on the subject.

Reaching the end of the hallway in the bedroom wing, she called him again. "Jack? Where are you?"

"Here, damn it!"

She spun around and found herself looking at the door of Jack's bedroom. It was closed.

"In your room?" she called.

"Sort of."

"Do you need help?"

"I need a hell of a lot more than that."

Curious, she opened the door. And froze.

Because there, hanging from the ceiling, was a leg that looked unmistakably like Jack's. And not too far from it was a hand.

She stared, not quite certain what to say. Finally, "You fell through the ceiling?"

"Sort of."

"That was a stupid thing to do," she said, as horror filled her. "The ceiling's ruined!"

"No shit, Sherlock."

"What the hell happened?"

"Never mind," he roared. "I've got to get out of here before I bring down the whole damn ceiling. You can yell at me later."

"As if you'll listen. Pull yourself out of there, now."

"If I could," he said, "don't you think I'd have done so?"

"Oh, God, Brigitte is going to be so mad at you, Jack." Tess could just envision one of her mother's explosions. She didn't do it often, but when she did, wise people ducked and ran. "Why in the world were you up there? I told you she wouldn't hide a clue in the attic."

"People hide plenty of stuff in the attic," he said impatiently. "It's a great hiding place because no one thinks they'd actually get up into one of these squirrelly little warrens on these damn Florida houses with the low hip roofs, vaulted ceilings, and an attic that's nothing but a narrow conduit for wiring and pipes!"

"Okay, okay. Sheesh. I didn't mean to make you so mad."

"I'm not mad, I'm frustrated. Now will you help me get out of here?"

"Why can't you do it yourself?"

"I'm off balance. I can't get any leverage. And my leg is stuck. Enough reasons?"

"I guess so," she allowed. "Just how am I supposed to help?"

His hand disappeared back up into the ceiling. She heard another thud, followed by a groan. Drywall flaked down onto the rug as his leg twisted.

"You're making the damage worse," she said.

"Tell me something I don't know."

"Okay. The rug's a mess now, too."

Suddenly his face was poking out the hole where his hand had been. "Somehow I think the rug is the least of my concerns. Get the stepladder from the garage."

She looked up at him, wishing she had a camera, because as sure as she was standing here, in five years a picture of him coming through the ceiling was going to be hysterically funny. On the other hand, judging by the thunderous expression on his face, he might kill her for taking a photo of him right now.

"It's going to cost a fortune to fix this ceiling," she couldn't help saying.

"I'll fix it myself, damnit. It'll be just like new by tomorrow night."

"Is that what you do for a living? Drywall?"

"Will you just get the stepladder?"

"What are you going to do, come all the way through the ceiling? And what did you mean about people hiding things in the attic? Do you search a lot of attics? What are you? A jewel thief?"

His face, framed by the popcorn-textured ceiling, simply stared at her. "No," he said finally. "You've got me confused with David Niven."

"Hardly. You're not that suave."

"I'm also not a jewel thief. Will you kindly get the stepladder?"

"Not until you tell me why your mind is so devious that you think of searching attics for something hidden."

"Maybe a better question would be why it *doesn't* occur to you."

"Oh, that's simple," she said airily. "When I want to hide something I put it at the bottom of the dirty clothes hamper."

"Really?" His eyebrows lifted, and Tess found herself thinking how surreal it was to be talking to a face in the ceiling. "What kind of stuff do you hide? Drugs?"

She was shocked. "Absolutely not! When I was living with Mom, though, I had to hide my diary."

"How come? I thought you were always strait-laced."

"Will you stop saying that, please? You don't know me at all."

"Apparently not, since you had to hide your diary. So what was so awful in it?" He wiggled his eyebrows suggestively.

She glared up at him. "Nothing like that. In retrospect, nothing at all. But it was private and I didn't want her to read it."

He looked interested. "Would she have?"

"Of course. She thought I didn't know she was looking through my things when I was at school, but I could tell."

"Why in the world would she do that?"

"I don't know. I never got into any trouble."

"Maybe that's why. She was hoping like mad that you really weren't perfect."

She sighed. "Oh, come off it, Jack. Nobody's perfect. I just didn't do any really bad stuff, like drugs and drinking. And I followed my curfew. As a rule, I didn't even lie about where I was going or who I was seeing."

"As a rule?" He started to grin. "Now, that's an interesting admission. What *did* you lie about?"

"None of your business. Just kid's stuff, anyway. Now, what do you want the stepladder for?"

"Just get it for me."

"And you never explained why you check out attics."

"It's a great place for people to hide drugs."

"Oh." She started to turn away. Then she froze a moment, a strange hurricane of emotions sweeping through her. Jerkily, she turned back and looked up at him. "You're kidding, right?"

"Hell, no. If you want to stash a dime bag, you can put it in the toilet tank, but if you want to stash a few kilos, that wouldn't work. So you use the attic."

"Oh." She felt leaden. Absolutely leaden. She couldn't believe this of Jack. "*Are* you a drug dealer?"

The words came out almost tentatively, and she closed her eyes and clenched her fists, hoping against hope that he wouldn't answer affirmatively. Then she realized how ridiculous she was being, because whether it was true or not, he was going to deny it.

"You just don't give up, do you?" he asked. "You're determined to make me into some kind of major criminal. In a single conversation you've suspected me of jewel thievery and drug dealing. What's next? Hit man for the mob?"

His sarcasm merely made her stubborn. "That's a possibility I hadn't considered. I'll have to think about it."

"Oh, for Pete's sake, will you please just get the stepladder?"

"You still haven't told me what you're going to do with it."

"I'm not going to do a damn thing with it. *You* are."

Well, that sounded safe enough, she supposed. It wasn't that she wanted to be difficult, but he *had* just fallen through the ceiling, and at the moment she had serious questions about his judgment . . . which was perfectly understandable under the circumstances. Surely he must see that.

But if she was the one who was going to do

something with the stepladder, then he couldn't get into any more trouble.

Satisfied, she went to the garage to get it. It was aluminum, six feet tall. Not really as high as she would have liked, considering the ceiling was at ten feet. But it at least reassured her that he wasn't proposing to step on it and break his way out of the ceiling.

When she reentered the bedroom with the ladder, he said, "Thank God. My leg is going numb."

"Move it, then."

"I can't. That's the problem. The way I'm lying, I'll wind up putting another hole in the ceiling."

"But you said it was no problem to fix."

He scowled. "Do you always remind people of everything they've said to you?"

She craned her neck to look up at him. "Only when they seem to be self-contradictory. So which is it? No problem to fix the ceiling, or something you wouldn't want to do on a bet?"

"It's no problem, but I still wouldn't want to do it on a bet. It's miserable. Boring. Time-consuming. A pain in the butt. But not a problem. Satisfied, Shorty?"

She was. "Thank you. Now, what am I supposed to do with this ladder?"

"Put it about where my leg is. Then climb it."

"And then what?"

"I'll tell you when we get there."

She didn't like the sound of that. "What aren't you telling me?"

"Nothing you need to worry about. Come on, Tess, the circulation is cut off. I'm going to wind up with gangrene if you don't step on it."

The awful possibility galvanized her. She moved the stepladder to the foot of the bed, opened it, then positioned it until it was almost directly under his foot. "You're not going to get gangrene. And I hate ladders."

"Are you telling me you can't do it?"

"No, I'm just telling you I hate ladders. Actually, I hate heights, but mostly I hate ladders."

"Why?"

"They wobble."

"Oh." He was silent a moment, then he said very gently, "Thanks for telling me that, Tess."

"Why?"

"Because I'm sure it wasn't easy to admit weakness to me."

She wanted to bean him. She wanted to climb that ladder, grab his foot, and tug until he came tumbling through the ceiling. She was halfway up the ladder when she realized how ridiculous she was being. He hadn't said that nastily, he'd said it kindly.

Of course, kindness could be even worse. "Don't feel sorry for me, Wright."

"I'm not. It's just that you always try to seem so sure of yourself, so tough and capable, I'm kind of touched that you trusted me enough to tell me you're afraid of something."

"Don't be ridiculous," she said sharply, when actually she suddenly had the most ridiculous urge to cry. Because . . . because nobody had ever said anything genuinely sympathetic to her in a long time. Most of the time people were yelling at her, arguing with her, or trying to undermine her. Since going to work for the IRS, she'd noticed that her social circle had been shrinking steadily, until it included only other employees of the IRS. Why? Because no one else understood what it was like. And everyone else seemed to think that IRS agents had a contagious disease.

Of course, working for Internal Revenue had made her even feistier than she had been before, because she had to be. Every day she went toe to toe with taxpayers who were angry with her. She had naturally developed a bit of attitude.

But that was neither here nor there. What was here was that a simple kindness from Jack had her ready to blubber.

Maybe it was time to seriously consider a career change.

"No big deal," she muttered. "How high do I have to climb here?"

"Until you can grab my foot and shove."

"What good is that going to do? Why can't you just get up on your other knee?"

He sighed. Now that she was on the ladder and closer to the ceiling, she could no longer see his face very well. "Because my other knee is between the rafters, right over more drywall. I need to move about six more inches forward, but the drywall is dragging on my leg and I can't get a grip on the other rafters at an angle that will let me push or pull hard enough to make the move without assistance. Got it?"

"I think so." She was having trouble envisioning it, but it seemed to make sense. "Which way do I push?"

"Upward and forward. I hope it's enough to make a difference."

"I'll give it my best shot."

"I'm sure you will." And he sounded as if he meant it.

This close to his leg, though, she could see it was scraped from having come through the ceiling. "You're bleeding."

"But not enough to call 911. Come *on*, Tess. I can barely feel the leg now."

It was a nice leg, she thought. Dusted with fine golden hairs that she suddenly had an overwhelming urge to run her hand over. The unexpectedness of the feeling shocked her back to her senses.

"Ready?" she said briskly. She refused to look down, refused to consider how wobbly the ladder felt under her.

"Ready. On three. One . . . two . . . three . . ."

She shoved and felt his foot move. She also felt the ladder move. Well, actually, it tipped. A small shriek escaped her, and she jumped, just in time, because the ladder tipped over onto the floor.

"Tess? Tess, my God, are you okay?"

She looked up and saw that instead of a face in the ceiling, there was the throat of a polo shirt.

"Tess? Tess, answer me!"

"I'm fine," she said. "Honestly. Really."

Barely, she thought, looking at the ladder. "Um, Jack?"

"Yeah?"

"Don't ask me to do that again, okay?"

"No need," he said, his voice muffled. "I'm on the move." The last of his leg slid out of the hole, and she could hear him inching his way across the ceiling.

"I'll be down in a minute," he called.

"Okay." She looked up at the two big holes and the crack that was running along the plaster between them. "Brigitte," she said to the empty room, "is going to kill us."

An hour later, Jack was carrying a four-foot by eight-foot piece of drywall into the house. Apparently it was heavy, because he was sweating profusely. Tess held the door open for him, surprised to feel the outside air was cooler and drier now. "What happened?" she asked as he passed. "Did the weather forget this is Florida?"

"Actually," he answered, "it's late November, Tess. The weather we've had for the last couple of days is not the norm."

"Really? Arranged for my benefit?"

"Probably. The state is doing everything in its power to persuade you not to stay."

"I believe that. I honestly believe that."

He carried the drywall back to the bedroom and leaned it against a wall.

Tess, who had followed, stood looking at it, then at the holes in the ceiling. "What are you going to do? Cut out most of the ceiling to fit that in?"

He glanced at her, a superior male grin on his face. "Reverse the process, Shorty. I cut the drywall to fit the holes."

"Those holes?" She had to laugh. "Good luck, Jack. You'll never be able to do it. They're all ragged."

"Right," he said. Putting the stepladder back up, he grabbed an L-shaped metal ruler and a pencil. Then he climbed up and measured a square on the ceiling around the biggest hole.

"Oh," said Tess, understanding. "Duh."

"Duh," he agreed.

"You didn't have to agree with me."

He looked down with a grin. "It's such a rare occurrence that I don't want to miss a single opportunity to be agreeable."

"You're an absolute stinker, you know that?"

"Really? But I shower every day."

She groaned but couldn't think of a comeback. So often, Jack got the last word while she floundered around for exactly the right retort. So she asked a question.

"Why are the squares so big around the holes? Why not smaller?"

"I need to make the cut from rafter to rafter so I can screw the drywall in place."

He descended the ladder, then picked up a small saw. Tess's heart clutched when he carried it back up the ladder. "You'll be careful, won't you? You won't make it worse?"

"Tess, I've done this before. Professionally."

"Professionally? Really?" She'd never thought of him as someone who was handy like that. "When?"

"When I was in college, over the summers. I worked on a drywalling crew."

"Wow." It had probably been the last legitimate job he'd had. "Can I help?"

"Take the pieces as I hand them down, will you?"

She had to admit it was kind of enjoyable to watch him standing up on the ladder, sawing away at the ceiling. What was it about a man doing this kind of labor that was so intrinsically sexy? Or maybe there wasn't anything instrinsically sexy in it at all. Maybe it was just her own particular fantasy.

Whatever, it was a nice fantasy to watch him patch the holes. He appeared to know what he was doing, and she got a nice view of flexing shoulder muscles, flat belly muscles, and tight butt as he lifted and stretched.

Part of her couldn't believe she was allowing herself to enjoy a man's purely physical attributes. The rest of her just grinned and soaked up the view.

Jack, thank goodness, seemed totally unaware of the direction her thoughts had taken. He just kept calmly on, measuring the drywall, cutting the patches from it, nailing them to rafters, and taping over the cracks with the ease of a seasoned pro.

"Okay," he said. "I'll mud it later, after the tape has had a chance to dry."

To her dismay he was climbing down the ladder, the show over for now. "Mud it?" she asked.

"Yeah. Sort of like spackling. I even it out, let it dry, sand it, then texture it. It'll be ready for paint tomorrow."

"Yeah?" That kind of amazed her. Right now the ceiling looked as if it had been treated at a construction hospital, with the pale gray rectangles taped into place. All in all, she was impressed. Maybe Brigitte wouldn't kill them after all.

"Well, I need to go finish cleaning the fridge," she said, suddenly afraid that if she didn't find something to occupy her she might follow her recent admiration of Jack's physique down the wrong corridors. She'd managed to get to this stage in life without committing a mortal error with a man. Why start now?

Back in the kitchen, she hunted up the baking soda and made a solution to clean the inside of the refrigerator. She was still wiping it down when Jack appeared, fresh from a shower.

"Let's go out for dinner tonight," he suggested. "I don't know about you, but the last thing I want to do is cook. Or worse yet, go shopping for something to cook. I take it you threw everything out?"

"I didn't dare risk it."

"Yeah." He peered over her shoulder, and she was suddenly aware of the whisper of his breath in her ear. It made a delicious shiver run down her spine. "Looks good. You can clean my fridge anytime."

"Do you have a fridge?"

"Tsk." He pulled back and straightened. "I take it you think I camp on the beach and live out of a Styrofoam cooler?"

"For the six-pack, anyway."

"You know, that's really strange. Because I almost never touch alcohol. If I have a six-pack, it's either soft drinks or bottled water."

She glanced over her shoulder at him, and found he was serious. "Sorry. I didn't mean to offend you."

"You didn't. Well, yes, you did."

She sat back on her heels and twisted so she could see him better. He wasn't kidding, she realized. She really *had* offended him. And for some reason, that made her feel awful. "Jack, I was just teasing."

"Funny how your teasing always seems to involve implying that I'm some kind of good-for-nothing bum. What's even more amazing is that I've been laughing it off all these years. Well, you know what, Shorty? I'm not laughing it off anymore."

He turned and strode from the kitchen. Tess, dismayed and even a little shocked, was left kneeling on the floor, staring blindly at a receipt that had fallen off the fridge door. Ted's Cleaners. She reached for it and stuck it back behind the magnet, wondering idly why anyone would keep an old dry-cleaning receipt.

Then she started to cry.

14

Jack was cursing himself for an ass. He couldn't
believe he'd reacted to Tess's teasing that way.
What had come over him? For years she'd been
making comments like that to him, and he'd
been letting them roll right off his back because
they were so absurd. And if he ever got a little
irritated by her insistence that he was a bum,
he'd just toss the insult back, making some comment about her job with the IRS.

So why, all of a sudden, had her stupid remark
zipped right past all his defenses and struck right
where it hurt? He couldn't explain it. But regardless, he owed her an apology. She hadn't intended to hurt him, but he could see in her face
that he'd hurt *her*. And worse, he'd done it in-
tentionally.

What had gotten under his skin?

What had changed?

But he knew. He knew deep inside what had changed. He was noticing her in a different way. Seeing for the first time just how really attractive she was. Sensing, for the first time, that most of her sniping was a cover.

"Hell."

He didn't want this to happen. He didn't want this to happen with any woman at this point in his life, but he most especially didn't want it to happen with Tess.

Cripes, if it was dangerous folly to get romantically involved with a coworker, someone you'd have to see five days a week even if the relationship didn't pan out, someone who would then have enough ammunition to sink your career boat—how could it possibly be wise to get involved with a family member? Because, if he and Tess were to have anything more serious than dinner together, and things didn't work out . . . where the hell were they going to spend the holidays for the next fifty years? If Brigitte thought there was a problem right now, she ought to think about what could happen if Tess and Jack got together and then broke up. World War III would look minor by comparison.

Sighing, Jack went to look for Tess. What did he expect her to think about him when he wouldn't tell what his job was?

Not that he was free to bruit it about heedlessly. But Tess, being a family member, qualified as someone with a need to know.

Which led him to wonder why he'd kept her

in the dark all these years. Did he distrust her that much? Or was it something else?

Right now, he was having a powerful feeling that all his actions and thoughts about Tess over the years had been a screen for something else ... something he *really* didn't want to think about.

He found her in the kitchen, kneeling in front of the refrigerator, her shoulders shaking. Faintly he heard a gasping sob, and realized she was crying.

Oh, God, he'd done that to her. He'd made her cry. Somehow that felt like the worst thing he'd ever done in his life. Without a thought of how she might react, he drew her up from the floor and pulled her into a tight embrace, cradling her head on his shoulder, rocking her gently side to side.

At first she was stiff, resisting his touch, but after a few seconds she began to melt against him, becoming soft and pliant. The tears still fell, but her sobs seemed to be easing.

"I'm sorry, Tess," he murmured. "I'm really sorry...."

She nodded against his shoulder and hiccuped. "Me, too. I didn't mean to hurt you, Jack. I didn't, honest."

"I know ... I know...." He stroked her hair and tried not to think about how good she felt in his arms. How nice it was to have her this close. It was as if there had been an emptiness right there on his shoulder and in his arms, waiting for her to fill it. The sense of satisfaction was almost terrifying, because he knew that in a minute or two it would be replaced by emptiness. An emptiness he would now never be able to forget was there.

"Come on," he said presently. "Leave the fridge. Let's go sit down for a bit. I think we're both exhausted."

She let him guide her into the living room, and together they sat on the couch. He should stop holding her, but he couldn't quite bring himself to do it, so he kept his arm around her shoulders. Much to his surprise, she didn't object. She even let her head return to its perch on his shoulder.

"I don't know what's gotten into me," Tess said. Her voice still sounded thick, although her tears had dried. "I know we've always picked on each other, but I don't think I've ever been so *nasty* before. Have I?"

"We've both been nasty before, Tess. Our mode of relating sucks, if you come right down to it."

She sighed heavily. "I guess it does."

"But we've both always understood the parameters before. It's different this time."

"But why?"

He looked down at her, and found her brilliant blue eyes lifted to him. "I don't know," he admitted. "Maybe because of the way this all came about—first worrying that something awful had happened to our parents, then the hurricane, and having a house full of strangers last night. . . . I think we're kind of worn out, Tess."

"Probably." She closed her eyes and nestled a

little closer. "Would it be awful if we just forget about the whole thing until tomorrow?"

"No. The only reason I've been pushing so hard is that I don't like being treated this way. I want to find them and give them a big piece of my mind. But tomorrow's soon enough."

"Yes." She sighed again. "I'm sorry I keep saying you're a beach bum."

"What else are you supposed to think when I won't tell you what I do for a living?" He hesitated, waiting for the question, but she didn't ask it. That made him feel even worse about withholding. Sighing, he ran his fingers through his sun-streaked hair and made up his mind. "Okay," he said finally. "I have a real job. I'm a federal employee."

"Really?" That perked her interest. "Which branch?"

"The DEA."

"So what's the big secret been . . . ?" Then she realized. "Omigod!" She sat up straight and looked at him. "You're an agent."

"Well, yes."

"You don't sit at a desk."

"Uh . . . no."

"Oh."

He waited, not sure what kind of reaction to expect. Scorn? Awe? Indifference? No, it wouldn't be awe. Tess wasn't the type.

"You work undercover?" she asked finally.

"Yes. . . ." He said it almost hesitantly, suspecting that this might turn out to be the crux of her reaction. "So don't tell anyone what I do, okay?"

"God, no! It's so dangerous."

Completely without warning, she reached out with both hands, grabbed the front of his polo shirt, and yanked on it as if she wanted to shake him.

"You can't do that!" she said.

"Can't do what?" he asked, shocked.

"Work undercover."

"Shorty, I've been doing it for nearly fifteen years."

She blinked, those blue eyes bigger than ever. "You've beat the odds."

He shrugged. "Maybe."

"You know you have. DEA agents get killed all the time on the job. It's a war zone."

"It can be," he admitted, wishing she'd stop pulling on the front of his shirt. "Which is why you won't tell anyone else, right?"

"And that Ernesto—you put him in jail for drugs? My God, how could you let him in this house? What if he'd killed you?"

Jack was beginning to wonder if she had a fever. She was getting awfully steamed up over this. Maybe excessively so. "Not Ernesto," he said soothingly. "I got him on a minor possession charge. He was lucky. They gave him a slap on the wrist in exchange for information."

"You said you sent him to *jail!*"

"Briefly. Not for long enough that the guy's going to screw up the rest of his life by trying to get even with me. Besides, I know Ernesto.

Chickenshit from square one. He doesn't think that big."

But Tess was still gripping the front of his shirt, and she pulled on it again, as if trying to get his attention. "You can't do this, Jack."

"Can't do what?"

"Can't keep on doing this job. You could get killed. My God, don't you know how dangerous it is?"

He didn't exactly know how to respond. "Umm, yes, but . . . I've been doing it for a long time, Tess. I'm pretty good at it."

"Good doesn't stop a bullet. You've beaten the odds for too long. Damn it, Jack, you could get hurt!"

"There is always that possibility."

"Oh, God!" She let go of the front of his shirt and jumped to her feet. "You're crazy."

He didn't argue with her, although he was of the private opinion that *she* was the one who was crazy. He *had* been doing this for a long time, after all.

"I can't believe—" She broke off and turned away, then rounded to face him again. "No wonder Mom is always saying you're going to pay for the risks you take."

"She says that?"

"All the time."

"Hell, no wonder you've always had such a low image of me."

She gaped at him. "You *are* taking risks!"

"But not what that sounds like."

"Really?" She put her hands on her hips. "And

just how would you characterize the risks you take? Do you think they won't ever have to be paid for?"

"Jeez, Tess, not like that. I'm good at my job. Damn good."

"Well . . ." she said after a moment, then drew a long, shaky breath. "I guess you must be. You're still alive."

"That's right."

"But," she said, pointing a finger at him, "you're still taking ridiculous risks."

"What do you know about it? You sit behind a desk."

"I know enough. I have ears. Besides, I dated an FBI agent for a while."

He wrinkled his brow. "What does the FBI have to do with it? And are you kidding me? You really dated somebody?"

Turning, she grabbed a small pillow off the couch and threw it at him. "I've dated," she said stiffly.

"I'm surprised anyone could get close enough."

"You beast!"

He *was* being a beast, he realized. He wanted to divert her attention from his job, and he was seizing the quick and dirty way to do it. He felt the prick of shame. "Okay, okay," he said. "I'm sorry. It's not totally beyond the realm of possibility that you date."

She gave him a look that said she wasn't quite sure whether to accept his apology or take issue with the way he'd phrased it.

"Come on, Tess, we were doing so well for a few minutes there. Actually talking like adults. But if you want to become violent about my job, I might make a few comments about yours."

"I'm not risking my neck."

"That's purely luck. If you ask me, I'm surprised more people don't come after you folks with guns."

She shook her head and rolled her eyes. "Quit trying to divert me."

"That's exactly what I'm trying to do. Because it's not your place to tell me what I can or cannot do."

She flushed. After a moment she said in a muffled voice, "You're right."

"Of course. I usually am."

She looked sad, but then made an obvious attempt to rally herself.

"Except when you fall through ceilings looking for a clue that couldn't possibly be there."

"Low. Very low."

"So was telling me that I don't have a right to be concerned about the way you risk your neck."

Feeling a rising sense of frustration, he rose to his feet. Why was it that every time they seemed to be getting close to a meeting of minds, something would happen to blow it all up?

"You know," he said, "we're terrible communicators. Five minutes of rational conversation, and one of us develops an overload that causes us to go off on some outrageous tack."

"That's ridiculous," she said, even as he saw reluctant awareness on her face.

"What is it, Tess? You've spent the last fifteen years thinking I was something totally reprehensible. Now you find out I actually have a respectable job, and you're off the deep end about it. Is there *anything* I could do that you wouldn't object to?"

The flush in her face darkened, although he couldn't tell whether it was from anger or deepening embarrassment. After a minute she folded her arms tightly across her breasts and said, "I'm worried about you, Jack. That's all."

It surprised him to hear that she cared that much. It floored him, actually, because it was so unexpected. Then he realized that it also made him feel damn good. Which made him feel distinctly uncomfortable. So he grinned and said, "Aw, I didn't know you cared."

She should have flared again, drawing them both back from the precipice he suddenly felt they were teetering over. But she didn't, leaving him even uneasier.

They hung here, neither of them saying a word, while tension stretched almost unbearably.

Jack met those huge eyes of hers, and saw something that made him start to melt inside.

"Just be careful, Jack. Please?"

"I'm always careful."

She nodded. "Okay. Let's talk about something else. Wanna watch some TV?"

"That sounds safe enough." It would give them an excuse not to talk for a while, anyway.

There was no picture on the cable, though.

"Storm must've knocked it out," Jack remarked.

"Probably. How about a video?" She bent and looked at the machine. "Hey, there's a tape in here already."

Jack leaned forward with a sudden sense of excitement. "Turn it on. What if they left a message?"

"Oh, God!" Her hand started to shake and she had to hit the play button twice. The blue screen on the TV abruptly gave way to a view of Kurt Russell and a young woman who appeared to be standing on a sailboat. Russell looked pretty old and seedy, and the actress looked young enough to be his daughter.

"You heard of St. Croix?" Russell said to the girl, who immediately asked if they were going there. No, Russell told her, but added that they were going one island to the left. The island, he said, was called Ted's.

Jack and Tess looked at each other.

"Play that back," Jack said.

Tess hit the rewind, but argued, "It's just a movie, Jack. How could it be a message?" She hit the stop button with the movie cued up to that bit.

"Ask yourself, Tess," Jack said, "how likely it is that either of our parents would leave a tape in the VCR like that."

"Not very," she admitted. Both Brigitte and Steve were painfully good about putting things away—something that always made her wince when she was here and thought of her own apartment. "But still, it could happen."

"Sure," he said, turning on the couch so he could see her without crooking his neck. "It could happen. But what's the likelihood that it would happen to a tape at the exact spot where the film refers to a Caribbean island, and that it would happen at a time when they've apparently gone to the Caribbean? Too much coincidence, Tess."

Excitement was nibbling at her stomach, but she wasn't quite ready to give in to it. "So you think they went to St. Croix?"

"I don't know. Play it again, will you?"

She hit the play button and they watched the scene again.

"One island to the left," Jack said when she paused the film again. "Damn, that could be a lot of islands."

"And left could be a lot of directions," she pointed out. "Depending on where you're coming from."

"Yeah." He blew a heavy sigh.

"I take it there isn't a Ted's Island?"

"Nope. There's lots of little islands, some only a few acres in size, but I don't know of any really called Ted's."

"You've spent a lot of time down there?" It would explain that faint lilt to his voice, a lilt that she couldn't remember being there when they'd first met.

"Yeah," he said. "I've been working on some of the drug routes."

"Wouldn't the Coast Guard do that? I mean, if they're in boats . . ."

"First, we're talking about foreign waters in most places. The Coast Guard wouldn't be welcome. Second, a lot of stuff gets shipped island to island as it works its way up here. I've been trying to nail down exactly where, how, and who. And I keep tabs on shipments so we can be ready to interdict when they get here."

"Any success?"

"Actually, yeah." He drummed his fingers on the couch beside him and changed the subject. "This is exactly the kind of clue Brigitte was so fond of leaving for her treasure hunts."

"True." Tess sighed.

"Maybe all they wanted us to get out of this was that they're on some island right around St. Croix."

"Hmm." Tess was silent a moment. "Or maybe it has something to do with Ted. Maybe it doesn't have anything to do with St. Croix at all. Maybe we should watch the entire film."

"I don't think they'd have left it cued to a particular point if we were supposed to watch the whole thing."

"*If* they left it cued on purpose."

He flashed an unexpected grin. "They did. Ah, the accountant's mind. Refusing to take any intuitive leaps."

She smarted a little. "I take intuitive leaps all the time. It's how I generally smell out cooked books. What I *don't* do is leap to conclusions."

"You certainly leapt to them about me."

Her look should have killed him, but he was feeling wonderfully impervious at the moment. "Look, we've got two parental units missing in what appears to be an elaborate but not-too-well-planned scheme to force the two of us to work together to find them. Agreed?"

"I guess."

He guessed she was feeling contrary, because not too long ago she'd agreed with that assessment. "We've had the indirect message through Hadley Philpott that Brigitte wanted to lock us up in a room until we worked out our differences. Only I got the feeling from Mary Todd that we didn't get the exact message we were supposed to."

Tess suddenly spoke eagerly. "You got that feeling, too? I wondered if I was crazy, but she acted so odd when we told her what Hadley said."

He rubbed his chin. "We agreed we wouldn't be able to get any further information out of her, though," Tess continued.

"No, I don't think we will. She doesn't strike me as the kind of person who'd yield to pleas or bribes. But I'll be interested to see what info turns up next, because I have a feeling she's trying to figure out how to patch up Hadley's error."

He looked again at the TV screen, where Kurt Russell's frozen image was jittering. "One island to the left of St. Croix. Ted's. The clue's in there somewhere."

15

They went out to dinner, and for once they didn't have an argument. After they had ascertained that Jack wanted a steak and Tess wanted fish, it was easy to pick a place: the Paradise Beach Bar.

"They might not be open," Tess warned him.

Jack shrugged. "Then we'll find some other place. The storm wasn't that bad, though. I think if we were to watch the news, we'd discover it wasn't even a hurricane by the time it got here."

"Probably," she agreed. They were walking along streets that were still damp and puddled in places, where a few yellowed palm fronds and dead tree branches were still scattered around. But all in all, the damage looked minor, even at the beach as they strolled down the boulevard.

Tess glanced between the buildings for a view

of the gulf. This evening, with the sun sinking over it, it looked nearly as placid as a bathtub. "You know what I hated most about living here?"

He glanced down at her with a smile. "You mean besides the heat and humidity? And all the tourists?"

She had to chuckle. "Besides that," she admitted. "What I hated most was hurricane season. I hated these endless get-ready marches with the threat of death and disaster moving ever closer. I mean, you can spend *days* getting ready for something that never happens. It's awful."

"And worse now."

"How so?"

"All the weather on TV. You can spend a lot more than a few days worrying about it."

"Too true."

The beach bar was open, much to Tess's surprise. She'd exercised great restraint when Jack had suggested it, forbearing to tell him that she was sure *nothing* on the island was going to be open tonight. The place was open, but not very busy.

"On the deck?" Jack asked. "Or inside?"

"The deck," she decided. In the wake of the storm, the evening was perfect, dry and just warm enough, with a breeze that smelled of the sea and the sand. A crescent moon hung to the east, and the sun was just now touching its lower edge to the water, pouring a red river of light across the gentle waves.

They sat at a table for two near the rail and

barely got settled before a waiter appeared with the menus. Tess ordered a rum punch, leaving Jack looking a little surprised.

"What's wrong?" she asked when the waiter departed. "Do you disapprove of me having a drink?"

"No," he said hastily. "I'm just surprised. It doesn't seem like you, somehow."

She shrugged. "I have a drink occasionally. Tonight I want to pretend I'm actually on vacation. Which is what I'm using up, to be here hunting for . . . *them*." She said the word with disgust. "I could have been on the way to the lake with my friends."

"Instead you're getting ready to take a Caribbean holiday."

She lifted her eyebrows. "You think so? If this is a holiday, it sure hasn't been much fun."

He grinned. "Hey, a vacation doesn't have to be fun. It just has to be a change. Preferably something that makes going back to work actually feel good."

"I always suspected you were weird."

He spread his hands. "Hey, what's weird about it? Just think about it, Tess. We all want to be happy, right?"

She almost answered cautiously, sensing that she was about to be drawn into a verbal trap. Then she decided it didn't matter. She was going to have fun tonight if it killed her. "Okay."

"Okay? *Okay?* Is that the best you can do?" There was a twinkle in his eye that kept her from taking offense.

"All right," she said, entering into the spirit of the game. "We all want to be happy."

"I thought I just said that."

"You did."

"Then why are you repeating me?"

"Because when I said, 'Okay,' that wasn't enough for you."

"Just say yes from now on. Got it?"

She swallowed a giggle. Why was she suddenly feeling giddy? Her drink hadn't even arrived yet. "Got it."

He shook his head and shook his finger at her. "No, no, you're supposed to say *yes*. Not *got it*. Got it?"

"Yes."

"At last. Okay, to return to the initial point of all this. We all want to be happy, right?"

"Right."

He sighed and shook his finger at her again. "Hard of learning, are we?"

"Yes." Her attempt to keep a straight face didn't work. She burst out laughing. The waiter, who just then brought her rum punch and Jack's iced tea, grinned and asked if they were ready to order.

"Five minutes," Jack told him. "The lady and I are having an argument."

The young man slipped away.

"Good. Okay, for the umpty-umpth time, we all want to be happy. You agreed."

"Yes."

"Now, we spend all our time at work thinking

about how badly we want that spectacular vacation that makes us happy, right?"

"Right."

"But considering that vacation is only a small portion of our year, just a few days or weeks, wouldn't we be happier if we didn't spend all our time pining for something that is so rare?"

"I suppose."

He shook his finger at her again. "Ah-ah-ah! You're supposed to say *yes*, not *I suppose*."

"Okay, okay. Yes."

"All right. Now, a vacation is, by definition, any major change in the routine."

"Oh?"

He nodded solemnly. "It is. You can take a vacation at home if you want. You don't have to go somewhere, just change your routine—because routine is what gets so tiresome. Especially when we spend all our routine time wishing we were on vacation."

"Take it easy, now," Tess said, her tone humorous. "You're in danger of losing me."

"It's simple, Tess," he said mock seriously. "The idea of a vacation is to do something different. But I have this theory that if you spend your vacation doing something different that makes you miserable, then when you get back to work, you'll be so glad to be back you'll feel truly refreshed. And you'll spend the bulk of your life being happy instead of wishing you were happy and taking a vacation."

She sipped her drink. "There is a perverse sort of logic in that."

"What's perverse about it? It's the way the human mind works. So we should be grateful to Brigitte and Steve for their little escapade, because we're both going to be very glad to go back to work next Monday."

"Except for one thing."

"What's that?"

"I'm going to be very upset that I missed my week away with my friends."

"Hmm." He frowned. "A glitch in my logic."

She laughed. "It's okay. You're allowed to have a glitch. And no matter what you say, I'm going to miss my vacation."

"And here I had it all planned out that we were going to spend a week at a slave labor camp."

Laughter spilled from her again, and she found herself thinking how absolutely wonderful it was to be sitting here with Jack and feeling none of the uncomfortable tension she usually felt around him. She didn't know why tonight was different, it just was. And without the tension that always kept her on edge, she found herself actually enjoying his company, enjoying his humor.

Still smiling, she tossed her hair back and reached for her drink. Life could be great sometimes.

He had turned his attention to the sunset, and she took the opportunity to study his face in the ruddy light. Square, bronzed from the sun, with little crow's feet radiating out from the corners of his eyes. Laugh lines around his mouth. It was a face that seemed to invite good humor and trust. It was a face she could have looked at for a long time.

He glanced her way, caught her staring at him, and smiled. It was a nice smile, friendly, welcoming. It was also something more. Something zinged and sizzled in the air between them suddenly, something that left Tess feeling breathless. She couldn't drag her gaze from his.

And he felt it, too. She could see it in the way his eyes narrowed, and his smile faded just a bit. She could almost smell the ozone as her heat leapt and her nerve endings began to sparkle.

"Ready to order, folks?"

The chipper voice of the waiter intruded. Tess blinked and felt an almost physical thud as she returned to reality. Then she felt irritated and looked at the youth who had barged into the electric moment, wishing she could snap his head off.

Jack apparently had better control than she did, because he merely looked at the boy and nodded. "I am. What about you, Tess?"

"Uh, sure." On the other hand, she thought with a sudden sense of gloom, maybe he hadn't been feeling the sparks. Maybe she'd been off in some fantasy world of her own.

Which was probably for the best. Why in the world would she want him to be attracted to her, let alone be attracted to him? Man, she needed to get back to Chicago and get back on an even keel. Maybe the humid air down here was rotting her brain.

By the time they looked at the menus they had both changed their minds. She ordered the Cobb salad and Jack ordered a lemon shark fillet, and the waiter vanished again.

The ruddy glow of the sunset was beginning to fade away, and the sky overhead was filling with night. Waves lapped gently at the sandy shore, giving a quiet rhythm to the night.

"It's beautiful out here," Tess remarked. The confession was almost reluctant.

"Yeah," he answered. "It is. I like sitting on the water like this in the evening. It's one of the reasons I enjoy working in the Caribbean."

She glanced his way. "So you spend a lot of time sitting in beach bars."

His gaze laughed at her. "As much as I need to."

"Sounds like hard work."

"Hey, my elbow gets sore."

She laughed, but she didn't believe him—not after the way he had reacted to her remark about a six-pack. He might sit in bars because his job required it, but she doubted he would still be alive to talk about it if he overindulged.

He leaned toward her and idly touched the back of her hand, running his finger over it lightly. "You were right about one thing. I live the life of a beach bum."

Her gaze riveted to him as her heart began to speed up. "Oh, no, don't tell me you own a surfboard."

"Actually," he said, looking almost embarrassed, "I own four."

"Four? What in the world does anybody need four surfboards for? You can only use one at a time."

"Ah, the abysmal ignorance of the nonsurfer. There are different designs, different lengths. I prefer different boards for different conditions."

"Oh. Really?" Suddenly feeling impish, she batted her lashes at him. "So there's a whole scientific theory of the use of surfboards?"

"I don't know. To tell you the truth, I don't care. I just know what I like."

"Sort of like the Philistine approach to art?"

"I always feel sorry for the Philistines. Maybe they weren't the uncouth barbarians we take them for."

"Why doesn't that surprise me?"

"What, that I feel sorry for the Philistines?" He grinned. "Maybe because you detect a family resemblance?"

That cracked her up. He could be so charming when he wanted. But as she laughed, he withdrew his hand from hers, and she felt the loss of his touch deep within her soul. Her laughter faded away, and she found herself wishing she was back in Chicago with its hard edge of reality, and away from the tropical breezes and sunsets, away from beach bars and Jack, away from things that were beginning to make her feel like someone else.

By the time their dinners were served, night had settled fully on the world. Reggae and calypso music was playing quietly over the speakers now, just enough to create a nice background but not enough to stifle conversation.

Except that there was no conversation. She and Jack ate silently, and for some reason seemed to be spending a lot of effort trying not to look at one another. Finally Tess decided the avoidance was ridiculous—especially since they were stuck together until they finished their meals and walked home. Why had the tension come back, anyway?

"So you surf?" she said.

"Guilty."

"Why guilty? I think it's amazing that anyone can balance on a board on a wave that way. I'd drown."

A smile began to crease his face, and some of the tension fled. "I almost did when I was learning."

"Why did you learn?"

"Oh, it was something to do when I was in college. My best friend was into it, and we used to go out on Saturdays when we could get some waves. It turned out to be useful, though."

"It's your cover?"

"Kind of. It gives me an excuse to hang around the beach dives."

"That's amazing. Given how touristy the Caribbean's become, I wouldn't have thought there were any dives left."

"Oh, they're there. Tourism hasn't completely wiped out the remnants of the old ways. There are still people who make their living from the sea and need a place they can go to at the end of the day, stinking of fish. There's still the criminal element and all the unsavoriness that goes with some segments of humanity."

She nodded, picturing it. "So you hang out with those types?"

"Sometimes. Sometimes I hang out at classier places. Depends on what I'm looking for and where the leads take me."

She hesitated, her heart skipping uneasily, and asked, "Do you ever get tired of it?"

"Tired of what?"

"Living alone. Undercover. With your neck in a noose?"

"My neck's not exactly in a noose." But he grew thoughtful and didn't answer for a while. She left it alone, because she had the sense that she had touched on something very personal for him. And she wasn't the type to go barging into the private places of another without permission.

"Yeah," he said finally. "Sometimes. Sometimes I think about a desk job."

"Fair enough."

He flashed a sudden grin. "But hey, I'd miss the beach and all the beautiful women."

"Figures."

After dinner, he suggested they walk along the beach. Tess agreed readily enough, and reminded him of their search.

"We've still got to figure out what that videotape message means."

"I know, but how about we take the evening off? I think we've earned it. Besides, there's no Ted's Island, and to the left of St. Croix could be almost anywhere, as you so ably pointed out. So we need another clue."

"I still think we ought to badger Mary Todd."

"And do what?" he asked. "Stick slivers under her fingernails? That woman's not going to talk unless she wants to. Anyway, enough for tonight. We're entitled to an evening off."

"Just so long as we find them by Thanksgiving."

He stopped walking and turned to face her. She stopped, too, and looked up at him. "What difference does it make?"

Tess sighed, hating to admit this when she was so angry with her mother. "Because she'll be absolutely heartbroken if we miss the holiday."

"Yeah." He sighed and ran his fingers through his sandy hair. "Okay, okay. By Thanksgiving. But we can still take this evening off."

He seemed rather determined about it. "Pretty hung up on that, aren't you?"

"Yes," he said with exasperation. "I *am*. And if you don't mind, I mean to spend the rest of the evening walking on the beach with a pretty girl and holding hands."

So saying, he snatched her hand and began marching down the beach toward the pass. Tess trotted along with him, torn between delight that he had called her pretty and annoyance at the cavalier and unromantic way he'd taken her hand.

"You've been away from civilization too long, Jack."

He sighed audibly enough to be heard over the

murmur of the surf. "Tess, do me a favor. Don't call me any names tonight. In fact, just shut your yap. That's all I ask."

Shut her yap? Indignation filled her and she tried to tug her hand out of his, but he wouldn't let go. "Shut my yap?" she demanded. "How dare you!"

He stopped walking again and faced her until they stood face-to-face with no more than six inches between their noses and an inch between their bodies. "Tess," he said. "Shut up."

Then he kissed her. Which was really a cave-man thing to do, except that he didn't grab her, didn't grind his mouth against hers, or anything she could have taken genuine exception to. He didn't touch her at all, except for holding her hand, and the lightest wisp of sensation as his lips brushed hers.

It was unfair. Unfair that he gave her nothing to object to, nothing to fight back against, no reason to shove him away. Unfair that with the simple, light touch of his mouth against hers he could melt her, turn her giddy and light-headed, make her want more and yet more.

Her fingers twisted around his, holding on for dear life. She felt as if the world were turning upside down and at any minute she might fall off and drift away. Needing more than the teasing of his mouth, needing something firm to buttress her in the topsy-turvy whirlwind he had created within her, she leaned into him.

He was strong, firm. Unyielding. A rock to cling to in the maelstrom. And it was strange, so strange, but she had never imagined that every cell in her body could physically ache just to be held. Or that it could feel so absolutely wonderful to have strong arms close around her and hold her tight. Oh, God, it was *good*.

They stood like that for a while, wrapped in each other's arms. How long, she had no idea. It was enough just to hold and be held while night settled ever more deeply over the world. And it didn't even matter that he was her nemesis.

But finally she felt his arms loosening and she had to let go as he stepped back. She suddenly felt emptier than she'd ever felt in her life.

"Let's walk," he said. His voice sounded perfectly normal, as if nothing earth-shattering had just happened.

He took her hand again and they began walking toward the end of the island. Little by little she grew aware of the night around her again, of the sound of the waves lapping at the shore, of the breeze in her hair, and of the way the damp sand gave beneath her shoes.

He squeezed her hand gently, as if to let her know he was still there. The gesture surprised her and made her uneasy, leaving her to wonder what she might have betrayed or led him to think during their embrace. Surely there was no reason for him to think she needed reassurance?

But she didn't say anything. The last thing she wanted to do right now was get into another fight with him.

Apparently he was no more inclined to talk than she, because they walked all the way to the end of the island without speaking another word. It was a surprisingly comfortably silence, and Tess felt herself relaxing more and more, until it suddenly struck her that she must live in a perpetual state of tension. She couldn't remember the last time she had felt this relaxed.

There was a fishing pier at the end of the island, and even at night there were a half-dozen people out there with their rods.

Jack and Tess passed them, walking out to the end of the pier to lean against the rail and watch the moonlight sparkle on the water. He put his arm around her shoulder, tucking her up to his side.

Watching the silvery light splinter on the water, Tess leaned into Jack, just enjoying the closeness. She'd always imagined feeling like this someday, enjoying this comforting closeness with someone. It was disturbing to realize that Jack, of all people, was the first person to ever give her this feeling. But she refused to think about that. For now, it was enough to just be.

Jack seemed to be feeling the same way. He shifted his weight so that he leaned more heavily against the rail and drew her a little closer. Now his scent mixed with the sea smells, a heady brew, and she felt something inside her growing quieter and quieter. As if she were easing ever so slowly into another world where nothing existed but the two of them.

It was delicious, and she savored it, wishing the feeling could go on forever.

Presently Jack stirred. His finger touched her

chin, gently urging her face up. He looked down at her, his eyes unreadable in the moonlight. "Let's go home," he said.

She nodded, everything inside her certain. It was time.

16

They walked home down the shadowy streets. It wasn't far, but it was long enough for either one of them to experience a change of mind. Jack quite frankly couldn't believe he was doing this. This was Tess, for Pete's sake. The pain in the butt. The unwanted evil stepsister.

All those words sounded hollow to him now. For she was also Tess, a beautiful woman who wasn't related to him; Tess, who could drive him to the edge of madness. Tess, who made him want her more than he had ever wanted a woman in his life.

Tess, who, despite all her zingers, despite the prickly way she reacted to him, struck him as a very vulnerable woman. A lonely woman. Like him, she had the kind of loneliness that friends couldn't fill. A loneliness that went to the very root of the soul.

So even as he thought of all the reasons he ought to head the other way, such as the way she was probably going to want to kill him in the morning, he couldn't do it. If this was to only happen once in his life, he still had to know what it was like to be with a woman who could move him this way.

He just hoped she didn't hate herself for this. Because if there was one thing he knew about Tess, it was how easily she was wounded.

They reached the house. Jack unlocked the door with a hand that wasn't quite steady, then they stepped into the air-conditioned darkness inside. Lights? he wondered, then decided against it. He didn't want the harsh edge of reality on anything that was about to happen between them.

Still holding her hand, he guided her down the hallway. If she'd had any doubts about his intentions, he told himself, they must be plain now. There could be no other reason he was leading her toward the bedrooms in the dark. But still she came with him, her hand clinging to his.

He felt a shiver of relief and delight pass through him as he realized she was feeling the same otherworldly magic he was experiencing. He wasn't alone in this place she had brought him to with nothing but her presence and her merest touch.

He chose her bedroom and led her inside. He

didn't close the door because he didn't want her to feel trapped.

Then he remembered what she had hinted before—that she'd never made love with anyone. The thought gave him a pang of near panic. Never in his life had he made love to an inexperienced woman, and suddenly he was filled with qualms. What if he didn't do it right? What if he scared her, or hurt her, or embarrassed her? It seemed like such an awesome responsibility.

But almost as soon as the qualms filled him, Tess banished them. And all she did was take a tentative step toward him and say uncertainly, "Jack?"

Backing off now, would probably hurt her worse than any slip-up he might make while loving her. If he turned away now, she would feel rejected in the most personal way possible.

Then she took another step toward him, bringing herself to within an inch. She tipped her head back, and he could just barely see her in the dim light that seeped around the curtains from the street lamps. "Jack?" she whispered.

It was a shivery, shuddery sound of longing, and it so perfectly echoed the longing in him that all his concerns vanished. Nothing would ever be this right again. Nothing.

He was a man who lived most of his life on the edge. This was a new edge, and it was heady.

Gathering her close with his arms, Jack gave her the kiss he had only hinted at on the beach, a kiss that dove all the way to the depths of her soul, carrying him with it. Colors seemed to swirl behind his eyes, colors that were at first cool and soothing, then gradually grew hotter and brighter. He wanted her, and the ache was growing in his every cell.

She tore her mouth from his, gasping for air, then her fingertips found his lips, touching them lightly, almost wonderingly. "I never guessed . . ."

Neither had he. He'd felt the white heat of passion before, but this was something different, something deeper and richer. It was carrying him along every bit as insistently, but it was fuller. And he loved it.

Taking the first risky step, he reached for the T-shirt she was wearing and lifted the hem, pulling it gently upward. As if she had been waiting for this, she unleashed a sigh and lifted her arms over her head invitingly.

He obliged, feeling his heart begin to hammer. Now he wanted light, light by which to see her every charm, but he feared its intrusion would break the spell. So he contented himself with the pale glow of her cotton bra to remind him of what he was looking at. And contented himself even more with the movement of his hands as they stroked over her shoulders, down her arms.

She seemed to want the same as he, because when his hands reached her fingertips, her arms leapt upward again, this time to work at the buttons of his polo shirt. When she found the hem and began to tug it upward, he felt a sense of fierce exultation.

Then his shirt was gone, too, and he reached

for her, drawing her close, giving them both the opportunity to savor the marvel of skin against skin. There was no rush, he reminded himself. They had all night, and no one to disturb them. It was a good night to savor every single touch.

Soon, though, as if they had a mind of their own, his palms began to wander over her back, learning the satin texture of her skin, the delicate ridge of her spine. He felt a shiver pass through her, then she was clinging to him tightly, her face pressed to his chest, her body writhing ever so slightly under his touches.

Delight exploded in him as he recognized the passion in her, and it fueled his own simmering need, fanning the coals to flames. The spell that had been pulling him to her took on a more primitive throb, and what had been tugging him gently along began to drive him.

But he refused to let go of his self-restraint. He took his time about unclasping the hook of her bra, and after he did, he slid it slowly down her shoulders, letting her feel the whisper of the cloth against her skin as it fell away.

In the dimness he could barely see her breasts. The mystery of the moment enthralled him, as if he were trying to peer past a veil to see riches untold. But his hands weren't blinded, and they reached out to cup her, causing her to gasp, causing an electric thrill to run through him. Soft and firm all at once, with hard little nipples that cried out for more touches. He was only too willing to oblige.

Gently he brushed his thumbs back and forth

over the taut peaks and felt another surge of delight as she groaned and let her head fall backward. Then she reached up with both hands, clinging to his shoulders as if she might fall.

He scooped her up then, hearing her soft gasp of surprise, and carried her to the bed. He laid her down carefully, then knelt over her, straddling her. Without a word, he gently caught her wrists in his hands and held them over her head.

"Just lie still," he whispered roughly. "Just lie still."

If her eyes grew bigger he didn't notice, because as he held her captive, he bowed over her, running his tongue lightly along her neck, tasting the pulse that throbbed there. He took a detour back up to her mouth, tasting a hint of the rum she had drunk earlier, then brought his tongue lower again.

He trailed it over her collarbones, leaving a damp, chilly trail in his wake. He felt her chest begin to rise rapidly, as her breath came in shorter and shorter gasps. Still he teased her, running his tongue down the valley between her breasts, as she shivered and then moaned.

Her hands tugged, trying to break free of his grip, but he tightened his hold. "Uh-uh," he said. "Be patient, Tess."

She relaxed, accepting his decision, but only for a moment because his tongue returned to her skin, now tracing a trail beneath her breasts, then around them, hinting at things to come. She gasped again and murmured his name, and it was the sweetest sound he had ever heard.

Then, after a foray lower to make her stomach muscles quiver, he brought his mouth back to her breasts. He took her nipple into his mouth and sucked, gently at first, then stronger, and felt the delicious tension fill her as moans escaped her.

Patience, he told himself. *Patience*. His entire body was throbbing, demanding surcease, but he forced himself to ignore it. Forced himself not to touch her with anything except his tongue and his hands, for fear he would forget his purpose and drive straight to fulfillment. All night, he reminded himself. They had all night.

Her hands gripped his back now, hanging on for dear life, and her body arched up toward him, begging for more and deeper touches. He was happy to oblige, nibbling gently on her nipples now, drawing gasp after gasp out of her.

She groaned his name and he answered by tearing himself away from her, by shoving to his feet and reaching for the button of his shorts.

He didn't know if she was watching; it was too dark to be sure. It didn't matter. All that mattered was that he get rid of the last of their clothing. When his own shorts and shoes were gone and he was naked, he stood over her and reached for the waistband of hers. No button, just elastic, making it easy for him to pull them down with one easy movement.

They caught on her jogging shoes, and he dispensed with those quickly. Then she was naked, and so was he, and the musky scent of their lovemaking filled the night.

This, he thought dimly, was how it was supposed to be. Nothing had ever felt so right.

He caught one of her feet in his hand and lifted it for a kiss on her instep, and another on her arch. He treated the other foot to the same consideration.

Then, little by little, he worked his way up her legs, tasting her with his tongue, teasing her until she could hold still no longer. Soft sweet skin, delicate scents, joy of joys.

He bypassed the dark thatch at the apex of her thighs, wanting to save that awhile longer. He blew a puff of air in her navel, then felt his heart thrill as a soft, surprised laugh escaped her. If she still felt like laughing, then he was doing something right.

Stretching out beside her, he took one of her hands and guided it to his body. "Delilah," he said, and this time she accepted the accolade. When her small hand closed on him, he sucked air between his teeth. The jolt of pleasure was almost too much to bear.

So was her eager curiosity about his body. Her touches were sometimes awkward, because she'd never done this before, but he'd never, ever known anything sexier in his entire life. His self-control was tested to the limit.

She also seemed to have an unerring instinct for what would drive him over the edge. He was clinging to the last tattered shred of his self-control when her mouth found the point of his small nipple, and her tongue taught him that he was as sensitive there as she.

For a few glorious minutes he lay nearly paralyzed by the overpowering pleasure she gave him, but finally other needs grew stronger. And when she tugged at him with her hands, as if she wanted to pull him over her, he was lost.

When he settled his weight between her thighs, she was open and ready. Her hands even gripped his hips as if to hurry him along.

But he still had one ray of clear thought in his head. "This might hurt, Tess."

"I know," she said hoarsely. "I know. . . ."

He thrust, filling her in one long movement, and felt a shudder of pleasure grip him, rippling through him from head to foot, shaking him to the center of his very existence. He heard her cry, a sharp, helpless sound, and it froze him.

Gently holding her head between his hands, he sprinkled kisses all over her face. "I'm sorry," he whispered. "I'm sorry. . . ."

She was stiff and holding her breath, and he encouraged her to breathe again. Finally she did, a long sigh followed by a deep gulp of air.

"Are you okay?" he asked, worried.

"Better," she whispered.

"I'll stop."

"No!" Her hands clutched at him. "No!" As if to make her point, she lifted to him, moving with an instinctive sensuality that made him forget everything else. He let her lead him, and it was as if she knew the way. Before too long, he surged hard against her and exploded into a million flaming pieces.

* * *

"You can cut my hair anytime," he said to her later.

She giggled into his shoulder, sounding happy. He was thankful, because that meant he hadn't hurt her, that she wasn't regretting what had just happened.

But she hadn't found her own satisfaction. He was going to have to remedy that, and he found himself wondering how much her sensibilities could handle before she became too embarrassed.

Man, life was easier with an experienced partner. On the other hand . . .

On the other hand, he would have hated like hell to miss this experience with Tess. And to be honest, he was enjoying her freshness, her pleasure in the newness of everything.

Then he had a brainstorm. "Be right back," he said, dropping a kiss on her forehead. Her hands trailed over him as he pulled away, as if they were reluctant to lose contact. That felt so good, in a way he'd never felt before.

In the bathroom he turned on the hot water and dampened a washcloth in it. Then he padded back to the dark bedroom and sat beside her on the bed, gently washing her between her legs.

She made a nervous little laugh at his first touch, but gradually she relaxed, letting him have his way with the warm, wet cloth. About the time it began to cool down, little sighs were escaping her, and her hips were moving slightly.

Jack took the invitation, tossing the washcloth onto the night table and sliding between her legs so that he could tease her with his mouth. Her first reaction was a sharp gasp, and she froze, but after another couple of laps of his tongue against her nub, she was lost, groaning deeply and arching wildly against him.

Higher and higher he drove her, enjoying her responses almost as much as if they were his own. All of a sudden her hands clutched at his head, holding him close as if she feared he might suddenly vanish. Moments later she shattered beneath him with a cry that pierced his heart.

Life could be so damn good at times. So damn good.

The shower was warm. Jack drew Tess into it with him, and held her close while the spray fell over them both. She was soft against him, warm and small, her eyes half-closed, her lips curved in a silly half-smile that wouldn't go away. He liked her this way. He wished she could always feel this good, because just looking at her was making him feel good all over.

Too bad it wouldn't last. The thought pierced his glow, reminding him that Tess was a prickly little thorn. And now she was probably going to get even more frustrated with him, because he'd seen her with her guard down. He'd seen the soft, delectable, sweet woman beneath the thorny exterior.

Great. If he'd made the situation worse, Steve

and Brigitte would never forgive him for that.

But he didn't want to think of that right now. Right now he didn't want to think about anything except how good it felt to hold this woman against him while warm water ran over them. How easy it would be to want this to be part of every day to come.

"This is so nice," Tess murmured. Her hands, wet and slick with soap, traced his back and buttocks lingeringly. He reciprocated, lathering the washcloth, then beginning a journey over every curve and hollow he could find.

Unfortunately, right about then, the hot water gave out. Ordinarily Florida's water was tepid at its coldest, but for some reason this water was cold enough to cause them both to jump.

Tess gave a small shriek, then started laughing breathlessly. They jumped out together, landing on the bath mat safely, and Jack reached in to shut off the water.

Cold, wet, and dripping, they stood looking at one another. The atmosphere in the bathroom began to thicken with need and suddenly the air didn't feel so chilly anymore.

A minute later they were cocooned in the bed again, while the world slipped away.

Morning came all too quickly. Jack peeled open one eye and looked around. He got the first inkling of trouble when he realized he was alone in Tess's bed.

She was hiding out in the kitchen, huddled

over a cup of coffee. She didn't hear his approach, so he spared a minute to study her unobserved. God, she looked miserable. In fact, she reminded him of a cold, wet kitten. Or a whipped dog.

Shit. He wanted to turn around and walk away from this right now. A beautiful night such as the one they'd just shared was rarer than diamonds, and it was cause for celebration, not regrets and hurts. They ought to be thinking of some romantic way to share breakfast, rather than getting ready for this fight that he was sure was coming.

Then he caught himself, realizing he was being ridiculous. Romantic breakfasts? Something about being around Tess must be rotting his brain. He *never* thought about such things.

Knowing that whatever was coming was unavoidable, only postponable, he headed for the coffeepot. From the corner of his eye he saw Tess look up quickly, then return her attention to her mug.

"Good morning," he said, hoping he didn't sound the way he felt, which was that he was stepping into a minefield with no idea at all where the trip wires were buried.

"Morning," she said quietly. Way too quietly. Heavily. Reluctantly.

Smothering a sigh, he pulled out a chair beside her. No matter how closed off she looked, he was determined not to put the entire table between them. Yet.

She didn't say anything more. He waited, believing that people who wanted to talk eventually got around to doing it on their own. It was a strategy that worked great with drug dealers, who sooner or later felt a need to talk, whether it was to brag or just to get it off their chests. Very, very few people could keep their mouths shut for long.

Apparently Tess was an exception. She just kept sitting there, staring glumly into her coffee, speaking not a word.

Hmm. "Uh . . ." he began finally, "is this the morning blues or did something terrible happen?"

She looked up from her cup and gave him a forced smile. "I'm not a good waker-upper."

"Oh." Nor did he believe that was the truth. Great. Really great. They had spent the night making the most fabulous love he had ever known, and certainly that she had ever known, given her lack of experience, and the morning after she was sitting here looking as grim as death. That was sure good for his ego. And for his heart. At least he assumed that was what was aching in the center of his chest.

Old instinct told him just to walk away. He had avoided getting entangled with women for years simply by avoiding getting involved in their emotional lives. It was an easy self-defense, one he'd practiced scrupulously because his job wouldn't have made him a good mate. The way he figured it, some woman would *think* she was capable of putting up with his long absences and the danger he faced, but when push came to shove, she wouldn't like it and life would go to hell for both of them.

So there was a certain amount of nobility in the way he avoided the gentler sex—or so he liked to tell himself. Although he knew damn well they were neither gentler nor weaker. In fact, when you came right down to it, he figured women were a hell of a lot stronger than men gave them credit for. But they were also far more emotional, and a guy needed to take that into account.

Which was something he'd neglected to do last night, and now that he sat looking at her, he felt pretty rotten about that. He should have known better.

"So," he said cautiously, "are you upset about . . . what we, um, did last night?"

Her eyes widened a hair, then she colored faintly. "No."

"Oh." Now he was flummoxed. If she wasn't having regrets about last night, then what *was* she feeling so gloomy about? Maybe he'd made a mistake by not giving her a kiss and a hug when he came into the kitchen first thing. He hadn't because he'd thought she was upset about their lovemaking, but since that wasn't the case . . . His thoughts sputtered to a stop.

Finally he said, "You know, it's too early in the morning for all this heavy-duty thinking."

"What do you mean?"

"I'm sitting here trying to work out what I did that made you feel so damn bad, and what's the best way to act so I won't make you feel any worse, and I'm going around in circles until my brain hurts. So if it's okay with you, can we put off any emotional crisis until I finish a couple of cups of coffee? Just to let my brain get into gear?"

She looked amused. "That's fine by me. That's all I'm doing."

So maybe she *was* just a lousy waker-upper. It was possible.

"Okay. I'll shut up."

"And don't burn those brain cells too much before they warm up."

"I won't." He raised his coffee cup, giving her a little toast, then carried it to his lips. As soon as he did that, her head lowered again, and he saw the gloom settle on her.

She was a good liar, he thought, but not good enough. Last night was bothering her. And he wished to hell she'd tell him why.

She'd never tell him why last night had been a major mistake, Tess thought. Not because it hadn't been wonderful. Not because she regretted making love for the first time in her life. But because she regretted what it had done to her feelings about Jack.

Suddenly he looked like someone she wanted to reach out and hug, and hold close to her forever. Which was an impossibility, and she knew it. Heck, he didn't even like her. Then there was the problem of his job. However he might legitimize it by working for Uncle Sam, he was still a pirate at heart, a man who hung out with smugglers and dope dealers and risked his neck on a regular basis. Three hundred years ago, he would have been sailing the Caribbean under a black flag.

But however she argued with herself, and however much she knew it was going to hurt, she couldn't look at him this morning and see the old Jack, the Jack who had perpetually irritated her. All she could see was this incredibly attractive man with sun-streaked brown hair and a golden tan who had the most devastating smile. Even the Caribbean lilt that had once irritated her as an affectation now seemed to her to be part and parcel of his attraction.

And he did look good sitting there in a loose white collarless shirt with the sleeves rolled up, and khaki shorts. Good enough that she ached to reach out and touch him and bring him close. Ached to tumble into bed with him and know that marvelous closeness again.

And that aching was the biggest danger sign she'd ever encountered.

He sighed and turned to one side, leaning back in his chair and crossing his legs loosely, ankle resting on his knee. She had a sudden, sharp memory of how that fine dusting of golden hair had felt beneath her palms last night.

"Heh," he said.

"Huh?"

"Heh," he repeated.

"Meaning?"

"Just that: heh. Coincidence."

"What coincidence?"

He pointed toward the refrigerator. "Ted's Island. A dry cleaning bill from Ted's Cleaners. Haven't you ever noticed how that happens? Something will come to your attention, then suddenly it seems like it's everywhere?"

"I guess so." Now that she thought about it, she had indeed noticed that from time to time. "A couple of months ago I ran into three women named Laryssa on the same day. That struck me because it seemed like such an unusual name. But it's just coincidence."

"Synchronicity," he said. "That's what I call it. Anyway, I guess we're in sync with Teds. Hey, isn't Mary Todd's boyfriend a Ted, too?"

"Yeah," said Tess after thinking about it. "I think she did." Sudden shock jolted her. "Jack? Jack, you don't think Mary's Ted knows where they are, do you?"

But Jack was already rising from his chair. "I'm getting my shoes. And I'll tell you right now—I'm leaving no Ted unturned."

17

"My kingdom for a car," Jack said as they set out toward Mary's house.

Tess agreed. Even though Paradise Beach was small enough to be a walking community, right now she didn't want to waste the time. "Maybe we should have called to make sure she's there."

"What, and give her a chance to hide? I don't think so."

"I forget I'm dealing with a DEA agent."

He glanced at her. "What do you mean by that?"

"Just that you're used to cornering criminals. Mary isn't a criminal. Why should she run if we simply call and say we'd like to stop by for a minute?"

He shook his head. "You're thinking like

someone with nothing to hide. Mary's in this up to her neck."

Tess thought about that. "Probably," she agreed. "But what makes you think we're going to get any information out of her? Not so long ago you were saying that, barring a threat of mayhem, she'd keep her mouth shut as long as she wanted to."

"I don't plan to ask her about Steve and Brigitte. I just want to find out where we can locate her friend. Then I'm going to question *him*."

"You think he'll be more amenable?"

"I have the feeling he's not in this by choice."

"Ah." Remembering the few minutes they'd spent with him, she was inclined to agree. "He told us his last name. I remember him saying it when he introduced himself. But I'm darned if I can remember it."

"Me, too. The thing was, I wasn't really interested in him."

"Me neither. And I've always been terrible with names. I can remember somebody's social security number or employer identification number from seeing it just once, but not a name."

He looked at her, lifting one eyebrow. "Now, *that's* weird."

"I know." She shrugged as if it didn't matter, but she wasn't exactly happy about it. She didn't like being weird.

But he wasn't giving up on the subject yet. "So numbers are your friends, huh?"

She gave him a sour look. "Well, it's better to

have numbers for friends than drug dealers."

"You may have a point. Except drug dealers aren't my friends."

The universe was laughing at him that morning, however, because as soon as he spoke, Ernesto popped out of a door right in front of him.

"Hey, man," Ernesto said.

Jack drew up short. "Where's the wife and baby?"

"At the hotel." Ernesto scowled at him. "You sound like my probation officer, man. It's none of your business. I'm clean."

"Yeah?" Jack looked past him at the store he'd just come out of. "Why do I think they sell screens and pipes in there?"

Ernesto shrugged. "I don't know. I bought a cigar." He held up a bag. "Wanna see?"

Jack shook his head. "I'm on vacation. But if you like cigars, go to Ybor City. They hand roll some of the best there."

Ernesto put his hands on his hips and thrust his chin out. "Why you tryin' to get rid of me, man? I got a perfect right to be here, just like anybody else."

"Did I say you didn't?"

"Then why you telling me to get out of here?"

"I'm not." Jack rolled his eyes with exasperation. "Look, I'm on my way to see a friend, so just let us pass, will you?"

But Ernesto wasn't about to budge, and his chin was sticking out even more pugnaciously. "You told me to go to Ybor. That's the same as telling me to get out of here."

Tess watched in disbelief. Ernesto hadn't seemed like the brightest bulb the other night, but he hadn't been such a pain, either. He was being deliberately obstructive right now.

"I owe you one, man," Ernesto said, pointing a finger at Jack. "I owe you a big one. You put me behind bars."

"No, you put yourself behind bars," Jack said. "You're the one who was selling the drugs."

"That's what I meant."

Jack sighed. "Look, what the hell do you want? Because you're extraneous."

"Extraneous? What's that?" Ernesto looked suspicious. "I ain't doin' nothin' but enjoying my vacation."

"Extraneous," Jack repeated. "Having no vital part in my current problem. Unnecessary."

Tess looked at Jack. "What do you do? Read the dictionary?"

"When I'm bored."

"Hey," said Ernesto, clearly offended. "I'm plenty necessary."

"Not to me, not right now. You are irrelevant. And if I were writing a report about the problem that *does* concern me, I wouldn't even mention you. If I were an editor, I would remove you from the story."

Ernesto now looked more than offended. He looked hurt. "Hey, man, I'm sorry you're having a tough time. It's not my fault I keep running into you."

"It was your fault you came to stay with me the night of the hurricane."

The other man shrugged. "I didn't have no choice. And I'm sorry your old man and step-mom are missing. But I didn't make them take off. *You* did."

Then, with all appearance of being in a huff, he started to walk away.

"Hold it," said Jack, reaching out and catching Ernesto's arm.

Ernesto looked down at Jack's hand on his arm. "That's battery, man. Hands off."

Jack dropped his hand immediately. "What did you mean?"

"Mean? Mean about what?" Ernesto ostentatiously brushed his arm, as if to remove Jack's touch.

"About me making Brigitte and Steve go away?"

"That's what happened, ain't it? That's what *she* said, anyway."

"She? Which she?"

"Brigitte, man. Your stepmom."

"Damn it!" Tess exploded, frustrated by this elliptical conversation.

Ernesto looked at her. "What's *your* problem?"

"You! Will you just get to the point?"

"What point?"

"What were you doing talking to my mother?"

Ernesto drew himself up. "What? There's some kind of law against talking to people now? What's the matter with you two? I can see why you drove her crazy."

"God," said Jack to Tess, "I don't think I can

handle this. She was discussing her personal problems with a drug pusher?"

"That doesn't surprise me. I'm more curious about how she met him," Tess said. "That's too much of a coincidence."

"Coincidence?" Ernesto repeated. "Who said anything about coincidence? I came looking for this turkey." He jerked his thumb toward Jack.

Jack stiffened, and Tess felt a sharp twinge of apprehension. It somehow didn't sound very cozy when a man came looking for the guy who'd sent him to prison.

Jack apparently agreed. "If it hadn't been me, Ernesto, it would have been someone else."

The other man shrugged. "Could be. Could be I'd be dead right now, too. That's what Julia keeps telling me."

"A wise woman."

"She's pretty cool. And ain't the kid the greatest?"

"Yes, she is," Jack said, a little impatiently. "But what does Brigitte have to do with this?"

"Not a whole hell of a lot." Ernesto shrugged. "It was Julia, anyway."

"What was Julia?"

"It was her fault."

Tess was beginning to have visions of shaking Ernesto until his teeth rattled. Had they been wrong in their assumption that Brigitte had pulled a stunt? What if this man had actually hurt her? It was *Julia's fault*? That didn't sound good at all.

"Cut to the chase," Jack said impatiently. "Did you hurt Brigitte and Steve?"

"Hell, no!"

"Did you kidnap them?"

"I already told you, man! No! I didn't do nothin' to them. If that's what you think, then I guess I *am* extratemperous, or whatever it was."

"Extraneous," said Jack, who was no longer thinking that Ernesto was extraneous at all. "But you talked to them. Why did you talk to them?"

"I didn't talk to *them*."

"But you just said . . ." Jack stepped toward him, his hands curled as if he were going to strangle Ernesto.

Ernesto promptly stepped back. "Watch it, man."

"Just tell me what you talked to them about."

"I didn't talk to them about *nothin*'!"

Jack took a menacing step forward. Ernest squawked, "It was *Julia*!"

Jack froze. He looked at Tess. Tess looked at him. Then they both looked at Ernesto, saying in unison, "Julia?"

"Julia talked to her," Ernesto said hastily. "Julia wanted to thank you for savin' me. At least that's what she keeps sayin', sayin' that I'd be dead now 'cept you put me in jail. So . . ." Ernesto shrugged. "She found out where you lived. And when we came out here for—"

"Hold it, hold it, hold it," Jack said swiftly. "Julia found out where I *live*? How'd she do that? That's supposed to be secret."

"I don't know." He shrugged. "She finds out

lots of things. Didn't I tell you? Julia's a cop. Miami PD."

Jack swore. "I don't believe this. Where is she now?"

Ernesto pointed up the street. "At the café. I just came over here to get me a cigar."

"Let's all go see her," Jack said. "Right now."

Julia was sitting at a small table, the baby sleeping in her arms. Before her was a cappuccino. She looked a little surprised to see Jack and Tess, but her smile was welcoming. The greetings they exchanged were pleasant enough, but Jack was clearly not in the mood for small talk, and Tess couldn't blame him. She had no difficulty understanding why it disturbed him to discover that *anybody* had been able to track down his family.

"So," he said to Julia. "You're a cop."

She nodded. "I guess Ernie told you."

"Yeah. So how come you didn't mention it before?"

"You didn't ask. Besides, it embarrasses Ernie to be married to a cop."

Ernesto did indeed look embarrassed. "Nah, it doesn't."

Julia gave him a fond look. "It *does*," she countered firmly. But then she looked at Jack. "I didn't see any reason to tell you."

"But you looked me up. You don't think that makes me nervous?"

"Well, after I talked to your mother, I wasn't

going to tell you. And I figured what you didn't know wasn't going to bother you."

"When did you talk to Brigitte? And about what?"

Julia passed the fussing baby to Ernesto, who took his daughter with loving caution. Then she opened the diaper bag at her feet and brought out a bottle of juice, which she passed to him. "She's getting hungry, I think. You all want some cappuccino?"

"No, thanks," Jack said, and Tess echoed him. "Let's get back to Brigitte, okay?"

"Sure, no problem," Julia said. She sipped her coffee. "I came to look you up, it's true. I wanted to thank you for saving Ernie. I wanted Ernie to thank you himself, but I'm not sure he's ready to do that. He still gets kind of mad sometimes about going to jail."

"No kidding," Ernesto said.

Tess could well understand that he might.

"Anyway," Julia continued, silencing her spouse with a look, "we were in high school together, you know. I was sweet on him back then, but he was too busy being a big deal with the wrong crowd. So even if he had asked me, I wouldn't have gone out with him. But when he got out of jail two years ago . . . he was a changed man. So I wanted to tell you that you saved one life. And I wanted to thank you for it."

Watching Jack, Tess wasn't surprised to see that he looked faintly embarrassed. It was probably about how she'd feel if the wife of some guy she'd audited and charged with fraud had come to thank her for putting him back on the straight and narrow.

"It was a stupid idea," Julia said. "I know it was. But I found your mother and father about a month ago and came to ask them how I could get in touch with you. Your mom wouldn't tell me."

"Wise woman," muttered Jack.

"I even told her I was a cop," Julia said. "You can rest easy. She won't give you away to anybody. So I asked her to tell you all about me and Guadalupe and Ernesto. I figured it might make you feel good. A little bit, anyway."

Jack managed a nod. "I feel like Mother Teresa."

Julia laughed. "Okay. Like I said, it was a stupid idea. I think I was feeling a little high because of Lupe, you know? But your mother and I had a good talk. She told me how worried she was about you. And she told me how she didn't see you much anymore. Either of you," she added with a look at Tess.

Tess shifted uncomfortably and hoped she wasn't blushing.

Jack gave her a look of commiseration. "It seems," he said, "that the whole world knows we don't get along."

"It's beginning to feel like it," Tess agreed, sounding smothered.

Ernesto spoke. "I don't get what's the big deal. I fight with my sister all the time."

The three other people at the table simply

looked at him. He shrugged and returned his attention to the baby.

Jack looked at Julia. "Did she say where they were planning to go?"

Julia shook her head. "Just that they were taking a Caribbean vacation. Going to stay with a friend, I think."

"A friend?" Jack's eyebrows arched. "You're sure about that?"

Julia nodded. "Something about a friend's house. I remember thinking it must be nice to have a friend who owned a house down there that he'd let you use."

"Oh, yeah."

Ten minutes later, Tess and Jack were back on the street, headed for Mary's house.

"It's this Ted guy," Jack said. "Mary's friend. It's got to be."

"I'm inclined to agree." Her legs were shorter than his, and she was getting annoyed at him for forcing her to run to keep up. "Damn it, Jack, will you slow down? This isn't a race."

"Sorry." He immediately slowed his pace to something more comfortable for her. "I resent this, Tess. I resent the hell out of it."

"Me, too." Where did Brigitte and Steve get off, thinking they could pull a stunt like this, utterly disrupting the lives of their children? Part of her was tempted to just pull out of this whole thing right now and teach the elder Wrights a lesson by going home without finishing this farce.

But she couldn't do that. And somewhere deep

inside, she realized that the real reason she couldn't do it was that she didn't want to leave Jack. Maddening, arrogant, disturbing, *sexy* Jack. The guy who had only last night taught her things about herself that exceeded her wildest imaginings.

It was only a fling. It would be over in a matter of days and they'd go back to their regular lives. But until she had no further choice in the matter, she felt compelled to hang around.

She glanced over at Jack and noted that he was looking awfully annoyed and awfully determined. She had a feeling he wasn't going to slow down today until he had discovered their parents' whereabouts. And she found herself wishing he weren't quite so determined. That he *would* slow down and draw these hours out a bit longer.

She even found herself hoping that he was wrong, and that neither Mary Todd nor Ted had the least idea where Steve and Brigitte were. But while that might delay their inevitable departure for their separate homes, it wouldn't solve the real problem.

And just what was the real problem? she found herself wondering as they strode down the boulevard. Her mother's feeling that she and Jack squabbled too much? Or the fact that suddenly they weren't squabbling? That they were closer than they'd ever been?

Of course, she might be the only one feeling that way. Jack might be in a hurry to get rid of her, now that they'd had sex. By way of her girlfriends, she'd certainly seen enough of that behavior from men. It was one of the reasons she'd never had sex before. Men always left, sooner or later. Look at her own dad.

She found herself wishing that she hadn't been foolish enough to give in this time, because Jack was probably like all the rest of them.

How else had he managed to reach the age of thirty-six without getting married?

The gloomy thoughts dogged her all the way to Mary's front door. Then things got even gloomier, because Mary wasn't at home.

"I told you we should have called," Tess said grumpily. She sat down on the top step of Mary's porch.

"One of your most irritating habits is your willingness to say *I told you so.*"

"Oh, just shut up. I *did* tell you so."

"She probably just went out for a short while. She'll be back soon." He settled beside her on the step.

"So what do we do? Sit here until midnight? Come back again tomorrow, until the police finally arrest us?"

He looked at her. "Don't be such a pessimist. She probably just ran to the store or something."

"Hmph."

He sighed. "Look, why don't you just go on home? *I'll* wait for her."

"Yeah, right." But her heart squeezed. Already he was trying to get rid of her. "You're stuck with my rotten company."

"Did I say your company was rotten?"

"You implied it."

"I did nothing of the sort. I just can't see any reason why *both* of us should sit here and be bored. I was being chivalrous."

"You? Hah!"

"Shut up, Shorty."

"When hell freezes over."

This time he didn't say anything, leaving her with nothing to do but stare at the cracked pavement of the sidewalk, or across the boulevard, between two buildings to the water. "I wonder why Mary's house is on the wrong side of the boulevard."

"It probably wasn't, before they built the street."

"True."

"I can remember when there was no boulevard, no hotels, no beach businesses. . . ." He shook his head. "It was a different world then. There was just a handful of houses out here, like Mary's. No bridge, so the only people who lived out here were fishermen. Then they built the bridge. The beginning of the end."

"Depends on how you look at it."

"Of course. Anyway, back then folks built their houses far enough away from the water that they wouldn't get flooded every time there was a storm. It was no protection against a really bad hurricane of course. It wouldn't take much of a storm surge to put this whole island underwater. But a tropical storm . . ." He shrugged.

"I guess people today are stupid."

He shook his head. "I wouldn't say that. But

they don't respect nature as much. Of course, nowadays there's insurance. It may be expensive, but they won't be wiped out. They're more willing to take the risk of having to rebuild."

"Mary's family was willing to take the risk that a hurricane would wipe them out."

"True." He flashed a sudden grin. "You find holes in everything I say."

"I don't know about that. It's just that people have always lived at the foot of Mt. Vesuvius. And I don't think the Romans had insurance, either."

He cracked a laugh. "Fair enough."

But Tess's thoughts were rambling in a different direction now. "I'd be feeling really frosty if I'd lived in this house all my life and somebody blocked my view with those buildings over there."

"So would I. But maybe Mary feels differently."

"I can't imagine that she would."

"Some people are more easygoing than you are, sweetie."

Sweetie? Uncertain how to take that, she latched on to the other part of his statement. It was so much easier to argue with him than wonder what he really thought of her. "I'm as easygoing as anyone else."

"Yeah? When does that happen? When the pumpkin turns into a coach?"

She glared at him. "Have I told you lately what I think of you?"

His expression was unreadable. "Repeatedly," he said, silencing her.

She looked down at her toes poking out of her sandals, and wondered why it always came to this between them. Why did she feel compelled to say irritating things to him? And why did he apparently feel the same way about her? She didn't act like this with any other person in her life.

"Okay," he said presently. "What's wrong?"

"Not a thing," she replied, refusing to look at him. "Why do think anything's wrong?"

"Because you're staring at your feet and not giving me a hard time."

"Now I'm required to fight with you?"

"Hell, no. I'm just worried because you're acting strange."

"I'm just thinking."

"Okay." He fell silent for a while. Then, in a quiet voice that belied the weight and impact of the question, he said, "How come you've never been with a man before?"

The question knocked the wind from her. For endless moments she couldn't breathe, as if her solar plexus was frozen. Then, at last, she drew a harsh, gasping breath.

"Sorry," he said. "None of my business."

She turned her head and glared at him. "How come *you* never married?" she demanded.

Something in his eyes lit as if he rather liked the idea of a confrontation with her. As if this were something he wanted to have out. "You want the truth? Or do you want the answer you're hoping I'll give?"

"I'm not *hoping* anything."

"Sure you are. You want me to say something that will confirm my iniquity so you can go back to your virginal cocoon in Chicago."

"My *what*?"

"So what's it going to be, Shorty?" he demanded. "The truth or just what you want to hear?"

"The truth, of course!"

"If I give you the truth, are you going to be honest with me in return?"

Trapped. Awareness flooded her, filling her with trepidation. He was proposing a trade, truth for truth. And she'd waltzed right into it. Unfortunately, she really *did* want to know the true story about him.

Then she wondered why she should even hesitate. It wasn't as if she had some big, deep, dark secret. She avoided men because they were untrustworthy—it was simple. No reason she shouldn't be able to say that out loud.

"Okay," she said. "Truth for truth. Why haven't you ever married?"

"My job makes me a lousy marital prospect. I'm gone a lot, and it's dangerous. That's the off-the-shelf reason."

Oh, God, she thought, her heart stilling. He wasn't going to stop there. He was going to tell her something more. And she had an intuitive sense that she didn't want to hear it, because it would change her view of Jack forever.

His hands clenched, then relaxed. "That's not the whole picture, though. It took me a while to figure that out. You ever do any soul-searching, Tess?"

"Sometimes."

"Well, sometimes I have a lot of time on my hands and nothing else to do, and I probably think a lot more than I should. But a while back it occurred to me . . ." His lips compressed and he fell silent for several beats. "The truth," he said, "is that I saw how much it hurt my dad when my mom died. And I know how much it hurt *me*. So . . ." He sighed. "So, I'm a coward. I don't want to risk feeling that kind of pain again."

Tess ached for him. She knew what he was talking about, knew how it felt. And she had to admire his courage for admitting it. "I don't think you're a coward," she said.

He gave her a wry smile that didn't quite reach his eyes. "No? My dad even has more guts than that. He married again."

"Well," Tess said slowly, realizing something even as she spoke. "He fell in love again."

"Yeah." A couple of seconds passed, then Jack asked, "Are you saying I just haven't fallen in love?"

"Maybe."

"Maybe," he agreed. "Maybe. Okay." He expelled a long breath and visibly relaxed. "Your turn, Shorty. Spill the beans."

She opened her mouth to tell him exactly what she had planned to tell him, but after the raw truth he had just exposed to her, she couldn't bring herself to be superficial about it.

"I just don't trust men," she said finally, not sure how to continue, or if she could even make herself.

"Because of your dad leaving?"

She resisted admitting it. Bringing it out in the open like this made it seem so terribly juvenile. But deep inside, she knew it was the truth.

"I guess," she said finally, hoping he wouldn't laugh at her, even if what she'd said did sound laughable. But he didn't laugh. Instead he reached out and took her hand.

"I suspected that," he said. "We're a pair, aren't we?"

Turning her hand over, she squeezed his fingers. "I guess. It's just that . . . well, you know, he said he loved me. He said he'd always love me, that he'd always be my dad, and that divorcing my mom didn't mean I was going to lose him."

"But you did."

She nodded. "I never saw him again. Never. And I've never been able to forget the sight of him walking away from me and getting into his car. Sometimes I even dream about it."

He didn't respond right away. Then he stood up and tugged gently on her hand. "Come on, let's walk. We can come back to look for Mary later."

18

Tess was glad to go with him. Some part of her felt on the verge of cracking open, and she knew from experience that walking would help soothe her.

Jack didn't let go of her hand, though. He clung to it, and she clung back, glad of the contact and the closeness it implied.

They were on the beach and walking along the water's edge before he said, "Maybe something happened to him, Tess."

"No. The child support came like clockwork. He just didn't want anything to do with me. He lied." She shrugged as if it weren't all that important anymore, but she knew better. It was kind of embarrassing, though, to realize that the single act of one person had gutted her ability to trust half the human race. "This is kind of extreme," she said presently. "I'm making too much out of it."

"You think so?"

"I *know* so," she said firmly. "Not everybody is as untrustworthy as he was."

"Maybe not, but trust isn't the real issue, is it?"

Her heart jumped uneasily. She didn't know if she liked the direction this conversation was going. In fact, she was sure she didn't. There were hurtful things lying beneath the surface explanation she had offered him, and she didn't want to look at them. Not for any reason. Nor would it do any good. She wasn't one who believed that sharing these things was somehow beneficial for anyone.

"Basically," Jack continued, "your father destroyed your self-esteem."

Tess halted abruptly, dropping Jack's hand and turning to face the water. An incoming wave lapped over her toes, but she didn't notice its warm kiss. "Let's not go overboard," she said stiffly.

The sky was a clear, cloudless blue, the turquoise blue color that seemed so much a part of Florida. Beneath it, the gulf was a light, almost minty green, dotted with the whitecaps of gentle waves. It was a picture-perfect day, so why were dark things intruding? Why was Jack pressing her on something that was totally irrelevant to him?

He didn't speak for a while, though, and she felt herself relaxing, thinking she had managed to convince him to drop the subject. It was too pretty a day to expose the ugliness inside her.

Then he dashed her hopes. "Actually," he said in a considered tone, "I don't think I'm going overboard. We're being honest here, and in all honesty I don't think you're afraid that men are unreliable. I think you're afraid of rejection. And quite frankly, Tess, I'd be amazed if you weren't, after what your father did. How could you *not* feel as if he was rejecting you?"

She folded her arms tightly and drew a steadying breath, wondering why tears were suddenly so near the surface. He hadn't said anything terribly shocking or revealing. "He *was* rejecting me," she said. "He didn't want anything to do with me. Big fat hairy deal. Lots of kids go through that."

"Sure. And it affects them all. I had an advantage: when my mother went away, it was because she died. It never entered my head to wonder if she had wanted to leave me, because I was sure she *hadn't*. It was different for you. The son of a bitch discarded you. And what's more, he couldn't even respect you enough to be honest about it. He *lied*. That's a pretty serious wound."

"Sure." She blinked, forcing the tears back. "And it was seventeen years ago, Jack. I'm over it. I've been over it for a long time. The reason I don't trust men is because I've seen them treat my girlfriends the way my father treated me. And that's the *only* reason I avoid them."

"But it's not," he said gently. "You avoid them because you think so poorly of yourself you can't imagine that any man *wouldn't* abandon you. Somewhere deep inside, you believe your father had a good reason for rejecting you."

Tears were burning her eyes now, and her chest was so tight she felt as if a giant fist were squeezing her. She told herself there was no reason to react this strongly, but her emotions weren't listening. Regardless, she managed to say scornfully, "Oh, come on!"

"It's okay, Tess," he said in that same gentle voice. "It's okay."

"Of course it's okay," she said firmly. Then, turning sharply, she began to march back to the house. She was going to pack her suitcase and get the next flight to Chicago. Enough was enough. Brigitte had thoroughly upset her life, and now Jack was acting as if he knew her better than she knew herself. She didn't need this.

But Jack had opened something deep inside her, and before long her steps were faltering because she couldn't see through the tears. It hurt, she realized. And it hurt because he was right.

She hated him for that. She hated him for exposing her, for leaving her emotionally naked.

Jack caught her and turned her into his arms, holding her snugly. Part of her resented him so strongly for making her feel this way that she wanted to shove him away, but part of her needed him to cling to, needed to feel that at least one person in this world didn't find her to be a problem.

But it was a false haven, and even as she wept in his arms, she knew it. Jack thought she was a problem. He always had, from the day their parents had welded all of them into a unit. He hadn't liked her then, and hadn't liked her at any subsequent meeting over the years. She wasn't crazy enough to suppose that he suddenly felt differently about her.

Even though she felt differently about him. She'd never guessed he could be as patient and understanding as he had been last night and today. She hadn't thought him capable of comforting anyone this way, let alone *her*. He had weakened her defenses by showing this unexpected side of him. And she had to admit he wasn't the pain she had always told herself that he was.

But she had done nothing to change his impression of her. In fact, she had done everything possible to make him think she was as incorrigibly obnoxious as always.

She sniffled and drew a shaky breath. She really needed to pull back out of Jack's arms before she got any deeper into the emotional morass. She couldn't afford to be weak. She'd figured that out a long time ago.

But his arms felt so good around her, and the solidity of his chest was like a bulwark against the rest of the world. The deepest, tenderest part of her wanted to stay here forever.

It was a nice dream, but, as usual, life wasn't going to grant her wish. A larger wave rolled up the beach, drenching their feet. Tess felt sand settle between her toes, and even some small seashells.

"Damn," said Jack. "My shoes are full of water and sand."

"Yeah." She lifted her head and dashed away the last of her tears. "Mine, too."

"You have sandals. The water comes out."

"But not the sand."

Their eyes met, and for some odd reason they both laughed, she thickly. Jack stepped back, leaving her to stand on her own. Leaving her feeling abandoned. But he didn't abandon her— he kicked his shoes off, then had her balance on his shoulder while he tugged her sandals off.

Tess took her sandals from him and they started strolling again, barefoot now.

"Have you noticed," Jack remarked, "that we seem to be getting information in dribs and drabs?"

She felt a little disappointed that his thoughts had moved so far, but she also felt relieved, as if someone had stopped the clock on a ticking time bomb.

"Well, yes," she said, "if you mean about Steve and Brigitte. But why is that surprising? Apparently nobody knows the whole story."

He shook his head. "It's not that it's surprising that nobody knows the whole story. It's this feeling I'm getting that we're getting timed releases of information."

Tess thought about that. "You might be right."

"Of course I'm right. Why in the world wouldn't Ernesto have told us that his wife had met Brigitte right at the outset, when I accused him of having something to do with her disappearance?"

Tess hesitated, not wanting to offend him, then decided, *Why not?* "Um . . . maybe because he was afraid you were going to break him into little pieces?"

He halted and drew his head back, looking seriously annoyed. "I have never in my life broken anyone into little pieces. I haven't even broken anyone into *big* pieces. My job is to arrest them, not turn them into mincemeat."

"Maybe Ernesto doesn't know that. I mean, Jack, the circumstance wasn't exactly conducive to him admitting he knew anything at all about our parents."

"Maybe not the first time. But what about the night of the hurricane? He could have said something then. It wasn't like it was a big secret that we've been trying to find our parents."

"No, but maybe he didn't think what he knew was relevant then. It's hardly even relevant *now*. We didn't learn a darn thing from him and Julia except that apparently Brigitte's been complaining about us to everyone on the planet."

He looked gloomy. "It's embarrassing, isn't it?"

"To say the least. But it remains that Ernesto and Julia are still *extraneous*." She chose the word deliberately, trying to lighten the mood.

His lips twitched, and for a second she thought he was going to laugh. Instead, he sighed. "Yeah. Except this is just too damn much coincidence."

She kind of agreed with him. Ernesto *did* seem

like a great big coincidence in the middle of all of this, seeing as how he had to come here all the way from Miami. "Okay, it's a coincidence. But what else could it be, Jack? You don't think Ernesto and Julia came all this way just to play some stupid part in a plot of Brigitte's, do you? That stretches credulity."

"It sure does. And if Julia hadn't already talked to Brigitte, I'd chalk it up to coincidence without a second thought."

"Yeah." Tess was having trouble getting around that, too. "Yeah." She looked down at the damp sand. "They didn't tell us everything they know."

"You think?"

"I think. I wonder if we can still find them."

Leaving the shore, they crossed the dunes and stopped at a faucet near a parking lot to rinse the sand off their feet and shoes.

"This was dumb," Tess said. "I'm not going to walk very far in wet sandals before I have blisters."

He looked at his deck shoes. "Ditto. Damn it. Why do I feel as if the whole universe is conspiring to put us on hold?"

She couldn't help giving him a wry look. "Delusions of grandeur?"

He laughed. "Come on. There's a shop a little way up the boulevard where we can get some canvas shoes."

Tess got herself some Keds, which she'd been wanting for a while anyway. Jack couldn't find any in his size, so he finally settled on a wildly colored pair of water shoes. Tess didn't mean to giggle. Honestly she didn't.

He glared at her playfully, then shrugged. "Hey, it's a beach town. I'll fit."

He certainly did, she thought as they hit the boulevard again. Now that she noticed, everyone seemed to be rather outlandishly dressed in brilliant colors and ill-matched clothing.

They went back to the café where they'd met Julia, but she and Ernesto were long gone, another couple at the table in their place.

"Okay," said Jack. "Back to Mary's."

"We could run in circles like this all day."

"Don't remind me. My only hope is that Thanksgiving is the day after tomorrow. Someone has to give us the clue soon, or we're never going to make dinner on time."

Tess started to laugh. She couldn't help it, it just suddenly seemed so funny.

"Hmm," said Jack. He drew her to the edge of the sidewalk out of everyone's way and waited patiently. "You're not getting hysterical, are you?"

"Me? Nah. I'm just realizing how ridiculous this all is. All of it. What a way to get two people to come to Thanksgiving dinner!"

"Yeah. It's a genuine Brigitte idea, isn't it?" A grin was starting to work its way onto *his* face, too. "Have I ever told you how beautiful you are when you laugh?"

It was as if somebody had thrown a switch. Her laughter died instantly. All she could do was stand there and look at him while her heart did a flip-flop. "No," she said finally, rejecting the whole idea because in some strange way it actually hurt.

"Yes," he said. "You're beautiful. Especially when you laugh. And you have a wonderful laugh. Come on, let's get to Mary's."

He took her hand, tugging her gently along with him, and she gave up trying to think of anything rational to say. She was long past rationality. He just kept throwing her off balance, and she was beginning to feel as if it didn't matter whether she ever found their parents, or whether she ever got back to Chicago and her job. Right now she could easily imagine floating dazed in Jack's wake like this forever.

By the time they approached Mary's house, though, common sense was reasserting itself and the daze had worn off. So what if he was the first person who had ever told her she was beautiful? He didn't mean it. He couldn't possibly mean it. She'd been looking in the mirror for enough years to know she wasn't beautiful. Her eyes were her best feature, but they didn't make up for the fact that everything else about her was simply . . . plain. Ordinary.

So if Jack was saying she was beautiful, he was just being kind. Beautiful was Sharon Stone. Beautiful was Michelle Pfeiffer. Beautiful was *not* Tess Morrow.

But despite telling herself all these harsh, realistic things, she continued to float along in a daze beside Jack, aware of very little except his hand holding hers.

"Wait," she said suddenly. The word passed her lips, and she wondered why she had said it. Then she knew. Jack stopped walking and faced her.

"What?" he asked.

"Let's just say to hell with this."

"We already agreed we weren't going to do that."

"I don't mean go back to our jobs. Let's just take the rest of the week for *us*. Let Brigitte and Steve stew in their own juices, and let's . . . oh, I don't know. Rent a boat and go sailing away from the rest of the world?"

"Brigitte will be really pissed at us." But he stepped closer to her, mesmerizingly closer, so close she could smell the soap he'd used in the shower that morning. So close she could feel his warmth as if he were the sun shining on her.

"So? I'm really pissed at *her*. And Steve."

"Well, that's one way of taking it."

"What other way is there?" Not that she was especially interested. Right now she couldn't seem to get past the wounding awareness that he hadn't leapt at a chance to run off into the sunset with her.

"Well, I could look at it as an opportunity to thank her."

Tess decided that the strain of the past few days must have knocked him off the precarious tightrope of sanity into the abyss of madness. "Thank her. *Thank* her?"

"Sure." He was smiling now, but more than the smile, the gleam in his eyes made her uneasy.

He was teasing her again. Which meant that in thirty seconds they were going to be at each other's throats once more. And strangely, she was utterly reluctant to do that right now.

She couldn't, however, keep herself from asking the deadly question. "But why?"

"Oh . . . how about thanking her for the fact that we've just been forced to spend a few days together? We'd never have done that otherwise."

It was true. Even back when they'd been coming home for holidays, they'd spent their time at opposite ends of the house when they couldn't find excuses to be out somewhere. "Okay," she said dubiously. "I guess."

"No, think about it, Tess. We've spent the last few days together. Yes, we've had our tiffs and our squabbles. But you know what? I've been getting to know you at the same time. And amazingly enough, I'm realizing that I actually like you. Sometimes."

In spite of herself, she had to grin at the qualifying *sometimes*. It quite accurately reflected how she found herself feeling about him. "Yeah," she said finally. "Yeah. I kinda like you, too."

The truth was, she more than *kinda* liked him. But admitting more than that might prove to be embarrassing. She didn't want him to know, or even guess, how much she longed to fling herself into his arms. She never wanted him to realize just how badly she'd love to sail away with him and abandon all the rest of the world. How much she wanted to crawl right back into the bed they'd shared last night and forget about all the rest.

And now that she thought about it, she wondered if *she* was the one who had tumbled into the abyss of madness.

"See?" he said. "So I figure I owe Brigitte some thanks, even if it will gall me to tell her so. I'm not real fond of being manipulated this way."

"Me neither."

"So we'll find the two of them, give them our thanks, have dinner with them, and *then* we'll sail away."

But she was sure he didn't mean to sail away *with* her. No, he meant sail away back to their jobs and their real lives.

And he was right. It was just the tropical sea air she'd been breathing lately. Her brain was missing its daily dose of auto fumes.

Once again they climbed the steps of Mary's porch and rang her bell. And this time, after a wait, she actually opened the door to them.

"Well, hello," she said in her dry voice. "Come to visit an old lady?"

Tess found herself wishing Mary hadn't phrased it that way. It would seem so crass to say no.

But before she or Jack could say anything, Mary was waving them inside. "Come in, come in," she said. "It'll be nice to have company while I take my midmorning tea."

Midmorning? Tess glanced up at the sun and realized that, indeed, it *was* only midmorning. Certainly no later than ten-thirty or eleven.

"Why don't you stay for lunch?" Mary suggested. "It would give me an excuse to order out for pizza. I can never do that when I'm alone because even one of the small ones they make for individuals is far too much for me, and I loathe it once it's grown cold."

As they followed her through the house to the patio, Jack said, "I don't think we can do that, Mary. We're on something of a quest."

Mary stepped out onto the patio, leaning heavily on her ebony cane, and turned to give him an amused look. "Don't you mean wild goose chase?"

"I hope not. I'd be singularly irate if I found out there's no Brigitte or Steve at the end of this hunt."

"Hmm." Mary's dark eyes were bright, full of humor. "I trust you're not planning to throttle them when you find them."

"I'm not feeling even the slightest impulse to violence."

"Good."

This conversation was surreal, Tess thought as she sat in the chair Mary indicated. Jack sat beside her.

Mary reached for a tall glass pitcher of iced tea and filled three glasses. Tess looked at the pitcher and the glasses and said, "You knew we were going to be here, didn't you?"

"Of course," Mary said. She passed them each a glass, then offered a plate of sliced lemon and lime. Tess helped herself to lemon. Jack passed.

"I saw you this morning, sitting on my porch.

At a very improper hour, if I do say so."

"It wasn't that early," Jack pointed out. "And when have you ever been proper?"

She *tsk*ed at him. "Where are your manners, young man?"

"The same place you left yours." He smiled.

Mary laughed delightedly. "I'm being mannerly, offering you tea when you arrived unannounced."

"Not really. Your curiosity got the better of you."

"Perhaps." Mary lifted her own glass to her mouth and sipped. "So what is it you want to know? And by the by, I may as well tell you straight off, I *don't* know where your parents are."

Tess felt a stab of disappointment. Part of her had been hoping Mary was in on the entire scheme and could sort it all out in a few sentences.

"I'm supposed to believe that?" Jack asked. "I'm supposed to believe you aren't in this up to your neck?"

"I'm not." Mary set her glass down and held the head of her cane in both hands. "Brigitte's quite capable of hatching her own schemes. My part is the most peripheral."

"And what might that be?"

"Sending Hadley your way."

"Really." Jack didn't sound very impressed, a fact which apparently wasn't lost on Mary, because she frowned at him. "It's not *my* fault," she said, "that he apparently didn't give you the correct piece of information."

Jack turned to Tess. "I knew it."

"Knew what?" Mary said irritably.

"Knew that Brigitte had planted clues. I'm willing to bet the whole reason Mrs. Niedelmeyer called me was because Brigitte put her up to it."

"I wouldn't know about that," Mary said with a dismissing wave of her hand. Tess thought she was lying, though; something in Mary's dark eyes belied her words.

Jack didn't look as if he believed it, either, but he didn't say so. "But you knew about Hadley."

"Well, of course I knew about Hadley. I was the one who sent him to you. And, of course, I was the one who told him what to say." She shook her head. "Dear Hadley. He's always been singularly poor at memorization. He believes it's enough to recall the *sense* of something."

"And in this case the sense wasn't the point?"

Tess was beginning to think that the number of people with whom she was never going to speak again was soon going to encompass nearly every soul in Paradise Beach. It was rather appalling to be faced with such a widespread conspiracy, all of which traced directly back to her mother—her own *mother*, for goodness' sake!— and all of it involving her mother telling the whole world that she and Jack couldn't get along. Her mother *appealing* to the whole world for help in making Tess and Jack agree. It was humiliating. She was also downright angry at her mother.

Mary's sharp eyes settled on her. "Won't do any good, gal," she said as if she could read Tess's mind. "Brigitte never let anybody put a damper on her that I could tell. One of her most charming qualities."

"In *your* opinion," Tess answered tartly. "Try having your mother talk to the whole world about you as if you were a misbehaving two-year-old."

"Aren't you?" Mary asked, her gaze sharp.

"This is none of your business."

"Maybe not, but that's never shut me up. The two of you *have* been acting like spoiled little children. Did either one of you ever consider your parents' feeling about all this? Did either one of you ever care enough about *them* to behave as if you were happy about being a family on just three or four occasions a year? Or were you so dead set on letting them know how *unhappy* you were with their marriage that you couldn't let them have a single holiday in peace?"

Tess felt as if she'd been slapped. "I'm not unhappy about their marriage!"

"Then why is it you can't manage to spend seventy-two hours at home without turning it into World War III between you and Jack? Consideration alone for your parents should be enough to create a cease-fire, don't you think?"

Mary turned her attention from Tess to Jack. "Don't you?" she asked him.

Jack looked at Tess. "She's right."

She was. Even Tess was able to admit that she'd been showing a remarkable lack of consideration for Brigitte and Steve. "Okay. She's right."

"Good," said Mary. "Now, what Hadley was supposed to tell you was that Brigitte wanted to lock you up on a *boat* until you found a way to get along."

Jack lifted his brows. "Well . . . we've kind of figured out they're on an island in the Caribbean." He looked at Tess. "I guess when we figure out *which* island, we'll get there and she'll lock us up on a boat."

"I don't like boats," Tess said.

"Why not?"

"I just don't. I keep thinking of all the cold, dark water underneath. It's creepy."

"Then I won't let her lock you up on a boat. But jeez, Tess, you really need to try sailing in the Caribbean. It might change your mind."

She didn't think it would, but with Mary's gaze intent on her, she wasn't about to disagree with Jack about anything, not even something she knew more about, namely her own fears.

"Well," said Mary, "I don't know if that's what the clue means."

"I suppose it could mean that we need a boat to find them," Jack said. "But we still don't know where we need to go. So . . . why don't you tell us the name of your boyfriend?"

"My boyfriend?"

"Yes, the gentleman who was with you the

other day when we came to visit. Ted Something."

"Ted Wannamaker," Mary said quickly enough. Then she cackled. "And I told her you'd never figure it out in time."

19

"In time for what?" Tess demanded as they hurried down the street toward Ted Wannamaker's brand-new condo at the southern tip of the island.

"My kingdom for a horse," Jack muttered. "You know, walking is great except when you're in a hurry."

"Why are we hurrying? If we're late for Thanksgiving dinner, it'll be Brigitte's fault for not just being up-front with us."

"Up-front? How was she supposed to do that?"

"Oh, I don't know. How about a phone call saying something like, 'Tess, I am sick of your squabbling with Jack, and I'm even sicker of you not coming home for holidays, so be a good little cabbage and come home and behave'?"

Jack looked curiously down at her. "And would you have?"

Tess sighed, but was too honest to say otherwise. "Probably not."

"Me neither. Which, considering that I stopped resenting you years ago, is pretty ridiculous. Except that I did get tired of being sniped at all the time."

"I would have stopped sniping if you hadn't sniped back."

"So it's *my* fault now?"

"I didn't say that." But she felt herself trying to repress a smile.

"You implied it." She could see the same smile start to dance around his own eyes.

"Okay, okay," she said. "I'll shut up."

"No." He reached out and snagged her hand, giving it a squeeze. "Don't ever shut up."

"Not in this lifetime," she agreed, feeling unexpectedly pleased and warmed. Although he would probably be absolutely astonished to know that in her other life—her real life, she reminded herself—she was considered quiet. Around him, she never had been, though. Not from their very first meeting.

The condo complex where Ted Wannamaker lived was a half-mile past the Paradise Towers. A newer structure, it looked considerably less institutional than the Towers, being faced with wood rather than concrete. It also stood on pilings which lifted the living quarters above all but the most catastrophic storm surges. Beneath was parking for residents.

They found the elevator in the parking garage, and went up to Ted's apartment on the fifth floor.

"He won't be home," Tess said gloomily. "I just know we're going to be standing in this hallway for hours."

"No, we won't. Be a little less pessimistic, will you?"

"I can't. I'm exhausted. And I'm ticked."

"I'm actually starting to have a good time. In fact, I'm fully prepared to forgive Brigitte for everything."

She looked up at him. "Traitor."

"Sorry." He grinned.

He punched the doorbell on Ted's apartment, and was rewarded thirty seconds later by the sound of the deadbolt being turned. Then the door opened, and Ted Wannamaker stood there smiling at them.

"Come in," he said, seeming not at all surprised to see them.

"I take it," Jack said, "that Mary called you."

"She did."

He ushered them into a glass-walled living room with a breathtaking view of the Gulf of Mexico. "Can I offer you refreshment?"

Tess, who was tired and thirsty after running up and down the entire length of Paradise Beach this morning—or afternoon, as it now seemed to be—would have loved a glass of water. Her stomach was telling her that it might even be time to eat something. But she also didn't want to waste any more time.

"No, thanks," she said. "Let's just get to business, shall we?"

Jack looked at her, but she couldn't tell if he was disapproving of her bluntness or cheering her on.

"Certainly," said Ted, taking a seat on the chair facing them. "First let me apologize. I usually stay far clear of these schemes of Mary's. I've made it a life practice never to let her draw me into it."

"Wait a minute," Jack said. "We were under the impression that this was Brigitte's scheme."

"Oh, it might well be," Ted said. "I really don't know who conceived the whole thing. All I know is that Mary drew me into it before I had any idea what was going on."

"What I want to know," Tess said, feeling impatient—and definitely feeling the lack of sleep from last night, something she didn't want to think about right now because if she did, she was going to break out in a brilliant blush and turn into a blathering idiot—"is whether you own an island."

Ted looked astonished. "An island? Me? I'm comfortable, but not that comfortable."

Tess felt her heart sink, and looking at Jack she suspected he wasn't feeling much better from hearing that news.

Ted shook his head. "I hope someone didn't tell you that. My involvement in this has nothing to do with owning an island. Good gracious."

Jack sighed heavily. "Well, I guess we're coming up against another blank, then. Sorry to have bothered you."

Ted hesitated. "Don't leave so quickly. Uh . . . why *did* you come to see me?"

"Our parents had left a videotape cued up in the VCR," Tess explained. "It was a scene from a movie, *Captain Ron*, I think, where one of the characters says something about going one island to the left of St. Croix, an island called Ted's."

"Oh, well," said Ted, "there's no island called Ted's that I know of. Quite a coincidence, isn't it?"

Tess and Jack exchanged looks, and Tess found herself wondering if he was feeling the same stomach sinking sensation that she was.

"Well," said Jack after a moment, "you can see we've troubled you needlessly."

"One island to the left," Ted said, ruminating. "What an odd way to describe it. I mean, it would depend upon which direction you were facing, wouldn't it? To the left of St. Croix? My word."

"We did think it was a little strange," Jack agreed.

"However," Ted said slowly, "I suppose one *could* put it that way. But Ted's Island? I don't think so." He laughed.

"Thanks for your time," Jack said, starting to rise. "We're sorry to have bothered you."

Ted held out a hand. "But wait," he said. "Don't you want to know what my involvement was?"

Jack sank slowly back onto the seat. "Do you know where they are?"

"Well, of course I do. They're staying in my house."

Tess slid forward in her seat, hardly daring to look at Jack for fear she would discover she'd misheard Ted.

"Your house?" she asked.

"Yes, of course," Ted answered. "That's how I got dragged into this entire abominable affair. Mary's quite persuasive, you know. Steve and Brigitte mentioned they wanted to get away for the holiday, but everything was already booked, and Mary gave me one of her looks—well, if you've never seen one, trust me, you'll do whatever she wants. And besides, I like Steve and Brigitte, so I was only too happy to let them have my house for the month. It seemed like such an innocent thing to do, you know, and I wasn't planning on using it. In fact, I haven't used it much at all these past couple of years—getting too old to want to travel that way, I suppose. In any event, I'm spending a small fortune on upkeep, and I thought your parents might as well enjoy the advantage of it."

Ted shook his head, then continued. "However that may be, I thought it was a perfectly innocent thing to do, to offer them my house. I didn't even realize that I was getting into something considerably smokier when Brigitte asked me if I would promise not to tell anyone where they were."

"She did?" Tess asked, even though she was sure Brigitte had done exactly that.

"It didn't seem like such a big thing at the time. I assumed they just didn't want to be bothered with the cares of daily life while they were away. I had no idea I was entering a conspiracy to keep their whereabouts from their children." He paused and frowned. "Can't say I approve of that at all. But I gave my word, you see, thinking that I wouldn't even face the problem. I should have known with Mary involved it couldn't be that simple."

Tess stirred. "What you're saying is that you got your first inkling of what was going on when we came to see Mary?"

"Well, yes, that's when I knew the enormity of what was going on. Up until then I thought the tickets I'd been given to pass on to you today were a surprise gift. I didn't realize that you were going to be tortured as well as surprised. I felt quite guilty about it, but I'd given my word not to give you the tickets before this afternoon, no matter what, and not to tell *anyone* where Steve and Brigitte are until I gave you the tickets. I should have realized something at that point, but not I. No, I thought it was a clever surprise for you."

Jack looked sympathetic. "Please don't feel bad about it. It wasn't your fault. Just give us the tickets and tell us where they are, and we'll be on our way, out of your hair."

Ted was shaking his head again. "Ridiculous,

isn't it? I'm not supposed to give them to you until four o'clock."

"Oh, come off it." Jack's impatience propelled him to his feet.

"I quite agree," Ted said after a few moments. "I'll get them now. And by the way, your parents are on a small island called Montmismo."

"So we just fly down there and look them up, hmm?"

Ted, who was walking toward another room, paused and turned around. "Oh, no, it's not that easy, I'm afraid," he said. "There's no landing strip on Montmismo. After your flight to St. Croix, you'll have to take a charter boat out there. But it's all in the travel package. The charter is expecting you."

Tess looked at Jack as Ted disappeared through a door. "A charter boat? I'm going to kill her. Do you hear me? I'm going to absolutely, positively kill her."

By six o'clock that afternoon, Jack felt he'd accomplished a monumental task just by managing to get Tess on the plane. She was so put off by the entire idea of having to take a boat that she initially refused to have any part of the trip.

But Jack had a few persuasive skills, developed over the years as he'd had to dance his way through difficult and potentially deadly situations with smugglers, dealers, and informants, and he brought them to bear now.

He didn't plead with her to go. No, he simply

started talking about what she'd be missing.

"A romantic trip," he said. "Most people would give their eyeteeth to get a Caribbean vacation. Just think about it. Sunshine, palm trees, aquamarine water—"

"We've that right here," she grumped at him.

"But it's not the same, trust me. This is . . . special. Special flavors, special sounds, special scents, and if what Ted said is true, an island paradise that most people can only dream of."

"Hmph."

"Tess, think about it. An island with nobody on it except a few thousand locals, most of whom fish for a living, and a few dozen extremely wealthy people. This is a true getaway. The type of getaway that's slowly but surely vanishing down there. No high-rise hotels. No pollution. No noise. Almost no people. A private beach. . . ."

It didn't take much longer after that. He could see the faintly wistful look coming over her face as he described the getaway. And having been all over the Caribbean for the last fifteen years, he knew how many of these hideaways had vanished under the onslaught of tourism.

She was weakening.

"There aren't many spots like that left," he said. "And just think, we'll be able to share it. Lazy afternoons on the beach. Long nights with soft breezes."

For an instant he feared he'd gone too far, presumed too much, that she was about to tell him that spending one night in her bed didn't mean he was entitled to expect another one. But after a moment, her face softened. A couple of minutes later she was packing.

When they at last touched down in St. Croix, there was a car waiting for them. A limousine, no less, and a driver who held the sign, MS. MORROW, MR. RIGHT.

He figured Tess was punchy, because when she saw the sign she burst into laughter. He felt a little stung, but didn't want to admit it. After all, he didn't want to be her Mr. Right, did he? Of course not.

There were two rooms for them at the hotel, which made *him* laugh.

"Stop it," Tess said as they got onto the elevator.

"I can't," he said, still chuckling. "I wonder what Brigitte would do if she knew I'd loosened your stays."

She gave him a disgruntled look. "I've never worn stays."

"Don't be so literal. You know exactly what I mean." How could she not, when he'd told her about his mental image of her? "She'll kill me," he said, and started chuckling again.

"No, she won't," Tess snapped. "She'll probably congratulate you on my downfall. She's always thought my standards were too high."

"That's a joke."

"What do you mean?"

"Brigitte's standards are so high I'm surprised my dad ever measured up."

"You think so?"

He thought she looked uncertain and a little hopeful. He found himself wondering what kind of an image she had of her mother, anyway. "I know so. Brigitte never settles for less than the best in anything. Including husbands."

"Then why—" She broke off, refusing to ask the question, apparently.

But he knew what the question was. "I guess she miscalculated about your dad. Or maybe, like a lot of guys hitting their middle years, he just went off the deep end. No way to predict that."

"Maybe not."

But now there was no way he could leave her alone in her hotel room. He hadn't been planning to. Hell, the last thing on earth he wanted after last night was to sleep alone in his own bed. In fact, if he had to do that, he'd probably lie awake all night feeling lonely and empty.

Which was a thought which should have terrified him, but somehow it didn't—probably because he was too busy trying to figure out how to make Tess feel better.

Because right now, she didn't look at all happy.

"Worried about the boat ride tomorrow?" he asked her as he followed her into her room.

"A little. I really do hate boats." She sat on the edge of the bed, testing its softness while he tipped the bellman and told him he'd let himself into his own room. Which, he suddenly realized, was adjoining. For just an instant he wondered about Brigitte, then dismissed the notion. She couldn't have planned this. No way.

He sat beside Tess on the edge of the bed. "What else has you down?"

"Oh, I guess I'm feeling deflated."

"Why?"

She looked up at him from the corner of her eye. "I'm not sure."

"Maybe it's all the letdown from the stress. After all, they had us going pretty good for a while there, and then we had that storm on top of everything else."

"Maybe."

He slipped his arm around her shoulder. "Or maybe you'd just like to know that last night wasn't a onetime fluke."

Her head snapped up, inadvertently banging him on the chin.

"Ow!" He grabbed his chin.

"Ouch!" She rubbed the top of her head.

"Forget it," he said, now feeling grumpy himself. "I'll go to my own room."

Getting up, he walked out of the room, aching because she didn't make any attempt to call him back. And then he wondered why he had even thought she would.

He was being childish, he supposed, but the way she had jerked her head up at his comment . . . well, it had told him how far off base he was. She didn't want to repeat last night at all.

In his own room, he took a few minutes to shower, and about thirty seconds to pull out fresh clothes for the morning. He was nuts. He was crazy. Why was he even doing this? He should have taken those tickets, mailed them to Brigitte, and told her to find another patsy next time she got a brainstorm.

Then he wondered why he was being so irritable. He'd actually been having fun until the instant when the top of Tess's head connected with his jaw.

And that was the whole problem. That hadn't been the reaction of a woman who was hoping for her lover's embrace. That had been the reaction of a skittish mare who was afraid of what might be coming.

He'd thought they'd both enjoyed themselves last night. He didn't exactly think of himself as a Casanova, but he *did* pride himself on leaving his partners happy and content. Apparently he'd really messed up here.

Which made him feel awful. It had been her very first time. Maybe that was the reason she had not had as wonderful a time as he'd thought. Perhaps it had all been too much for her.

Oh, man, what if he'd screwed up so badly he'd put her off sex for the rest of her life?

The thought galvanized him. He couldn't leave things like this. No way.

But her adjoining door was locked, and no matter how many times he knocked on it, she never came to answer it.

Hell. He had really, truly blown it.

* * *

In the morning Tess treated him distantly, as if he were a stranger she barely knew. His concern grew by leaps and bounds as he considered the magnitude of this disaster. It niggled at him that she hadn't treated him this way yesterday, but maybe she'd been in shock or something. Or maybe she'd been in denial until he opened his mouth. That was possible, because he sure hadn't treated her anything like a lover yesterday.

The trip today on the boat was hell. Oh, it was a nice sailboat, and the two crew members seemed to know what they were doing, and under any other circumstances he would have kicked back and thoroughly enjoyed the beautiful cruise.

But Tess was seasick, violently so, even though the waves were so gentle they hardly rocked the boat. She hung over the rail for so long that he finally feared she was going to turn into a crispy critter. When he tried to put sunblock on her, though, she jumped away from his touch.

"Tess, get real," he said impatiently. "We're in the tropics. I repeat, *the tropics*. This sun is going to burn the skin right off you, so either let me put the sunscreen on you or get your butt below."

"Okay," she said. "Okay." Sticking out an arm, she kept her head drooped over the rail. He started lathering sunblock on her.

"Do you have any Dramamine?" he asked her.

"No."

"I guess you had no idea you'd get seasick."

"I hate boats!"

"I can kinda see why." He dabbed lotion across her shoulders and upper back and began to massage it in. It was promising, that he could feel her relax a little under his ministrations. "You'll have to do your face, too," he said. "All the reflection off the water . . . you're not in as much shade as you might think."

"Okay."

Lotion down her other arm, in long, soothing strokes. "I'll ask our captain if they have any Dramamine."

"Does it work?"

"I don't know; I never get seasick. But I hear that it does."

"God, I hope so."

At least she was talking to him. Next her legs. That got a little tough for him, because he could think of a lot of ways he wanted to touch her legs, and rubbing all that sunscreen in along the length of those beautiful thighs, nearly all the way up to the apex where her secrets lay, was enough to drive him nuts. He loved it. And he wanted to toss her down on the deck right now and have his way with her. And might have, except for their crew.

Who, now that he thought about it, were watching him apply the lotion to Tess with a bit too much interest. He scowled at them and they quickly looked away.

"I can't believe," Tess said, sounding breathless, "that people actually think this is romantic."

Jack, who thought exactly that, kept his mouth

shut. Of course, he hadn't counted on having a seasick companion. That did take some of the romance out of it. He laid his hand on Tess's shoulder. "I'm so sorry you feel so sick."

"Me, too," she said. "But hey, I read somewhere that Admiral Nelson got violently seasick every time he went to sea."

"Yeah?"

"Yeah. So I'll make it, right?"

"Lotsa pluck there, lady. Hang on. I'll go see if there's any Dramamine on this charter."

They didn't usually carry it, but the last passenger had left a small suitcase behind which the captain searched for Jack. Lo and behold, there was a box of patches for motion sickness. Jack promptly brought a patch up for Tess and applied it to her back beneath her shirt, where there was no lotion to keep it from sticking.

"I hope this works," she said. " 'Cause I don't know how much more of this I can take."

"The worst that's going to happen is that we'll be at the island in a few hours and you'll be on dry land again."

"That long? God. And you know what's worse?"

"What?"

"The only way to get home will be on a boat." She groaned and he rubbed her shoulder soothingly.

He stood at the rail beside her, offering what comfort he could, which was actually very little. He found himself thinking sappy things, like he wished he could be the one sick instead of her.

Which was a really strange thought for him to have. And apart from being a sappy thought, it was also a stupid thought, since it didn't change the situation one iota. In fact, now that he thought about it, it was cheap, useless sympathy, because it was obvious that the wish wouldn't be answered.

All of which wasn't doing a thing to help Tess, who was looking green and miserable. But over the next fifteen minutes or so, she began to droop less and stand up straighter.

"It's helping," she said finally.

"Great!" He couldn't have asked for better news. "All better?"

"Not exactly. I'm still queasy, but I don't feel like I'm going to lose my cookies anymore."

"That's an improvement."

She gave him a wan smile. "I'll say."

Eventually she was even able to sit in one of the deck chairs and start to take in the scenery.

"It *is* pretty," she admitted finally, sounding reluctant, as if she didn't want to see any good in this voyage.

"It's gorgeous."

"I'll bet you've done a lot of this?" She looked curiously at him.

"Some, although not as elegantly. I love this boat."

"It's nice."

He almost laughed. *Nice* was the understatement of the year. This was the kind of boat he could actually salivate over.

Instead of starting a disagreement with her

over something so inconsequential, he pulled his chair closer to hers and reached for her hand. It worked like a charm. She smiled again and let her head relax against the headrest.

"So . . ." he said tentatively after a few minutes, "you were mad at me this morning? And last night?"

She opened one eye. "No-o-o . . ." She drew the word out, as if uncertain what he was trying to find out.

"Why didn't you answer when I knocked on the adjoining door last night?"

"That was you?"

He opened his mouth, then froze as he realized there would have been no way for her to know. He'd picked up the room keys and had never mentioned to her that their rooms were next to each other. Not once. He suddenly felt very stupid. "Umm, yes. God, I must have scared you."

"Just a little," she said grumpily. "I sat up for hours wondering why anybody would be knocking like that, and worrying that they might try to get in."

"Why didn't you call me?"

"Because I thought you were sleeping. I thought about calling hotel security, but then decided I'd feel really stupid if it just turned out to be some drunk who was mixed up."

"Why should that make you feel stupid? You should have called someone."

"In retrospect, I guess so. But I haven't had enough sleep, Jack. I wasn't thinking clearly. I'm not sure I'm thinking clearly right now."

"Not enough sleep. How much did you get last night?"

"Three hours? Maybe a little more."

"So . . . you weren't mad at me this morning, either?"

She shook her head. "Just exhausted."

He suddenly felt like doing a major leap and clicking his heels with relief. He contained himself, though, and squeezed her hand comfortingly. "Why don't you sleep now?"

She gave a little nod. "Maybe I will. I think the Dramamine is making me sleepy."

"Just go ahead and close your eyes. I'll watch over you."

It felt good to say that. And it felt really good when she took him up on the offer.

20

They arrived at Ted's island in the late afternoon. Tess had slept for four hours and was looking considerably perkier by the time they began to ease up near the private dock.

The light was golden, slanting across the green water and casting long shadows beneath the coconut palms on the sandy beach.

"It looks like a postcard," Tess said, her eyes wide and bright.

"It sure does." Behind the palms there was a garden and a large Mediterranean-style house. A white sand beach arced away from the dock, creating a protected area where the water was still and inviting.

And on the beach were Brigitte and Steve.

"You still going to kill her?" Jack asked.

"I'm thinking about it. Look at her, lounging

there with a drink in her hand. And we've spent days going nuts trying to find them!"

"It does rankle," he admitted.

"It more than rankles. I'm pissed."

"Ooh, another one of those words you never use."

She scowled up at him. "You're rubbing off on me."

"Pity."

"I couldn't agree more."

The crew tied the boat to the dock and put out the gangway. Tess was the first one onto the dock, and looked considerably relieved to be at last standing on a surface that didn't move. Although, judging from the way she sort of staggered, Jack had a sneaking suspicion that she was going to need a little while to stop feeling as if the ground were moving beneath her. She had a sailor's drunken roll. He managed not to laugh at her, though. The crew passed up their suitcases, waved, untied the lines, and sailed off into the aquamarine distance.

"They're not staying?" Tess asked with dismay. "How are we going to leave?"

"I guess we'll need to ask Brigitte."

Tess turned to look in her mother's direction. "Look at the two of them lounging there— they're not even coming to greet us! I guess I'm supposed to go kiss the ring, as it were."

He felt another bubble of amusement. "So it seems."

She looked askance at him. "Don't tell me you're enjoying this."

"Of course I am. It's hysterically funny. Who else has a family that would pull a stunt like this? Besides, I'm not going to quarrel with a beautiful Caribbean Thanksgiving holiday."

"Are you always such an optimist?"

"No."

"Thank goodness. I was beginning to wonder about your judgment."

He loosed his laugh then, and was relieved when she actually smiled back at him. Leaving their luggage on the dock, they set out for the trek around the beach to where their parents were sitting in beach chairs beneath the coconut palms.

Steve Wright, a tall, fit man in his middle sixties, rose from his chair as they approached, greeting them with a wide smile and a toast of his tall beverage glass. "About time you got here!" he called.

"As if we could have gotten here any sooner," Jack called back.

Brigitte, still lounging on her chair, sipping her concoction through a straw and looking twenty rather than fifty in her bikini—Tess thought that alone was reason to kill her mother—waved a languid hand. "How nice to see you, *ma petite chou*. And you, too, Jack." Only she said it *Zhack*.

"Hi, Brigitte," Jack replied, bending to kiss her cheek before shaking his father's hand. "I'd better warn you, Tess is thinking about killing you."

Brigitte frowned at her daughter. Her skin, Tess noted, was still as smooth as a baby's bottom. It was terrible to have a mother who would never age. Tess herself had already begun pulling gray hairs, and there were definite signs of fine lines beginning around her mouth and eyes . . . not unusual for a woman of thirty. But Brigitte . . . Brigitte would never face those things, apparently. Her surgeon must be wonderful.

"But *chou-chou*," Brigitte said, "haven't you learned the lesson?"

"Oh, we've *both* learned the lesson," Jack said, slipping his arm around Tess's shoulders. "Which is why *your* life is in danger."

Steve cracked a laugh and grinned down at his wife. "I told you it was too much scheming."

Just then two men in white polo shirts and blue shorts came hurrying up. One carried two more chairs, and the other carried a tray of drinks and canápes.

"Do sit," Brigitte said as the chairs were unfolded. "And join us, darlings. A drink will make you feel ever so much better, don't you think?"

Tess frowned down at her mother. "Actually, it'll take me more than a drink to make me feel better, Mother. In the first place, you scared me half to death. I didn't know whether you'd been in a plane crash or you'd been kidnapped. We both were worried sick after your phone call and Mrs. Niedelmeyer's phone call."

"But of course," Brigitte said with a wave of her hand. "There had to be some way to get you both to come together and stay together."

"A simple invitation might have worked,"

Tess said sharply. "An honest statement of your feelings."

"You think so? No, it would not. Sit down, it bothers me to have you hovering over me this way."

Tess sat but did not relax. "You could have just told me, Mother."

Brigitte shook her head. "But no. If I had said to you, 'Tess, I'm tired of the two of you fighting all the time,' you would have said, 'But I don't come to visit when Jack is there anymore.' And I would have explained that we would like both of you to be with us on holidays. And you might have grudgingly come to visit, and you and Jack would have walked around talking between the teeth like this." She illustrated. "No. It could not be. I wanted you two to get past your problem."

Jack looked at Tess. "Don't hate me."

She lifted her brows. "For what?"

"I think she's right."

Tess scowled at him, then turned her glare back to her mother. "I was terrified for you and Steve. That was a terrible thing to do."

"Perhaps," Brigitte said with one of her characteristic shrugs. "But how else to make the two of you actually stay together? Besides, it wasn't long before you knew that something else was going on. Which was all part of the plan." She looked very pleased with herself.

Jack spoke to Tess. "Give up. You'll never convince her she went too far."

"There is no such thing as too far," Brigitte said firmly.

"Good," Jack said, "because I accidentally put a big hole in your ceiling while I was looking for clues. I wouldn't want you to think I went too far."

Brigitte gasped. Steve's brow creased. Tess grinned.

"You destroyed my house?" Brigitte demanded.

"All in a good cause," Tess told her mother. "After all, we had to hunt for clues."

Steve looked at his son. "How bad is it?"

"Not bad. I didn't have a chance to finish patching, but all it needs is another layer of mud, some texture, and paint. It's no problem to fix it."

"Well," said Brigitte, "I can't believe you were so clumsy."

Jack manfully refused to respond. He wasn't going to get into a quarrel with Brigitte. Not now, not ever. The woman's mind had a strange way of working, and there was never any way to settle a disagreement with her.

"It's nearly dinner," Brigitte said presently. "Let's go up to the house and change. You children can do what you like, of course. Just keep in mind that dinner is at six and I insist we dress."

"Great," said Jack as he and Tess stood on the beach watching Steve and Brigitte walk up to the house. "Dress for dinner. All I brought was my beach bum stuff."

Tess, who had a couple of sundresses, was doing better. "Can you believe her? She honestly thinks she didn't do anything wrong."

"Actually," Jack said cautiously, "it wasn't *that* bad."

She faced him. "What in the world do you mean?"

"Well, she got us to work together. And I discovered that underneath that prickly exterior of yours, there's a very nice woman."

Suddenly Tess simply didn't have the will to bristle. Looking up at Jack, she instead felt herself smiling. "You're not so bad yourself."

"I'm glad to hear it." Reaching out, he took her hand again. "Let's go, Shorty. We'll shower and change, then astonish our parents with how incredibly well we get along together. In fact," he added with a comical leer and wiggling eyebrows, "we might even shock them."

Which was how Tess came to be laughing as they walked up to the house. She was still smiling ten minutes later when Jack slipped into the shower stall with her and began to teach her just exactly what could be done with a bar of soap.

But as they got more slippery with soap, the bar stopped cooperating and insisted on shooting out of their hands and bouncing off the walls of the shower enclosure. Before long, like a couple of kids up to mischief, they were stifling giggles and warning each other to hush. And Tess felt more beautiful, more cherished, and more alive than she had ever felt in her life.

Jack was addicting. Maybe at some deep level she had known from their first meeting that she would be at risk of losing her heart to him. Maybe she had been obnoxious to him because some part of her had realized what an emotional threat he was. Maybe the bruised heart of a fifteen-year-old who'd been abandoned by her father had warned her that Jack had the power to hurt her every bit as much.

Those thoughts flitted across her mind as they finally reached for towels, as he dried her from head to foot, the strokes of the towel a sinuous, sensuous invitation to the games of love.

Tess's laughter died even as her breath caught and came more quickly, even as fear tried to worm its way into her full awareness. But before she could decide which way to tumble, into Jack's arms or into the abyss of anticipated lone- liness, Jack wrapped a towel around his waist and used his finger to turn her face up to his.

He kissed her. It was a gentle kiss, a kiss that seemed to promise, but she didn't believe in promises.

"Later," he said thickly. "We have a date for a walk on the beach. Later."

Then he turned and slipped out of the bath- room, leaving her alone as she had known he would.

Later. All right, she told herself, fighting an aching urge to cry. Later they'd take that walk, and she'd let him tell her that it had been fun but now it was done. Or whatever. Because she was sure he was going to tell her they had no future.

Otherwise why would he have walked away now, when she would have tumbled right into bed with him?

There could be only one reason. He didn't want her anymore, now that he'd had her, and he was just trying to let her down easily.

She managed not to cry as she dressed for dinner in a backless blue sundress and sandals, but she hadn't felt this hurt since fifteen years ago.

Men. They were all the same. Somehow they could just walk away without a backward look.

They dined at an intimate table for four on an enclosed porch, with shutters open to let in the soft evening breeze. Palm fronds clattered gently, the sound of waves was soothing, and the fresh scent of the sea seemed to heighten the taste of everything.

The service was elegant, handled by the two men who had earlier brought them the chairs and canapés.

"Ted Wannamaker," said Brigitte, "certainly knows how to take a vacation. At first when he offered his house, I thought we'd find some small little place covered in mildew and neglect. I never imagined anything quite so wonderful. Or that he had a staff to look after things."

"It's wonderful," Steve agreed. "So, if he's still thinking about selling, do you want to buy it?"

"I'm tempted," Brigitte said. "Very tempted. And I'll keep the staff. They're marvelous."

"They certainly are," Jack said as a plate bearing a broiled swordfish steak was placed in front of him. "I could get used to this really fast."

Brigitte looked at Tess. "What's wrong, *chouchou*? You're so quiet."

Tess dragged her gaze up from her plate and managed a smile. "I'm just tired. The man in the room next door to me was beating on my wall last night. I didn't get much sleep."

"How awful. Did you complain?"

Tess shook her head. "It was too much bother."

"Well," her mother said, looking annoyed, "I shall speak to the hotel about it anyway. Perhaps they can discover who it was and see that he never stays there again."

"Not necessary," Jack said, his fork poised near his mouth bearing a flaky piece of fish. "The nasty man was me."

"You!" Brigitte looked appalled.

"Yes, me," Jack said. "I thought Tess was mad at me, and I wanted her to open the adjoining door so I could apologize for whatever it was that I had done."

Steve, who had been remaining largely quiet, looked up from his plate at his son. "You did? Will wonders never cease."

Brigitte didn't seem to hear him. "You didn't know what you'd done?" Brigitte frowned at Jack, then Tess. "Really, *m'petite*, if you're going to be angry at someone with effect, you *must* let them know why." She paused, then said with obvious perplexity, "But you never before had trouble telling Jack why you were annoyed with him."

"I wasn't annoyed," Tess said defensively. "Not at all. Jack imagined it."

"Yup," Jack said. "We're getting along these days, remember? I'm just a little slow getting used to it."

"Oh." Brigitte looked doubtful, but subsided. Steve looked as if he were sure they were up to something.

Tess picked at her fish. It was delicious, fresh and perfectly broiled, but her appetite seemed to have vanished, even though she hadn't eaten since last night.

She picked her way through the roulades, too, and finally through the fruit which was served for dessert. She really should kill Brigitte, she thought gloomily. Except for the woman's machinations, her defenses against Jack would never have gotten so low, and she wouldn't now be in this emotional hell.

Brigitte was apparently annoyed by her mood. "Why are you sulking?" she demanded of Tess after dinner. "For goodness' sake, you've been given a wonderful vacation."

"I had a wonderful vacation planned with my friends," Tess retorted. "I'm missing it because of you."

"Because of *me*? It's Thanksgiving. Where else should you be except with your family?"

Before Tess could think of a suitable response,

Jack appeared at her side. "Our walk," he said, just a shade too firmly. "You promised me we'd take a walk in the moonlight. If you'll excuse us, Brigitte?"

She hadn't promised him any such thing, but she wasn't prepared to argue about it. Bad enough that he was getting ready to dump her. She might as well get it over with. Although now that she thought about it, she wondered how she could possibly think he was *dumping* her. There was nothing to dump. They had no relationship. All they'd had was a one night stand. What's more, she ought to be tough-minded enough to separate sex and love. That's what modern people did.

And barbarians, too, she supposed. It didn't exactly seem all that enlightened to her when she thought about it that way. It actually sounded rather primitive.

Down near the water, they kicked off their shoes and began to stroll away from the house. The moon was huge in the sky, hanging low over the palms. It painted the world silver and sparkled on the water with a cool, colorless, soothing light.

"It looks like a silver highway, doesn't it?" Jack pointed to the ribbon of moonlight across the dark water. Reaching out, he took her hand. Tess didn't have the heart to pull it away. "Imagine what it must have been like here a few centuries ago, sailing a ship across these waters on a night like this, the only light the moon, and perhaps a lantern. Or standing on a beach just like this with no one else around for miles."

"It's beautiful," she agreed, although her lips felt wooden.

"Tess, there's something I want to tell you." He turned to face her, taking her shoulders in his hands.

Here it comes, she thought. *The boom.*

"I'm thinking about quitting my job," Jack said.

Her jaw dropped open in shock, as she tried to change mental gears.

"Why?" she asked. "I got the impression you like what you do."

"Sure. How many people do you know who get to pretend to be a beach bum in the Caribbean while collecting a great paycheck? It's been fun, but I think it's time to grow up."

"Whoa, there. That sounds like a serious thing to do. Are you sure you want to take the risk?"

He peered down at her. "Are you picking on me?"

She felt a reluctant bubble of laughter well up, and it tumbled over her lips. "A little. But I'm serious. Won't you be miserable?"

"I honestly don't think so." He tilted his head back a bit and the breeze ruffled his hair. "God, I love the Caribbean. I love the way it smells. I love the way the sea makes the breeze so soft. I love the people down here. I'll miss it."

"Then don't give up your job, Jack. Why in the world are you going to give up everything you love?"

"Not everything I love. I don't think my current lifestyle would agree with the lifestyle to which I'd like to become accustomed."

"What do you mean?"

He flashed a smile down at her. "Just that it's time for a sea change."

"But why?"

"I figure no woman wants a man in my profession. Too dangerous, too many long absences."

"Oh." Well, she thought, it had happened. They'd gotten past the animosity, and now she was going to be his *sister*. He was going to confide everything to her, including the fact that there was a girl on one of these islands somewhere that he'd been crazy about for a long time, and didn't Tess think it was time for him to settle down?

"Yup," he said. "It's time to grow up."

Yup, now she was going to hear about Marla, or Tawnee, or some other tropical beauty with beaded black hair and coffee-colored skin and a brilliant white smile. Someone absolutely gorgeous. A woman with an exotic lilt in her voice, like Jack's. A woman he didn't think of as a Victorian lady in too-tightly-laced stays. Someone as colorful and vibrant as Jack himself.

But he was looking at her, and not saying anything. She felt as if his gaze were plucking at something in her soul, and her heart began to beat slowly and heavily.

Jack lifted his hand and touched her cheek

gently with his fingertips. "Are *you* ready to grow up?"

"I'm already grown up."

"Maybe too much," he said. "Too responsible. Too adult—until you get around me."

The corners of her mouth lifted a little, even as she felt something inside her teetering on the brink between despair and joy. She hardly dared believe what she felt was happening. "Maybe," she agreed.

"I bring out the worst in you."

"Sometimes."

"But if that's your worst, sweetheart, you're a saint. And your best is . . . well, your best is wonderful. So tell me, can you stand me?"

Could she stand him? What a silly question. "Of course I can." She was crazy about him. She didn't even mind it when he called her Shorty now. She even kind of liked it.

"Well," he said, appearing to brace himself, "I have a question for you, but you have to promise not to respond by calling me names."

"Sure." Her heart was beating harder now, and she was terrified that he was going to ask her if she thought some woman would ever want him. When what she wanted him to ask was if *she* wanted him.

"The thing is," he continued slowly, his fingers making slow, hypnotic circles on her cheek, "I seem to have fallen in love with you."

"Me?" The word was disbelieving, because she was braced for anything else.

"You," he said. "And all this time we've been

fighting our private little war, the feeling has been getting stronger and stronger. Fighting with you was my attempt to get over you. But it didn't work, Tess. I'm crazier about you than ever."

"Oh, wow . . ." She didn't know what else to say. She was having trouble wrapping her mind around the magnitude of what he was telling her.

"I knew," he continued, "that if I fell in love, I'd have to give up my job. And I loved my job. But that doesn't seem so important anymore. I can settle behind a desk. I can run a business. I can do anything else, if only I can have you in my days for the rest of my life. So . . . am I crazy?"

Joy burst in her, a great sunburst of it, filling her with light and a happiness so intense that for a few moments she couldn't speak.

"Um . . . did I appall you that much?"

"No!" The word burst from her, and she vaguely realized that he had misunderstood her, and he was looking rather crushed. Before it could get any worse, she jumped on him, throwing her arms around his neck, wrapping her legs around his hips, and burying her face in the curve of his neck, feeling a gratitude so intense that she had to squeeze her eyes closed and let it just envelop her. He wrapped his own arms around her and held her tight.

"I take it," Jack's voice rumbled in her ear, "that I haven't dismayed you."

Drawing a long, shaky breath, she lifted her

head and looked straight into his eyes. "I'm *thrilled.*"

He drew a long, deep breath, as if steadying himself. "Thank God."

 *Epilogue*

"**W**ell," Steve said, looking at Brigitte, "you got a little more than you bargained for."

The sun was setting in a glorious explosion of red, casting its last warm light over the wedding guests who clustered laughing and talking on the frangipani-strewn beach beneath the coconut palms.

Brigitte, barefoot in lavender silk with a magnolia blossom in her champagne-colored hair, looked up at her husband, who, she thought, looked absolutely magnificent in a Hawaiian shirt and red shorts. "What makes you think that?" she asked archly.

"Oh, don't expect me to believe that you planned from the outset that Jack and Tess would marry."

"From the outset?" Brigitte arched her brows,

tapped her fan against her lips, and looked out across the swirling crowd toward the happy couple, who were dancing on the sand to music provided by a six-piece reggae band. Jack looked quite charming in a white shirt and slacks, she thought, and of course her daughter was stunning in a white silk sarong. "No, my dear," she said, remembering Steve's comment, "not from the outset. I'm not sure exactly when I realized that their antipathy was far too strong for two people who only rarely saw one another. But even so . . ."

"Even so," he prompted, when she fell silent.

She turned to him with a bright smile. "Even so, I couldn't be sure. And all I wanted, truly, was to be able to have holidays with my children."

"So you got more than you bargained for?"

"Oh, no." She laughed, a sound that lifted above the music and drifted away on soft tropical breezes. "I always bargain for more than I get. Ask me again when the grandchildren come."

He nodded and looked at Jack and Tess. "I'm glad they're living in Miami now. And I'm glad Jack gave up his undercover work. Now I only have to worry about the ordinary things parents worry about."

Brigitte laughed. "With those two? Never. Now, do you suppose that after the honeymoon we can get them to finish fixing the ceiling in the guest bedroom?"

Steve laughed, too, and shook his head. "I

think Jack's got his mind on one thing."

"Good," Brigitte said, tucking her arm through his. "I want my daughter to have all the same wonderful things you give me."

"Really?" His eyes seemed to sparkle in the last glow of the setting sun.

"Really." She hugged his arm. "I have my Mr. Wright. And now Tess has hers, too."

"If you're looking for passion that sizzles, you've come to the right place . . ."
Jayne Ann Krentz

Now, don't miss CAIT LONDON's
newest contemporary love story

IT HAPPENED AT MIDNIGHT

It's been said that when the wild heart of a Langtry is captured it will remain true forever, and Michaela Langtry's heart has not escaped this fate. And when she returns to Wyoming to face Harrison Kane—she knows that their love will overcome all obstacles.

Coming in November from Avon Books

Discover Contemporary Romances at Their Sizzling Hot Best from Avon Books

SLEEPLESS IN MONTANA   by Cait London
80038-1/$5.99 US/$7.99 Can

A KISS TO DREAM ON   by Neesa Hart
80787-4/$5.99 US/$7.99 Can

CATCHING KELLY   by Sue Civil-Brown
80061-6/$5.99 US/$7.99 Can

WISH YOU WERE HERE   by Christie Ridgway
81255-X/$5.99 US/$7.99 Can

IT MUST BE LOVE   by Rachel Gibson
80715-7/$5.99 US/$7.99 Can

ONE SUMMER'S NIGHT   by Mary Alice Kruesi
79887-5/$5.99 US/$7.99 Can

BRIDE FOR A NIGHT   by Patti Berg
80736-X/$5.99 US/$7.99 Can

HOW TO TRAP A TYCOON   by Elizabeth Bevarly
81048-4/$5.99 US/$7.99 Can

WISHIN' ON A STAR   by Eboni Snoe
81395-5/$5.99 US/$7.99 Can

Avon Romantic Treasures

*Unforgettable, enthralling love stories,
sparkling with passion and adventure
from Romance's bestselling authors*

HAPPILY EVER AFTER   *by Tanya Anne Crosby*
0-380-78574-9/$5.99 US/$7.99 Can

**THE WEDDING
BARGAIN**   *by Victoria Alexander*
0-380-80629-0/$5.99 US/$7.99 Can

THE DUKE AND I   *by Julia Quinn*
0-380-80082-9/$5.99 US/$7.99 Can

MY TRUE LOVE   *by Karen Ranney*
0-380-80591-X/$5.99 US/$7.99 Can

**THE DANGEROUS
LORD**   *by Sabrina Jeffries*
0-380-80927-3/$5.99 US/$7.99 Can

THE MAIDEN BRIDE   *by Linda Needham*
0-380-79636-8/$5.99 US/$7.99 Can

A TASTE OF SIN   *by Connie Mason*
0-380-80801-3/$5.99 US/$7.99 Can

**THE MOST WANTED
BACHELOR**   *by Susan K. Law*
0-380-80497-2/$5.99 US/$7.99 Can

LION HEART   *by Tanya Anne Crosby*
0-380-78575-7/$5.99 US/$7.99 Can

THE HUSBAND LIST   *by Victoria Alexander*
0-380-80631-2/$5.99 US/$7.99 Can

Available wherever books are sold or please call 1-800-331-3761
to order.   RT 0600

ELIZABETH LOWELL

THE NEW YORK TIMES BESTSELLING AUTHOR

LOVER IN THE ROUGH
0-380-76760-0/$6.99 US/$8.99 Can

FORGET ME NOT
0-380-76759-7/$6.99 US/$8.99 Can

A WOMAN WITHOUT LIES
0-380-76764-3/$6.99 US/$8.99 Can

DESERT RAIN   0-380-76762-7/$6.50 US/$8.50 Can

WHERE THE HEART IS
0-380-76763-5/$6.99 US/$9.99 Can

TO THE ENDS OF THE EARTH
0-380-76758-9/$6.99 US/$8.99 Can

REMEMBER SUMMER
0-380-76761-9/$6.99 US/$8.99 Can

AMBER BEACH   0-380-77584-0/$6.99 US/$8.99 Can

JADE ISLAND   0-380-78987-6/$7.50 US/$9.99 Can

PEARL COVE   0-380-78988-4/$7.50 US/$9.99 Can

And in hardcover

MIDNIGHT IN RUBY BAYOU
0-380-97405-3/$24.00 US/$36.50 Can